The King's Esquires
Or, The Jewel of France

by

George Manville Fenn

Double 9
BOOKS

The King's Esquires
Or, The Jewel of France
by George Manville Fenn

Copyright © 2023

All Rights reserved.

ISBN: 978-93-61158-96-4

Published by

DOUBLE 9 BOOKS

2/13-B, Ansari Road
Daryaganj, New Delhi – 110002
info@double9books.com
www.double9books.com
Tel. 011-40042856

ABOUT THE AUTHOR

George Manville Fenn was a very productive author of novels, a writer, an editor, and an educator from England. He was born on January 3, 1831, in Pimlico, London. He mostly learned on his own; he taught himself Italian, French, and German. During the years 1851–1854, he went to Battersea Training College for Teachers and then became the head of a state school in Alford, Lincolnshire. In the early 1850s, Fenn started to write short stories and pieces for newspapers and magazines. The Old Forest Ranger, his first book, came out in 1856. Afterward, he wrote more than 100 books, many of them for teenagers and young adults. He was one of the most famous writers of his time, and his books were well-liked and read by many people. He also worked as a reporter and writer for Fenn. Among the newspapers and magazines, he worked for was The Boy's Own Paper, which he ran from 1866 to 1874. He worked hard to make children's books better and was a strong supporter of education and reading. The Englishman Fenn passed away on August 26, 1909, in Isleworth.

CONTENTS

Chapter One
How young Denis kept guard

His Most Christian Majesty King Francis the First had a great preference for his Palace of Fontainebleau among the many places of residence from which he could choose, and it is interesting to glance into that magnificent palace on a certain afternoon in the year 151—. In a special apartment, from which direct access could be obtained to the guard chamber, where a detachment of the favourite musketeers of the King of France was on duty, and which also communicated with the monarch's private apartments, a youth, nearly a man but not quite was impatiently striding up and down. He stopped every now and then to glance out of the low window, from which a view could be obtained over the great Forest of Fontainebleau, where Philip Augustus in the old days, centuries before, loved to go hunting. It seemed as though to the young man there was a chafing disquietude in the silence, the inaction, of the afternoon, when the inmates of the palace, like the inhabitants of the tiny little white town, retired to rest for a time in order to be ready for the evening, when life began to be lived once more.

It was a very handsome chamber in which the young man was evidencing a species of disquietude, as of awaiting the coming of somebody, or a summons. As he stopped once in his feverish pacing up and down, a massive clock was heard to strike three. Rich mats lay on the polished floor, and the *salon* was so lofty that high-up it seemed almost grey dusk by contrast with the bars of sunshine which came through the window.

From outside there came the challenging clarion note of a trumpet.

"Changing guard," he muttered, "already!" And then he fell to thinking of other things, for there was beneath the thud of horses' feet, the baying of a dog and a loud shout.

He turned away from the window at last and tapped the dark arras with which the walls were draped.

He was a tall, dark-eyed, well-made lad, looking handsome enough in his rich velvet doublet, evidently one who spent a large part of his time in the open air, in the chase, or perhaps in sterner work still.

"How much danger?" he murmured, and he went to one side of the room, raising the heavy folds of a curtain which concealed a door, and listening intently a minute, before dropping the drapery and then impatiently springing on to a chair. The chair stood before a long, narrow, slit-like window, and from it likewise there was little to be seen but forest, all deep green and silent, and a strip of blue sky. He sprang down again with a sigh, crossed to the other side of the chamber, lifted the curtain again, opened a door, and looked out, before closing the door, dropping the curtain, and resuming his restless walk, as if saying, "What shall I do with myself?" Somehow the answer seemed to come to that question, for he suddenly clapped his hand to its side, drew a long, thin, triangular-bladed sword from its sheath, and admiringly and caressingly examined the beautiful chased and engraved open-work steel hilt and guard, giving it a rub here and there with his dark velvet sleeve. Then he crossed to the great open carved mantelpiece, took hold of the point of the sword, passing the blade over so that the hilt rested beyond his right shoulder; and, using the keen point as a graver, he marked-out, breast high upon one of the supporters of the chimney-piece, which happened to be a massive half-nude figure, the shape of a heart—the figure being about four inches in diameter. Apparently satisfied with his work, he drew back a few feet, turned up his right sleeve, and grasping his rapier by the handle, made the thin blade whistle as he waved it through the air and dropped gracefully at once into position, as if prepared to assault or receive an enemy, the enemy being the dark oak, chipped and much rubbed, semi-classic figure, the work of some wood-carver of a hundred years before, and whose grim aspect was rendered grotesque by the want of a nose. The next minute the polished floor gave forth sounds of softly shuffling feet, and stamps, as the lad, page or esquire, and evidently for the time guardian of the ante-chamber, began to fence and foin, parry and guard, every now and then delivering a fierce thrust in the latest Italian fashion right at the marked-out heart upon the grim figure's breast. It was warm work, for the lad put plenty of spirit and life into his efforts, and before long his clear, broad forehead and the sides of a rather aquiline nose began to glisten with a very slight dew. But the efforts were quite unsuccessful, bringing forth softly uttered ejaculations of impatience as the keen point of the rapier stuck into the solid wood above, below, to the right and left, never once within the ellipse traced out to represent a heart. But evidently under the belief that practice makes perfect, and regardless of coming shortness of breath, the lad kept on thrusting away, so intent upon his work that he did not bear the faint smothered click as of a latch behind him, nor note a white hand from one of whose fingers glistened dully the stone *en cabochon* of a big ruby ring.

This hand looked thin and ghastly against the dark curtain which it grasped and held on one side for some minutes, while its owner, hidden by the arras, seemed to be watching the sword-play of the lad. This went on vigorously as ever even when the tapestry was lightly brushed aside and a rather short, keen-looking, grizzled-bearded man appeared, in square black velvet cap and long gown, which half hid a closely fitting black velvet doublet and silken hose. He was armed, according to the custom of the time, with a long rapier balanced by a stiletto at his girdle, and as he dropped the curtain, his hands moved as if involuntarily to these occupants of his belt and rested there. It was not a pleasant face that watched the sword-play, for the wrinkles therein were not those of age, but deeply marked all the same.

They showed, fan-like, in two sets of rays at the corners of his eyes, and curiously about the corners of his mouth and beside his nose, as if he were about to laugh, the sort of laugh that one would give who enjoyed seeing a fellow-creature in pain; while his dark right eye seemed to glow beneath the grey shaggy brow, at one moment in a strange fiery way, while the next, as its owner made some slight movement, it literally flashed as if sending forth scintillations of light, giving to his countenance a weird, strange aspect, emphasised by the peculiar fixed stare of his left optic, which suggested that it was doing the fixed, quiet, patient work of its master, while the other searched and flashed and sought for fresh subjects upon which its fellow might gaze. Whatever value such a pair of eyes might be to their possessor, they had one great drawback, and that was that they caused distrust in a stranger who met him for the first time, making him involuntarily feel that this man must be having him at a disadvantage, for it was as if one eye held him in play and took up his attention, while that other with its strange fixed stare searched him through and through.

His was not a pleasant smile, and there were people about the Court who said sinister things about Master Leoni, the King's physician, and who would not have taken a dose of his medicine even to save their lives, for he had acquired a bad name, and Saint Simon had once half laughingly said:

"He knows too much about poisons to please me."

It was no wonder, then, that taking into consideration his quiet and unexpected approach, and the grim aspect of his face, the fencing lad should, when he became aware of his presence, give a violent start and slightly change colour, his exercise-flushed face turning for the moment pale. It was just after one of his most vigorous attacks upon the supporter of the great mantelpiece, one which ended in a really successful thrust delivered with a suppressed "Ha, ha!" followed by a dull thud, and a tug on the lad's part to extricate the point of his sword from its new sheath, quite a couple of inches being firmly thrust into the hard old wood right in the centre of the marked-out heart.

"Humph! At last!" said the watcher, as the boy faced round. "You won't kill many of the King's enemies, Master Denis, if you can't do better work than that."

"What!" cried the boy, flushing. "You've been watching?"

"Of course, I watch everything," said the other, smiling. "That's the way to learn. You must watch, too, my boy—good fencing masters—and learn how to parry and thrust. It's of no use to carry a fine blade like that if you don't master its use. Some day you may have to draw it to defend the King, and aim its point perhaps at an assassin's heart; and that will be a harder target to hit than that motionless mark. You seem to have drawn upon the King's furniture to the great damage of the carving. Denis, my lad, you ought to be able to handle a sword to better purpose than that. Why, even I, old man as I am, who have not held a blade in my hand this many a year, could make a better show."

"At binding up wounds perhaps," said the boy scornfully.

"Ay, and making of them too.—His Majesty is not in his chamber, I suppose?"

"Yes, he is," said the lad shortly; "asleep."

"Soundly, then, or the noise you made must have aroused him. Go and see if he is yet awake. I want to see him."

The boy frowned, and gave a tug at his weapon, which refused to leave the wood.

"Gently, my lad," said the doctor. "That is a very beautiful weapon, too good to spoil, and if you use it like that you will snap off the point, or drag the blade from the hilt."

"But it is in so fast," cried the lad impatiently, and he pulled with all his might, his anger gathering at being dictated to and taught.

"Let me," said the doctor, raising one hand; and the lad resented the offer for the moment, but on second thoughts gave way.

"Perhaps you will find it as hard as I do," he said, with a malicious smile.

"Perhaps I shall," said his elder; "but I should like to try. Sometimes, my boy, the *tactus eruditus* will succeed when main force fails."

"I wish you wouldn't talk Latin," said the boy impatiently, and he snatched his hand from the sword-hilt, leaving it vibrating and swaying up and down where it stuck in the wood.

"Worse and worse," said the doctor quickly, as he caught it by the guard. "Why, Denis, you don't deserve to possess a blade like that. There," he continued, as, apparently without an effort, he drew the rapier from its imprisonment and handed it back to the owner. "There; sheathe your blade, and if his Majesty is awake, tell him that I beg an audience."

"And if he is asleep?" said the lad.

"Let him rest," replied the other, with a smile. "Let sleeping—kings lie. They are always better tempered, my lad, when they have rested well. Take that as being the truth from an old philosopher, Denis, my boy, and act accordingly. You and I don't want to lose our heads through offending the master we serve."

"I don't," cried the boy sharply.

"Nor I," said the doctor, with a smile that was more unpleasant than ever. "There, go softly."

"Yea, I'll go," said the lad; "but I am sure he's asleep."

"If he is, make haste back and while I wait till his Majesty has ended his afternoon nap, suppose I give you one of my prescriptions on the proper way to use a sword."

"But will you?" cried the lad eagerly, his whole manner changing.

"To be sure I will. There was a time when I used to fence, and had sometimes to wound or take life to save my own. But of late years my work has been to heal."

The lad nodded sharply, rested his left hand upon the hilt of his now sheathed sword, drew aside the arras to the right of the fireplace, and passed through the door that faced him, one which closed behind him with a soft click.

Chapter Two
A fencing lesson

"Pert—impudent—all over the young courtier," said the doctor thoughtfully; "but I like the boy for his father's sake. Yes, all that was good and true. Now then, what will he say to me this time? I moved him a little yesterday, and I think that his love of adventure will make him think well of my proposals."

He stood thoughtful for a few moments, bent of form and dreamy of eye. Then with a sudden movement he drew himself up quick and alert, and looking ten years younger, as he swung back his long gown from his shoulders, grasped his rapier by the sheath, brought round his right hand to the hilt, and drew forth a glistening blade, to hold it at arm's length, quivering in the rays of light which came athwart the room from the high-up narrow window. Then falling into position, his whole body seemed to glide forward following the blade, as he made a thrust in the most effortless way, the point of his weapon passing into the hole made a few minutes earlier by the young esquire; and he was in the act of drawing it forth to thrust again, when the arras to his right was plucked aside and the boy stood before him.

"What, you trying!" he cried.

"Yes.—But the King?"

"Asleep, and he will not awaken for an hour yet. No one can hear us," continued the lad eagerly. "Do give me a fencing lesson, Master Leoni. I remember how Saint Simon once said that you were the finest swordsman about the Court."

"Did he say that?" said the doctor quietly.

"To be sure he did," cried the lad, drawing his sword and putting himself on guard.—"Come on."

"Better not now," said the doctor. "We may awaken the King."

"Don't I tell you he's fast asleep?"

"Yes; but the guard may hear."

"Not they; and what matter if they did? Now then; shall I attack you?"

"Yes," said the doctor quietly. "Would you like a place marked-out upon my chest?"

"There, now you are mocking at me."

"Yes: I was."

"Well, you shall attack. But had I better get some buttoned swords? I shouldn't like to hurt you, sir."

"I'll take care you do not," said the doctor quietly; "and there will be no need, for I will not hurt you."

The lad coloured slightly as the thought flashed through him that he should like to humble the other's confidence and pride. The next moment he was looking on, half astonished, as his adversary slipped off his long robe-like gown and stood before him in his tight doublet and hose, upright, keen, and active as a man of half his years, ready to fall into position the next moment and challenge him to come on.

The lad required no second invitation, for, calling up all he knew of fencing, he crossed swords and attacked vigorously, with the sensation the next moment that he had received a sharp jerk of the wrist as his rapier described a curve in the air and the doctor leaped up, making a snatch with his left hand, and catching it by the middle of the blade as it fell, to hold it to its owner with a smile.

"Bad," he said. "Don't let me do that again."

"You can't," cried the lad defiantly, as, tingling with annoyance, he attacked once more, to feel his adversary's blade seem as if endowed with snake-like vitality, and twine round his own, which then twitched and fell with a sharp jingle upon the oaken boards.

"Oh," cried the lad impatiently, "I can't fence a bit! But tell me, doctor; is there any— no, absurd—stuff! I don't believe in magic. I'd give anything, though, if you would teach me how to do that."

"You must learn to fence first, my boy, and work hard. I did not learn to do that in one lesson. Now attack again, and keep a good grip of your hilt. There, come on."

"No, not now, sir," said the boy huskily. "This has made me hot and angry, and one ought to be cool when handling pointed weapons. I shouldn't like to hurt you, sir."

"Neither should I, my lad," said the doctor calmly; "but you need not fear doing that. Come on, I tell you. There, I'm not speaking boastingly, Denis, my lad. I am no master of fence, but I can do precisely what I please with your weapon, disarm you at every encounter, or turn your point whichever way I choose. There: you see." For nettled by his words, and in a futile effort to prove that they were untrue, the lad attacked sharply once again, made about a dozen passes, to find himself perfectly helpless in his adversary's hands, and at last stopped short, lowered his point to the floor, and stood with both hands resting on the hilt.

"You are right, sir," he said. "It's horrible. I thought I could; but I can't fence a bit."

At that moment there was a sharp click of the outer door, and the doctor hurriedly began to sheathe his rapier, but not quickly enough for his action to be unseen. The arras was thrown aside, and a tall handsome young cavalier strode into the ante-chamber and stopped short in astonishment.

"Words and wonder!" he cried. "A duel? or young Denis defending his Majesty from an attempted assassination on the part of Master Leoni with a sword instead of physic?"

"Does it ever occur to you, Saint Simon, that your tongue runs at times somewhat too fast?" said the doctor coldly.

"Oh yes, often," was the laughing reply; "but it's a habit it has. What have I interrupted, though?"

"Master Leoni was giving me a fencing lesson, Saint Simon," cried the lad eagerly.

"Then you are the luckiest fellow at Court," cried the new arrival. "Why was I not here? There, pray go on, and let me stand by and learn."

Chapter Three
His Majesty

Denis glanced at the doctor, grasping his hilt tightly the while, and ready to spring into position for a fresh encounter; but at the same moment he noted the change which came over his adversary, who from being tense, erect and active, suddenly seemed to grow limp of body, though his face was more animated than ever. He hung his head till his chin rested upon his chest, his eyes literally flashed, and he gazed up through his bushy brows at the young courtier who had just joined them, while for answer to his request he slowly finished sheathing his rapier and then took his heavy gown from where he had thrown it upon a chair, and held it out to Denis.

"Help me," he said. "I am growing old and stiff."

The lad looked at him wonderingly as he recalled the marvellous activity of a few minutes earlier, and then helped his instructor to resume his garment.

"What!" cried Saint Simon warmly. "You will not go on? Why, doctor, I want to learn."

The doctor gave him a peculiar, double sinister look, and said, with his unpleasant smile playing about his thin lips:

"The time to bend and train the wand is while it is young and green. You, sir, have grown too old and tough and stubborn to learn."

"At five and twenty?" cried the young man, flushing.

"Yes, at five and twenty. The soil of a court makes a tree old before its time, and—hark! Did I not hear his Majesty ring?"

"Yes," cried Denis quickly, and hurriedly smoothing his hair, which hung loose from his late exertions, and then, readjusting his doublet and seeing to the hang of his sword, he hurried through the arras, those who waited hearing the click of the door latch as he passed into the King's chamber.

"You don't like me, doctor," said Saint Simon, as soon as they were alone.

"I don't dislike you," said the other, smiling. "Have I ever treated you as an enemy?"

"No; but—"

"Hist!" whispered the doctor, as voices were heard beyond the hangings; the door fastening clicked again, and the lad appeared, carrying himself in stiff and formal fashion.

"Gentlemen," he said, "enter. His Majesty will give you audience."

"Both? Together?" said the doctor.

"Yes. His Majesty asked who waited. I told him, and he bade me show both in."

"There, doctor," said Saint Simon; "it is not my doing, so don't visit this upon my head. I daresay he will soon send me away."

Then, following their young escort, the two men stepped into the darkened chamber where his Majesty, heavy-eyed, as if he was hardly yet awakened from sleep, lolled back in a short fur-trimmed robe in the corner of a couch, his left hand behind his neck, his right resting upon the shaggy head of a huge boar-hound which glanced suspiciously at the new-comers and uttered a deep muttering growl.

The King's fingers closed tightly upon the animal's ear, and he gave it a jerk.

"Quiet, Tonnerre!" he said. "Can't you see they are friends?"

Ugh! grunted the dog.

"Brute!" cried the King. "You see, gentlemen, he seeks the company of the wild boar so much that he has acquired his uncouth expressions. Well, Saint Simon, you want to see me?"

"Always, your Majesty," said the young man lightly. "You told me to wait upon you this afternoon."

"Did I? Well, I don't know that I want you. But to return your compliment, the place seems dull when you are not here."

The young man smiled and darted a triumphant glance at the saturnine-looking doctor, before turning to give Denis a look, his eyes sparkling with pleasure the while.

"And you, Leoni," said the King, yawning. "Tut, tut!" he added impatiently. "I am hardly awake. I was tired, gentlemen. Tonnerre and his brother here led us such a race yesterday that I feel it yet. Well, Leoni, what do you want?"

"Your Majesty told me that I might come and continue our little debate of yesterday—"

"To be sure, yes," said the King, yawning again. "Let me see; it was a sort of historical, half prophetic discourse, very learned and hard for a hunting man to understand, about the past and the future, and the safety of my throne, and its depending upon the recovery of a certain mystic stone carried off—carried off—let me see, Leoni, who did you say carried it off?"

"The enemy and invader of your country, your Majesty: Henry, the English King. But, your Majesty—" The doctor ceased speaking and turned slowly, to let his eyes rest meaningly upon the two young men in turn.

"Eh? What? You mean this is secret, and not for other ears?"

The two young men made a quick movement as their eyes sought the King's, and mutely asked the question:

Your Majesty wishes us to go?

"My liege, what I communicated was of the gravest import to you and yours, meant for your ears alone."

"To be sure, Leoni, but kings need very long ears indeed to take in all that concerns them—and have them too, sometimes, my learned doctor, as I have no doubt you men of wisdom think. But to be serious; I find I cannot hear all I want for myself, and am glad to have the help of other ears that I can trust. You are suspicious, my good old friend."

"No, your Majesty: cautious in your service. Years of experience have taught me to trust no one in your Majesty's service but myself."

"Ah, but you are not a king. Where should I be if I trusted none?"

The doctor bowed.

"There, you see, I trust you; and what is more, I trust these two boys as thoroughly as anyone at Court. You know, old friend, that there are hundreds here who will say they would die for me. Now, those two lads would not say such a thing to save their lives."

"Your Majesty!" cried the two young courtiers, in the same tone of protest.

"Well," said the King, smiling; "I am right. I believe you would either of you die to save me, and without saying word."

The pair drew back, smiling and satisfied, each glancing at the doctor as much as to say, Do you hear that?

"There," said the King, "I trust you all; so now go on, Leoni, and say what you have to say; and, boys, mind this; we are in secret conclave now. There must be no chattering afterwards, or discussion."

"Your Majesty commands," said the doctor gravely. "Shall I continue from where we left off yesterday?"

"No; let's have it all again. My gallop yesterday through the forest gave me so much to do in managing a fiery horse and keeping him from breaking my neck amongst the boughs as he carried me into so many real dangers, that all your imaginary notions were swept away. Let's have it all again."

The doctor bowed.

"It will save me," said the King, "from making only a half confidence to my young friends here. But be brief. Put it if you can into a few words. You in your studies and porings over black books are convinced—of what?"

"That your Majesty's throne and succession—"

"Well, really, Leoni, I don't know that I care much about the succession. But my throne is not a safe seat unless—"

"Unless, your Majesty, that half sacred mystic balas ruby that was carried off by Henry of England is brought back and restored to its place in the French Crown."

"Yes, that's it," said the King. "I remember all now. But do you believe, Leoni, as a man who has long studied the secrets of nature, and the mysteries of life, that there can be such virtue in precious stones that they can influence our lives?"

"Yes, your Majesty," said the doctor solemnly; "and everything goes to prove it the wide world through; amongst the greatest and most civilised down to the most savage nations these talismanic gems have been preserved and treasured up. Prosperity and safety of life have always accompanied their possession; misfortune and destruction their loss."

"Well," said the King thoughtfully, "I don't think that I believe it. It sounds to me like an old woman's tale."

"If your Majesty would read and study the history of the past—"

"I haven't time," said the King. "But look here; do you mean to tell me that this present Henry—what is he—the Eighth?—of England believes all this?"

"Yes, your Majesty, and proves it by treasuring up the ruby that by right is yours."

"Then you think that the holding of this stone, reft from our crown, had something to do with the hold of these English upon our fair domains of France?"

"Certainly, your Majesty, and moreover, I hold that it is your sovereign duty to restore it to its place."

"How?" said the King, and his eyes rested upon those of the two young men, whose intent and watchful faces told how they were drinking in with intense interest the subject that was being discussed.

"That, your Majesty," said the doctor gravely, "is what I am here to urge upon you."

"But what do you want, man?" cried the King impatiently. "If Henry is more wise than I, and believes in all this mystic stuff, is it likely that he will give me back this talisman, as I suppose you would call it, that his ancestors plundered from our crown?"

"No, your Majesty. Efforts have been made by statesmen of the past, in previous reigns, to get the jewel back, but all in vain."

"Very well," said the King impatiently; "and France seems to have got on very well without it. We are at peace with England. Why should I disturb our friendly brotherly intercourse by raking up the past? I am quite content and happy to enjoy my hunting pursuits. Do you want me to go to war, invade England, and bring the jewel back?"

"Far from it, your Majesty."

"Then why disturb the pleasant present?"

"For fear of a troubled future, Sire. It is to ensure your long and prosperous reign that I speak like this. Believe me, Sire, I have no other aim."

"Well, Leoni, I believe your words. You have a good position here at Court, and a good master ready to give you anything in reason; and believe me, I want to enjoy a quiet prosperous reign. Mine is a very pleasant life. There are plenty of boars to kill, and I would rather slay them than Englishmen. War is very attractive and very grand. The clash of arms, the trumpets' bray, and the thunder of chargers' hoofs, all thrill me to the core; but I prefer it in the tourney, the mimic charge, and I don't much care for blood. But you as a wise and thoughtful man, you tell me that I ought to stir in this and get the ruby back?"

"I do, Sire," said Leoni sternly.

"Well, well, then I suppose it must be done."

The dog gave a sharp growl and showed his teeth.

"What, sir!" roared the King, snatching back his hand to grasp the dagger in his girdle. "Do you dare to turn upon your lord?"

"No, no, Sire," cried Denis excitedly. "It was not his fault."

"What do you mean, sir?" said the King angrily.

"You were pulling his ears so hard, Sire, and dragging his head to and fro."

"Was I?" said the King.

"Yes, Sire. He bore it as long as he could."

"Poor old Tonnerre!" said the King, clapping his hand upon the dog's head again; and the dog whined with pleasure at the caress. "I was growing excited, I suppose. Well, never mind the hound. Now then, Leoni; we must have this ruby back?"

"Yes, Sire. I shall never rest till I see it safely in the ancient crown."

"And I suppose I must say the same," said the King. "But how is it to be done? There: speak. You have studied all this out, I suppose? How is it to be done?"

"By a trusty mission to England, Sire."

"Absurd! I am sure King Henry would never give anything up."

"And I, Sire. He must be forced."

"Send force?"

"No, Sire. The force must be that of one strong, daring envoy who would seize upon the gem and bring it back."

"What, steal?" cried the King.

"Can one steal that which is one's own, Sire?"

"True. No," said the King. "This is ours by right."

"Your Majesty speaks well," said the doctor triumphantly. "This gem belongs to France's ancient crown, from which it was wrenched, plundered, stolen, carried away as spoil. And now it must be recovered."

"Openly," said the King.

"No, Sire. That means war. My plan is that you should send a trusted envoy to watch his opportunity, seize the gem or gems, and bring them back."

"Hah!" ejaculated Denis, in the excitement of the moment; and Saint Simon turned upon him sharply, and with a resentful look which was returned.

"But it means a deal," said the King thoughtfully. "That ambassador would risk his life."

"Hah!" ejaculated Saint Simon, giving vent to his suppressed excitement in his turn; and Denis now gave him back his resentful jealous look.

"Yes, Sire," continued Leoni; "the envoy would risk his life, of course—in the service of his King. But there are men who would do this for their master's sake, to ensure his long and peaceful reign."

"And if he fails?" said the King.

"He would not fail, Sire. He would be carried forward by the knowledge that he was fighting in the cause of right and duty towards the master that he loved. Have no fear of that, Sire. He would succeed."

"But I have fear," cried the King. "Find me such a man as that, and I should look upon him as a treasure whose life I would not risk."

"There would be no risk, Sire. It would be a question not of force but guile. He would make his way to the Court of your brother of England in a way which I have planned."

"With recommendations from me?"

"Perhaps, Sire. I have not settled that."

"No," said the King angrily. "Why, man, when the gems were missed, the theft would be laid at my door. I would sooner march my people across English ground and take them honestly by force."

"That could not be done, Sire. Leave that to me. Your messenger must go, and carry out his ambassage by guile."

"And who is to be the man?" asked the King.

"I!" cried Denis, springing forward, to sink upon one knee before Francis, and so suddenly as to rouse the dog, which leaped towards him, barking furiously.

"You, my boy!" cried the King.

"No, Sire," cried Saint Simon excitedly, following Denis's example, to spring to the King's feet. "I will go. It is work for a man grown, not for a puny boy."

"Ha, ha, ha!" laughed the King merrily. "Quiet, Tonnerre! Quiet!" For the great hound, roused by the excitement, was filling the chamber with his deep-toned bay, his eyes glaring redly, and his glistening white fangs bared, as he gazed in his master's face as if asking for orders as to whom he should seize by the throat and pin.

"Down, sir!" cried the King again. "Quiet! There, Leoni, was I not right in letting these boys share our confidence? Who says that Francis of Valois has not followers in whom he can trust?"

"Not I, Sire," said the doctor grimly; "but this is no work for them."

"Not for Denis here," cried Saint Simon excitedly, "but, your Majesty, for me. I would strike, and strike now. Mine be the task to do or die!"

"Silence, boy!" cried the King, laying his hand on Denis's head as he dumbly looked up at him in protest, his eyes appealing the while that his monarch's favour should be awarded to him alone. "No, no; emphatically no! Neither of you will go alone. You hear, boys? I will not send you on this quest."

Francis turned to Leoni as he spoke, and the doctor bowed his head in acquiescence.

"Yours are the words of wisdom, Sire," he said. "The work is not for such as these—these two gallant followers of their King."

"Who then is to follow out the task?" said Francis. "For I like it well, and it must and shall be done. You hear me, Leoni? I have spoken now, and I will not rest, since you have roused me to this task, until this jewel glistens once more in its rightful place above my kingly crown."

"Spoken like the King of France!" cried the doctor, drawing himself up. "And now, Sire, it will be done."

"By whom?" cried Francis sternly.

"By your servant, Sire, who has dwelt upon this for years, thought out and nurtured the plans until the fruit is ripe. By the man who possesses the energy, the guile, and the determination to serve his master in this great duty to his King."

"And who is that man?" cried Francis, rising to his feet and standing proudly before his three courtiers kneeling before him; for as he uttered his next words Leoni sank in turn upon one knee and bent his head, to say in a low deep tone, almost a whisper, but which seemed to fill the silence of the place:

"I, Sire—your faithful servant. I am that man."

The silence for the next few moments was profound, while a cloud that had eclipsed the sun for some time past floated slowly from before the glowing orb, which poured its full beams through the gorgeous panes of the stained-glass windows of the chamber, and flooded the standing monarch with its glowing light as he made reply. His words were quick, sharp, and decisive, and fell upon the listeners like a thunderbolt, stunning them for a moment with the astonishment they felt; but they were only these:

"Neither are you the man to carry out this quest. I will go myself."

Chapter Four
The Doctor's eyes

For some moments the trio remained kneeling and staring up at the King in absolute wonderment; for in a few brief words he had swept away, as by the touch of a magician's wand, the gathering feeling of jealous annoyance which was forming in each breast. Leoni was the first to find the use of his tongue; but it was in a hesitating way quite foreign to his usual speech that he faltered out:

"You go, Sire?"

"Yes, I said so," said the King sharply.

"But it is impossible, Sire. You could not stoop to do such a thing as this."

"Then what's the use of being a king," cried Francis, "if one cannot do what one likes?"

Leoni slowly rose to his feet and shrugged his shoulders.

"That is a question I cannot answer, Sire. It forms part of the scheme of life. I have lived fifty years in the world, thirty of which have been spent in thinking and in study of my fellows. I never met one man yet who could do exactly as he liked."

"Well, if you come to that," said the King, "I don't think that I ever did; but I mean to do this all the same."

"But how could you, Sire? If the King of England chose to play you false he might throw you into prison."

"What!" cried Francis hotly.

"And hold you to ransom, Sire."

"Ah! I didn't think of that; but if he did it would give young Denis a chance to come and rescue me. You would, wouldn't you, boy?"

"Yes, Sire, or die in the attempt."

"Don't you be so fond of talking about dying," cried the King. "Who wants to die? Here, with all France at my feet, one wants to live and enjoy oneself. But let's see, Leoni; that wouldn't do at all. What's to be done?"

"Your Majesty will have to stay at Fontainebleau and let your servant do this duty, as he has said."

"No!" shouted the King. "I told you I would go myself."

"With a powerful following, Sire," cried Saint Simon, giving Leoni a triumphant look. "Let me choose and lead your bodyguard."

Denis frowned and set his teeth hard in his annoyance at being passed in the race by his companion; but he brightened directly on hearing the King's next impatient words:

"Hang your bodyguard! Leoni is right."

"Yes, Sire," said that individual, just loud enough for the young man to hear.

"This must be done with guile."

Denis's eyes flashed.

"Pardon, Sire," he cried eagerly. "You might go in disguise." And the next moment the boy's heart swelled within his breast, for the King slapped him heartily on the shoulder.

"Good!" he cried. "That's it! Do you hear, Leoni? That's the idea: I'll go in disguise."

"Sire! It is impossible!" cried the doctor.

"Quite," said the King, laughing; "but I like doing impossible things. Let me see, what's the proper way to go to work? I have it! As a learned doctor like you. H'm, no. They'd want me to cure somebody, and I should be killing him perhaps. Here, Saint Simon, how should I disguise myself?"

"Well, Sire, if I were going to undertake the task I should dress myself like a—like a—like a—"

"Minstrel, Sire," cried Denis excitedly, "like the English King Alfred."

"Or Richard Coeur de Lion," shouted Saint Simon, striving not to be beaten in the race.

"Here, hallo!" cried the King, "that won't do! I do know better than that. It was Richard's minstrel who went in disguise."

"Yes, Sire," cried Denis eagerly, while Leoni, with his eyelids nearly closed, glanced from one to the other with a look of contempt.

"That will not do," said the King gruffly. "There is no instrument that I could play; but I must go as something."

"Is your Majesty seriously determined to go in disguise?" said the doctor.

"Yes, old Wisdom. Now then, what do you propose?"

"I can only think of one way, Sire, and that is that I should go as what I am—a doctor—a part, I believe, that I could worthily play."

"Of course," said the King. "There is not a better doctor in the world."

Leoni's eyes flashed, as he bowed his head gravely.

"But you are not going," said the King decisively.

"No, Sire, unless your Majesty thought it wise that I should go, and take you as my servant."

"What!" shouted the King.

"In disguise, of course, Sire."

"That I won't!" cried the King. "Either in disguise or out of it. Bah! Pish! The idea is absurd. Go as your servant! Are you growing into your dotage, man?"

The two young men exchanged glances, brothers once again in combination against their rival for the King's favour, who seemed to be coming to the front and leaving them behind.

"Pardon me, Sire," said the doctor humbly. "I proposed that, as it seemed an easy way to achieve your ends."

"I would sooner give up the project, Master Leoni," said the King haughtily. "Propose something else."

The doctor spread his hands apart in the most self-abasing way, but the King was not appeased.

"Picture me, the eldest son of Holy Church, His Most Christian Majesty, masquerading as the servant of a leech! Have a care, Master Leoni. You have a way of handling a lancet and letting your patients' blood. Recollect that kings have a way too of treating patients so that they never bleed again."

"I am your Majesty's humble slave," said Leoni, in low, deprecating tones; but Denis noticed that there was no humility in the half veiled eyes as they were lowered to the ground; "You are forgiven," said the King. "But have a care. By the Faith! It brought the blood hotly to my eyes! Now then, speak again. In what habit shall I go?"

There was silence in the chamber, broken the next moment by the impatient trampling of the monarch's feet as he paced up and down, while for a time nobody ventured to speak. And then in his excitement lest he should be supplanted, it was Denis who sprang into the gap.

"I have a plan, Sire," he cried. "Go as a powerful French noble, travelling to see the Courts of Europe, and—and—"

"Yes, go on, boy. That notion likes me well."

"Your Majesty might take me as your esquire, or page," added the boy, trembling lest he should have brought his master's wrath down burning upon his head.

"Hah!" shouted the King, and for a moment the boy's heart sank, for the King's hand came down upon his shoulder in a painful grip; but the next moment the sinking heart rose with a bound, his eyes flashed with excitement, and for the life of him he could not keep from darting triumphant glances at his fellow-courtiers. "There, Master Leoni! There, Saint Simon! Who dares tell me we haven't got a young Solomon of wisdom in our Court? Hear him! That's the very idea I had in my own breast, only I couldn't think it then. Yes, Denis, that's the plan, and we will go at once."

"But your Majesty will want other followers," cried Saint Simon excitedly. "I could—"

"Select a score of quarrelsome, fiery young blades like yourself, to pick quarrels with the English courtiers and spoil our plans? No, sir; that will never do."

"Oh!" groaned the young man, so despairingly that the King laughed merrily.

"Well, you're not a bad fellow, Saint Simon, and I might get into some trouble and want the help of your sword as well as my own. Denis, boy, shall we take him with us?"

The lad flushed deeply at the "shall we?"

It was his moment of triumph. He was called upon to say yes or no, and he turned his eyes, which flashed with pride, upon his elder companion, who gazed at him imploringly, and generosity prevailed.

"Oh yes, Sire," he cried. "He will be a splendid follower to have with us at such a time."

"Then he shall come," cried the King; and Saint Simon sprang forward to kiss his sovereign's hand, while as he rose he turned his eyes upon Denis, and the boy react in them, as it were, the extinction of rivalry, for they seemed to say, I shall never forget this.

"Then that's about all," cried the King, with a sigh of mingled relief and content.

"Sire, may your servant speak?" said Leoni humbly.

"Yes. What is it?" was the impatient reply.

"You are going into a strange country to encounter many perils."

"Pooh! Adventures."

"And adventures," said Leoni—"and may meet with injuries, suffer in your health. Would it not be wise to have the leech in your train?"

"My faith, no!" cried the monarch. "I know you of old, my plotting, scheming friend. You would be having me ill, stretched upon a pallet, within a week, and then it is the doctor who becomes the King. I think we three can manage without your help; but I won't be forgetful of old services, and I'll trust you in this. There is no such scribe about the Court as you, so you shall keep a chronicle of everything that happens here while the cat's away, and read the record of the sporting of my mice to me on my return. I can trust you to see twice as much as any other man about the Court, in your double-sighted way."

"Double-sighted suggests duplicity, Sire," said the doctor.

"No, no; I don't mean that," cried the King, "and you know it. If I thought that you were guilty of duplicity, Leoni, do you think that I should trust you as I do? There," he continued impatiently, "don't look at me like that, man. It worries me."

"It is my misfortune, Sire, not my intention."

"Of course. I know; I know. But you look sometimes as if you were keeping me in conversation with one eye, while the other was seeking how to take me at a disadvantage."

"That's what people about the Court say, Sire," said the doctor, with a grim smile.

"Yes, I know," replied the King. "I have heard Saint Simon say so. I shouldn't have thought of it myself. But it is quite right, all the same."

"In appearance, Sire; but it is not true."

The King laughed.

"My dear doctor, yes, of course; I know that. Do you know what I lay and thought once when I was ill?"

"No, Sire; but something wise, no doubt."

"Bah! None of your subtle flattery. No one knows better than I do, Leoni, that I am not a clever man. What I lay and thought was that you had studied your two crafts so well that one eye was the window from which the clever doctor's brain looked out, the other that of the calm, quiet, thoughtful statesman. I should long to have two such eyes as yours, Leoni, only that there are the ladies, you know. I don't think that they would approve, eh, doctor? What is your experience?"

"That your Majesty is quite right," replied the other, with his cynical smile. "I have never been a ladies' man."

Chapter Five
A King at sea

"Well, boys, we are fairly started," said the King, "but this vessel moves about a great deal. I hope we are not going to have rough weather."

"Well, I'm sorry to say, Sire—" began Saint Simon.

"Ah!" cried the King, in a low angry voice. "Four days since we started, and I have been giving you lesson after lesson, and you begin at once addressing me like that. Once more, both of you, I am the Comte de la Seine, on my travels, and you, Saint Simon, are my friend, and you, Denis, my esquire. Now look here, Denis, do I look at all like a king now?"

"Not in the least, Comte."

"And now you, Saint Simon; what have you got to say about the weather?"

"That I have been talking to the shipmaster, and he says the weather is going to be very fine—"

"That's good," cried the King.

"—but very windy."

"That's bad," said the King—"for the poor horses," he added hastily. "I wish we had had them fastened up below."

As he spoke he glanced forward at where, a good distance apart, three very beautiful chargers were doubly haltered to the rail, and whinnying uneasily and pawing at the deck, and then made an uneasy gesture, for a puff of wind filled out the two big sails of the clumsy vessel and made it career, so that the royal passenger made a snatch at a rope which was hanging loose and gave to his touch, when he made another snatch and caught at Saint Simon to save himself from falling.

"A bad, a clumsy vessel!" he cried angrily. "Here, I'm tired with our long two days' ride. I think I'll go into the cabin and lie down. Give me your arm, Denis." And, steadying himself by the lad, he went below, lay down at once, and dismissed his attendant, who returned on deck, to be met by Saint Simon.

The two young men, gazed silently at each other, and with mirth in their eyes.

"The sea doesn't respect kings," said Saint Simon merrily.

"Nor anybody else," replied Denis; "so don't let us holloa till we are out of the wood."

"You mean across the water."

"Yes," said Denis. "It may be our turn next. I wish we were over in England now."

"What, are you afraid?" cried Saint Simon.

"Yes—for my poor horse. I'm afraid of his breaking away. Look how he is straining at his halter, and how rough his coat is. It looked like satin yesterday. If he broke loose what should we do?"

"Try to tie him up again," said Saint Simon bluntly. "But if one gets loose the others will follow, and then—"

He stopped short and spread his legs as wide as he could, for the vessel was beginning to dance in the chopping sea.

"Well, and what then?" cried Denis.

"Our wild-goose journey would be at end, for those horses would go overboard as sure as we stand here."

"What!" cried Denis excitedly.

"What I have said. My charger is safe to make a dash for the side, and rise at it; and he'd go over like a skimming bird, and the others would follow at once."

He had hardly spoken when the skipper of the vessel, a heavy, sun-tanned-looking man in scarlet cap, high boots and petticoat, came up to them.

"Look here, young masters," he cried, "I don't often take cattle in my boat, and when I do I have them slung down into the hold. My deck isn't a safe place for beasts, and if those three don't break loose before long I'm no shipman."

"Then what is to be done?" cried Denis hurriedly.

"If the—" He stopped short, for Saint Simon gave him a sharp jerk with his elbow and continued his speech.

"—Comte's horse were to be lost overboard he'd never forgive us."

"No," said Denis, recovering himself. "Look here, you have plenty of ropes. Call some of your men to help; we must put slip-knots round above their hoofs and tie them in different places, so that they couldn't get away."

"Yes, that's right," said the skipper. "But won't they kick?"

"No," replied Denis; "we can manage that if your men will help."

No time was lost, for the need for doing something grew more and more evident; and with the young men standing by to calm and caress each beautiful steed in turn, running nooses were placed round their fetlocks, and the ropes' ends slipped through ring-bolt and round belaying pin, to be made fast, so that before half an hour had passed the horses were thoroughly secured, and stood staring-eyed and shivering, ready to burst out into a piteous whinnying if the young men attempted to move away.

It was a rough passage, growing worse hour after hour till nightfall, and the cares that had come upon them were so onerous that the two young men were too busy and excited to feel any qualms themselves. Not only were there the horses, but their companion below made no little call upon their attention, and in turn they descended into the rough cabin to see what they could do. But the second time that Saint Simon approached the spot where his suffering sovereign lay he was ordered back.

"Send Denis," he said. "You go on deck again and mind that nothing happens to my horse."

"He's very ill," said Saint Simon, who did not look at all sorry, but more disposed to laugh, as he joined Denis, who was dividing his attention among the three horses, and patting each in turn.

"Then why did you leave him?"

"Because he wants you. He's ashamed to let me see how bad he is."

"Is he so very ill then?" said Denis.

"He thinks he is; but you had better make haste down."

Denis hurriedly went below, to find that the sea entertained not the slightest respect for the stricken monarch, who uttered a low groan from time to time, and grew less king-like in his sufferings.

"This is very bad, Denis," he said, "and it doesn't seem fair. Why am I ill, and you going about as if we were on dry land?"

"I wish I could suffer for you, my master," said the lad earnestly.

"Thank you. That's very good," said the King; "but unfortunately you can't. Denis, my lad, it takes all the bravery out of a man when he is like this. Do you think the shipmaster would call it cowardly if I were to send word for him to turn the vessel round and make sail back for Havre de Grâce?"

"I don't think he would notice it, my—Comte," said Denis earnestly; "but I don't think he could do it now."

"Why?" cried the King.

"Because the wind is growing stronger, and blowing hard from behind, driving us fast for the other coast; and even if he could turn we should not get back."

"No," said the King. "But this is very horrible, Denis, my lad.—Are the horses safe?"

"Yes, sir, quite."

"Ah! that's right," moaned the King. "Say sir, not Sire, on your life."

Boomp! Rush!

"What's that?" cried the King, in a startled voice, sitting up, but falling back with a groan. "Oh, how my head swims! Can you swim, Denis, boy?" he moaned.

"Yes, sir; but no one could swim in a sea like this."

Boomp! Crash! Rush!

"What's that, boy?" groaned the King again. "Why don't you tell me? Didn't I ask before?"

"It was a big wave, sir, leaping at the vessel's bows, and curling over and rushing along the deck."

"How dreadful!" said the King. "Why is it so dark? Is it the sea flooding the ship?"

"No, sir; it is nearly night."

"Oh yes, I forgot. I think I have been asleep. Are we almost there?"

"No, sir. It is a long way yet."

"If I could only go to sleep! Why didn't I let that doctor come? Denis, my boy, if I die, or if we are drowned, or— go up and ask the shipmaster how long it will be before we get across."

In no wise troubled by the pitching and tossing of the clumsy vessel, Denis climbed on deck; but it was some moments before he could make out where the captain stood, and then only by the help of one of the men, who pointed out the dim figure in the semi-darkness lightened by the foam, standing beside the man at the rudder beam; and then it needed no little care to pass along, holding on by the bulwarks, to ask the question the lad was sent to bear.

"How long, my lad?" said the skipper. "Oh, very soon. We are flying across to-night. This is the fastest run I can remember to have made."

"But are we nearly there?"

"Nearly there! No, not halfway; but if the wind holds on like this we shall be across in time for dinner at noon to-morrow, and perhaps before."

"So long as that?" cried Denis.

"So soon as that," said the skipper, laughing. "There, I see how it is. You are afraid—"

"I'm not!" cried Denis sharply.

"Don't be in such a hurry, my lad. You don't give a man time to speak—about your horses, I was going to say. But they're all right. I have another rope passed from neck to neck, and as soon as the poor beasts felt it it seemed to give them comfort, like being more in company. Don't you be afraid. They're noble animals, but not fit for work like this. Go and see."

Denis hurried to where Saint Simon was standing with the horses, drenched with spray, and growing impatient at his task.

"Oh, there you are!" he cried. "Why didn't you come before?"

"I couldn't leave him. He sent me up to ask how soon we shall be across."

"Well?"

"The skipper says at noon to-morrow."

"Not till then?" said Saint Simon.

"No."

"Well, I'm glad of it. Serve him right. It will finish this wild-goose chase and send him back quite satisfied, ready to settle down again."

"I hope so," said Denis. "How wet you are!"

"Yes, I don't mind now," said Saint Simon. "It was very horrible at first, but I can't get any wetter, and that's some comfort after all."

"I'd stop and keep guard myself so that you could go into shelter," said Denis; "but I must go down again to tell him what I have learned. But why couldn't you go?"

"Because he sent you, and he'd be furious perhaps. There, go and tell him."

"Yes, I had better go," said the lad thoughtfully; "but—I am sorry to leave you, all the same."

"Hah! That makes me feel warm," cried Saint Simon—"that and the knowledge that the horses can't get loose. There, go on down. After all, he's worse off than we."

Denis crept along by the bulwarks till he could reach the cabin hatch, lowered himself down to where a vile-odoured lamp was swinging from the cabin ceil, and then, moving slowly, having hard work to keep his feet, he reached the spot where the suffering monarch lay, to find to his great relief that Francis had sunk into a deep sleep, and was breathing heavily, leaving him nothing to do but sit down and watch.

Chapter Six
How to land horses

It was a long and dreary night, full of suffering; but, like the worst, it slowly came to an end. The grey dawn began to creep through the dim skylight, grew stronger and brighter, and at last the sun arose, with the King still sleeping profoundly, and Denis standing at the top of the cabin ladder, gazing out over a glorious foaming sea, all purple, orange, and gold, wide awake to the beauty of the scene, and ready to wonder what had become of the horror and darkness of the night.

There was a fresh breeze blowing and the sea was rough, but the clumsy craft rode more easily and had ceased to pitch and toss. Far ahead too the sea looked smoother, and so Denis said to the rough-looking skipper, who came up with a nod and smile.

"Only looks so," he said, "because it is so far off. But the wind is going down, and in a couple of hours we shall be in smooth water. How's your master?"

"Fast asleep still," replied Denis.

"Best thing for a man not used to the sea. Well, you see, we shall get your horses over safely. Poor beasts! They are worse sailors than men. How are you? Feel as if you could eat some breakfast?"

"Yes, I'm getting horribly hungry."

"That's right. You are the best sailor of the lot. There will be some in an hour's time."

The skipper passed on, leaving Denis with a look of disgust upon his features, for he was thinking of the roughness of the common vessel upon which they had been obliged to take their passage, and the pleasant meal of which he would have eaten at Fontainebleau.

Just then Saint Simon turned, caught sight of him, and signalled to him to come. Denis started, hesitated, and then ran down into the cabin again to see whether the King had awakened. But far from it: he was flat on his back and looking far from king-like, for his mouth was open and he was giving forth sounds which in a common person would have been called snores.

Hurrying back to the deck, Denis ran forward, awakening to the fact that the sea was much smoother, for he could not have progressed like that over-night.

"Well, how are you?" he cried.

"Beginning to get dry," was the morose reply. "Look here, boy, if I had known that I was going to play horse-keeper all through a night like this I wouldn't have volunteered to come. I shall want a week's sleep to put me straight."

"Why didn't you ask one or two of the sailors to come and help you?"

"Why didn't you come and help me?"

"You know: because I was obliged to be in attendance on the—"

"Comte!" shouted Saint Simon. "You will be spoiling the expedition before you have done."

"Yes, it is hard work to remember. I am sorry, though, Saint Simon. You know that I would have come and helped you if I could."

"Oh yes, I know," said the other. "I couldn't trust anyone to help, for the poor beasts knew me, and at the worst times a word or two and a pat on the neck seemed to calm them, and they left off shivering with cold and fear; but I have had a night such as I don't want to have again."

"You must have had. But the skipper says that we shall soon be in smooth water, and that there will be some breakfast in an hour."

"Heugh!" ejaculated Saint Simon. "Breakfast here! I don't want anything till we get on shore—if we ever do. Here, look behind you."

Denis turned sharply, to see a familiar face in the full sunshine peering over the edge of the hatchway and looking about, but apparently not seeing what was sought till a hand appeared to shade its owner's eyes, sending forth a flash or two of light from a ring upon one of the fingers.

"Why, it's the—"

"Comte!" said Saint Simon quickly. "Stop here, and lay hold of his horse."

Saint Simon said no more, and Denis obeyed, grasping his companion's reason, while the next minute the King had mounted to the deck, and came forward to join them, after making a rush to the bulwarks and grasping the rail.

"Oh, you're here, gentlemen," he said sharply. "Why was not somebody in attendance—oh, I see; you're minding our steeds. It has been a very bad night for them. Not injured, I hope?"

"No, sir," replied Saint Simon; "but during the worst part of the storm we had to have extra ropes. I was afraid at one time that we should lose them all."

"But they are safe," said the King, "thanks to you, gentlemen. Poor boys," he continued, as he passed amongst the ropes, each charger in turn uttering a low, piteous whinny, and stretching out its muzzle to receive the King's caress, each too snorting its satisfaction the next moment, and impatiently pawing the deck.

"Morning, master!" cried the skipper, hurrying up. "Been a windy night, but it will be all smooth directly. Wind's veered round to the north, and coming off the shore. Sha'n't be getting on so fast now."

"But these horses," said the King; "they ought to have water and food."

"Not they, master. They wouldn't touch it if you gave them of the best. They want to feel solid ground under their hoofs."

"And how soon will they get that?" asked Denis quickly.

"Two or three hours if the wind doesn't drop," replied the skipper; "and," he continued, as he held up his hand and shouted an order or two to his men to stand by the sheets, "it's chopping round again to the south. Give us an hour like this, and we shall be in shelter, sailing between the island and the mainland. You can't say but what we have had a splendid run."

There was such a quaint comical expression upon the King's countenance that Denis felt obliged to swing swiftly round and bend down to make believe to loosen the slip-knot about his charger's leg.

"If I hadn't done so," he said afterwards to Saint Simon, "I should have burst out laughing in the Comte's face. There," he added quickly, in triumphant tones, "I have got it now!"

"Yes, and you would have got it then," replied Saint Simon, "for my lord will forgive a good deal sooner than being laughed at."

This was some time later, when they were gliding gently on through the smooth water on a bright sunny morning with their port close at hand and full prospect of being, some time during the next half-hour, close up to the landing-place; and before long so it proved, for the King, quite recovered now from his indisposition, was in eager converse with the skipper as to the best means of getting the horses ashore.

"Well, master, you see this: Southampton isn't Havre de Grâce."

"Bah!" ejaculated the King impatiently.

"We had nothing to do there but walk the horses straight from the wharf over the planks, and down through the gangway on to the deck; but you see it's different here."

"Nonsense!" said the King. "There are landing-places here, for I can see them. Work your vessel up quite close, and then boards can be laid from the deck, and the same thing can be done the other way on."

"Yes, master, that's what I meant; but I forgot all about the tide. You see, we are coming in just at low water, and I sha'n't be able to get within fifty fathoms of the shore till well on towards night."

"What! And we have to stop here all day?" cried the King angrily.

"Yes, that's about it. I'll get in as close as I can, and then we shall be in the mud."

"But is there no other way farther along?" cried the King.

"The only other way is for me to hail a barge or a flat, and swing the horses down into that; but I shouldn't like to undertake the job."

"It must be done," said the King. His words were law, and, in his impatient eagerness to get clear of the vessel where he had passed so many uncomfortable hours, he promised to hold the skipper free from responsibility.

Taking advantage of the King going aft with Saint Simon, Denis went up to the skipper.

"Do you think there will be any danger," he said, "to the horses?"

"Shouldn't like to promise, my lad," was the reply, "but if they were my horses I should go to your master and say, What's the use of being in such a hurry? It's only waiting a tide, and then we could get close in."

"But you don't know him," said Denis. "He will have his own way."

"Yes, I can see that," said the bluff skipper. "It'd do him good to be six months aboard my vessel under me. I'd make another man of him. Ah, you may laugh, my young sharper. You think I'm a quiet, good-tempered sort of an old chap, but a ship's captain has to be a bit of a Tartar too. Do you know what he is aboard his ship? Well, I'll tell you. He's a king."

Denis gazed sharply in the man's face, wondering whether he had any suspicion as to who his passenger really was, as he went on talking.

"You see, my boy, I'm used to this sort of thing. Sometimes it's cattle, sometimes it's pigs and sheep. Well, they don't like going down into a flat-bottomed boat; but," he added, with a chuckle and a nudge, "they have to go, and if they won't go decently like passengers, we just shoves them overboard and lets them swim ashore. But with horses like these it would be spoiling them to treat them roughly."

"But you need not treat them roughly," said Denis. "You could sling them with your ropes and tackle into the boat."

"Yes, you could," said the skipper; "but they wouldn't let you."

"Oh, they would," said Denis.

"Well, sir," said the skipper, "you wait and see."

Chapter Seven
Only a boy

The rough old skipper was right, for after getting in as close as he could, the vessel took the ground, and some time was spent in hailing and getting a large flat barge close alongside to the open gangway.

A big spar with its blocks and tackle was run out, and proceedings were commenced with the men for slinging the horses off the deck and lowering them down; but everything was of the roughest kind and perfectly unsuitable, while the horses, which were recovering fast from their stormy journey, grew more and more restless, and after several attempts with the King's charger, which was to be the first, it resented the handling of the men, lashed out, and then began to rear, proving in a short time that disaster must follow the attempt, for plainly enough, if the horse began to struggle when raised from the deck, it would free itself from the badly fitted on ropes and be seriously damaged and maimed before being finally lowered down.

The worse matters grew the more the King lost his temper. He bullied, raged, and stormed, called the skipper and his men clumsy idiots and imbeciles, till temper was lost on the other side, the skipper's face, always ruddy and brown, grew red and black, and he ended by telling his Majesty that he would have to wait, for the men should do no more.

"This will be the end of our travels," whispered Saint Simon, "for the King will now betray himself."

"The Comte, you mean," said Denis quietly; for he had been standing very thoughtful and quiet, thinking over his conversation with the skipper hours before, and starting forward suddenly just as the King was clapping his hand to his sword, he whispered to him quickly:

"I think I can get the horses ashore, Sire."

"How dare—here—how?"

"Will your Majesty let me try—I mean, Monsieur le Comte, will you let me try?"

"Hah! That's better, boy. But speak; what do you mean to do?"

"Let me show you, sir," cried the boy excitedly, and going to where his steed was tethered, he patted and tried to soothe it for a few moments before taking bit and bridle and fitting them on. Then he called to the skipper.

"What do you want?" said the man gruffly, as he came up scowling.

"Have that flat hauled away," said Denis quickly, "and then give me a clear space on the deck. There isn't much room, but I think I can manage."

"Hah!" cried the skipper. "Well done, youngster! I see what you mean, and if you can do that there will be no trouble with the others. Well done! Good idea!"

The anger against the King seemed to die out at once, and giving his orders sharply, in a very brief space of time the shallow barge had been allowed to drift astern, there was a fairly clear space on deck, there was the open gangway on the side of the vessel nearest the shore, and the time had come for the young esquire to act.

The next minute Denis cast loose the halter which tethered his charger to the vessel's side, turned it round, patted the arched neck once more, and then, bridle in hand, sprang up, threw over one leg, and the next moment was seated upon his barebacked steed.

The sailors gave a cheer, which startled the horse, but a few words from Denis quieted it again, and in obedience to the pressure of the rider's heels it paced forward along the deck as far as the hamper of the vessel would allow, turned in obedience to the pressure on the rein, and paced back again in the other direction, to be turned once more.

Everyone else on board was turned into a spectator now, the men in the flat watching as eagerly as the rest. "He will never do it, Saint Simon," said the King.

"Think not, sir?" was the reply. "I believe he will. Look!"

For after walking his beautiful steed to and fro again, Denis waited till they reached the open gangway, and then turned the noble animal's head and let it stop to stretch out its muzzle towards the shore to gaze with starting eyes at the solid land and moving people there.

It snuffed the air loudly, and then a loud neigh rang out like a challenge, which was answered by one of the horses attached to a trolley high-up on a wharf.

This had the effect of setting the other two chargers challenging in turn, and as they ceased, Denis spoke to and patted his steed, bending well forward the while. Then he turned its head again and rode a few yards up and down the deck once more.

"Well done, my lad," cried the skipper, coming to his side. "You will do it. Go on."

"How deep is the water here?" said Denis eagerly.

"About a fathom. Plenty of room for you to swim."

Denis set his teeth, walked his horse up and down once more, turned it sharply toward the gangway, and then with voice and heel urged it forward, but only to elicit a loud snort as it stood with all four feet pressed firmly on the deck.

Once more, half despairing now, Denis rode up and down again, before turning toward the open gangway, and it happened that just as he reached it a neighing challenge came afresh from the shore, sending a quiver through the charger, which snorted loudly, and then, in obedience to the rider's voice and the pressure of his heel, rose and bounded bravely forward from the vessel's side, out into the water, descending with a heavy splash, and then submerged all but the extended neck, and with the lad with the water rising above his hips, but firmly in his seat, bending forward and giving as if part of the brave animal that had begun swimming steadily towards the shore.

A ringing cheer rose from the vessel, was taken up by the men on the flat, and answered from the shore, while all watched the progress of horse and rider, who both seemed as if to the manner born.

"That means success, sir," said Saint Simon eagerly. "Will you go next?"

"But I shall be so wet, man. You had better follow with my charger now."

"Yes, sir, I will if you wish," whispered Saint Simon; "but—this is the beginning of our adventures, and—"

"Yes," said the King, in a voice full of vexation, "it seems so cowardly if I hang back. I am not afraid to do it, man, but I shall be so horribly drenched."

"You can get dry, sir, when we are ashore."

"Yes, of course," whispered the King. "Here, I'll go next. I am not going to be beaten by that boy."

He was in full earnest, and bitting and bridling his horse himself, refusing Saint Simon's help and leaving him to perform the same task on his own steed, almost as soon as Denis had reached the shore, for his steed to stand snorting and shaking the water from its flowing mane and tail, the King was mounted, barebacked too. He rode his charger to the open gangway, where the brave beast answered the neigh that came from its companion on land, and without hesitation made the splashing leap so suddenly that the rider nearly lost his seat, having an undignified struggle to get himself upright again; while as soon as there was a clear way Saint Simon followed without the slightest difficulty, his charger in a few strides getting abreast of the King's; and they swam together till the water shallowed and the swimming became a splashing wade to where, wet and triumphant, Denis was waiting their arrival.

Chapter Eight
Madame the hostess

A little crowd of idlers soon began to gather about the adventurers, who had dismounted to shake the water from their clinging garments and make much of their brave steeds.

"My faith!" said the King. "We are beginning our adventures indeed; but we are in a sorry plight, and ought to change."

"Here's the boat coming, sir," cried Denis, who turned away from a man who began questioning him eagerly as to who they were and why they had come ashore like this.

The fellow's manner had annoyed him, for though he pretty well understood his English he replied shortly in his native tongue. But the man was in no wise rebuffed, and turned now to Saint Simon, with whom he fared no better, in fact, rather worse, the result being that he addressed the King, who shortly told him to go and mind his own affairs.

The boat, which soon reached the shore, contained the skipper, who had thoughtfully brought on the travellers' light valises, their saddles, and the remains of the horse-gear, ready to offer them any further assistance, and praising their gallant swim; but warmed up by his excitement, the King made light of it all, seeming ready to forget the state of his garments; and eager to get away from the crowd, he joined with his young companions in saddling up and mounting, to ride away from the curious crowd and the hangers-on, several of whom seemed on friendly terms with the man who had first addressed Denis, and whose curiosity seemed in no degree abated.

"I did think of going to some inn to change and rest, and start forward later on for Winchester," said the King; "but we will start at once and get away from here. Do the people think we have come to make an exhibition for them?"

"But you will want rest and refreshment, sir, and to dry your clothes," said Saint Simon.

"No," said the King. "Do you?"

"I am ready—we are ready," said Saint Simon, "to follow you in everything."

"Are our valises fast in their places, and the saddles well girthed?" said the King. "Yes? Then we ride on at once till we are clear of this town. We shall soon dry in the hot sunshine, and be better ready to make a breakfast, for I feel as if I could touch no food. Follow, gentlemen," he continued, and putting spurs to his charger he cantered away along what seemed to be the main street, at the end of which a few inquiries put them on their right road and direct for the open country, where, once amongst green fields and hedgerows, they dismounted, to rest their horses by a river-bank and let them drink and graze.

But for this the brave animals, which had suffered more than their riders from the crossing, displayed no eagerness, and the travellers advanced again, walking each with his bridle in his hand, enjoying the glowing sunshine and the simple beauty of the country, and gradually growing more light-hearted and ready for any fresh adventure that they might encounter.

The road became more and more deserted, a village or two was passed, and later on in the day they were attracted by the appearance of a substantial farmhouse whose very aspect suggested that here was the spot to put an end to certain qualms connected with the fact that they had not partaken of food for a considerable length of time.

Here there was corn for their horses in a shady barn-like stable whose loft shed a delicious odour of sweet hay, and in the house a clean white scrubbed table with bowls of new milk, newly made bread, and freshly fried ham, the whole forming a repast to which the party paid ample justice, while it made the King declare that it was the most delicious banquet he had ever enjoyed.

Then with the horses quite recovered, the journey was recommenced and the travellers rode off, Denis turning in his saddle to wave his hand to the farmer and his wife, just in time to catch sight of another party riding up to the farm as if to take their places and enjoy a similar meal.

Winchester at last, with the square tower of the fine old cathedral standing up from amongst the trees, the river sparkling in the sunshine, the wooded hills and verdant plains rising on all sides making Francis draw rein to breathe his horse and half close his eyes as he gazed around.

"Well," he said, "France is France, but my brother of England, if all his country is like this, possesses a land that any king might envy; and I shall tell him so if we meet, as of course we shall. But after all, I don't like this task. I am a king, and it begins to look to me, boys, as if I am going crawling up to the back door of this palace of his like some lacquey. But there, I have said that I would do it. It is for France, and I will. What do you say, Saint Simon?"

"Oh, sir, you mustn't turn back now."

"No: I must not turn back now, though we have been rather damped at the start, eh?" he added, with a laugh. "But are you lads dry?"

They declared they were, and the conversation turned upon their proceedings.

"This is evidently a fine city," said the King. "I have read enough to know that it has been a home of kings, so we will sleep there to-night and start afresh in good time to-morrow, though we shall not go to the Palace for a bed. But there is sure to be some good travellers' inn."

And this proved to be the case as they rode through the city gate down the High Street, to check their steeds by the Market Cross, the observed of all observers, and they were many lurking about the place, for it had been market day.

It was not the costume of the three horsemen, for they were purposely very plainly clad, everything about them, however, looking good and soldierly. It was their beautiful horses that took the attention of most of the sturdy country-looking folks, and more than one keen-eyed man approached them with no little freedom, scanning their mounts from head to heel, one man giving the King a nod and stretching out his hand to run it down his charger's leg.

The King looked furious, darted a fierce glance at the intruder, and reined up his horse so suddenly that the fine beast reared and made the man start back, his discomfiture being greeted by a roar of laughter on the part of the uncouth people around.

"The insolence!" muttered the King to Denis. "These English islanders are brutal in their ways. If they knew who I was! Here, let's ride on."

His horse answered to the pressure of his knees and moved off upward through the crowd, Saint Simon following his track, and Denis coming last, having no little difficulty in closing up, for the increasing crowd obstructed his way, the people's curiosity being aroused by the strangers.

"These horses for sale?" said the man who had been rebuffed, pressing up to the young esquire's knee.

"No," said the lad, in fairly good English. "Why?"

"Hallo!" said the man. "You are a Frenchman. Then you have brought these over to sell. Look here, young man, I can help your master to find a buyer in some great English lord. I deal in horses, and I'll make it worth his while. Where are you going to stay?"

"I don't know," replied Denis. "Keep back, please. My horse doesn't like crowding, and he may strike out."

"I'll take care," said the man. "I understand horses. Yes, this is a nice animal you are riding too."

Denis made no answer, but pressed forward. There was some shouting, but the crowd gave way and he rode up close just as the King drew rein by a gateway and then passed into a great inn-yard, where a couple of hostlers hurried to meet them, and a buxom-looking landlady in widow's coif came smiling to the door of the comfortable-looking inn.

"Hah!" said the King, dismounting. "This looks like France. Here we can rest and dine. Denis, my boy, talk to the dame there, and tell her to get us quickly a dinner of the best."

Denis turned, meeting the pleasant-faced landlady's eye as he dismounted and threw his rein to one of the stablemen, noting, as he walked to where the landlady stood waiting, that the man who had accosted them was following into the inn-yard with three or four others of the same stamp; and the sight of the fellow made the lad hesitate as he thought of the possibility of the fellow's insolence raising the King's ire. But he had his task to fulfil, and the next moment the landlady was receiving him with bows and smiles, ready to show him into a comfortable old-fashioned room, and make his task easy by suggesting instead of taking orders, the only one he found it necessary to give being the simple one:

"Everything, and of the best; but quickly, for we have ridden far."

This was in French, but to the lad's great delight the hostess spoke his tongue, with a good accent, easily and well.

"Anyone would think you were French," he said, with a courtly bow.

"Oh no," she said, "I am English. I was in Rouen many years at school, and we have French travellers here sometimes. But let me show you the chambers for your lord and your young friend. He is a lord?" she said, with a pleasant smile.

"He is what you English would call a lord," replied Denis. "The Comte de la Seine."

"Ah," said the hostess, with a smile of satisfaction at the quality of her guests, as she led the way to the best chambers of the fine old inn, Denis selecting two, one within the other, which were exactly such as he felt the King would like—that is to say, a fine old bedroom with a double-bedded ante-chamber, which he immediately determined should be for himself and Saint Simon.

Within an hour, partly refreshed, the King and his two followers entered the room where their dinner was spread, unbuckled and laid by their swords, and took their places at the well-furnished table, as a couple of fresh-looking serving-maids, under the guidance of the hostess, brought in the soup and plates, the mistress seeing to the helping and then retiring, leaving the guests to their repast.

"Hah!" exclaimed the King. "My appetite is grand. What soup! Why, we might be in France. No, it is better, thicker and stronger. But what's this? The insolence of these Englanders! Here, Denis, boy, read it aloud." And he tossed a folded paper, one end of which was sticking out from beneath his soup bowl, across to the young esquire.

The lad's eyes flashed, as he read in a crabbed, clear hand the words: "*Imminent undique pericula.*"

"What's that, Leoni? Bah! He isn't here," cried the King, letting his spoon fall back into the bowl. "I thought it was the account. Latin. Read it again."

Denis obeyed, while the King's left hand began to play with his dagger, as he darted a suspicious look at the closed door, and then at the side dresser upon which he had thrown his sword.

"What do you make of that, Saint Simon?" he said, in a low, deep voice.

"Sir, I do not know Latin as I should," was the reply.

"Shame on you!" growled the King. "You, Denis, you were last at school. What do you make it to be?"

"In plain homely language, sir: Beware of danger."

"Yes, imminent danger," cried the King. "Poison! And I have eaten nearly half my soup!"

"No, no, sir," cried Denis. "I'll vouch for this. A woman with a motherly face like that could be trusted, I will vow."

"I don't know," said the King. "You are only a boy. Now I have grown old enough to think that it requires a very clever man to know exactly what there is behind a woman's pleasant smiling face. This one looks plump and comfortable and honest; but there's no knowing. Now, if we had Leoni here he'd fix her with that quiet eye of his, and search her through and through with the other. He'd know. And I am beginning to find out that I have done a very stupid thing in not bringing his Ugliness with us. By my sword, I wish we had brought him! I wished it last night too, over and over again, when I felt so—ah, hum—when I couldn't sleep for the creaking and groaning of that wretched vessel."

As he pulled himself up short he looked searchingly from one to the other of the two young men, giving each a suspicious glance, suspecting as he did that he would find a mocking smile upon their lips; but he was pleasantly disappointed, for Saint Simon looked stolidly stupid, and Denis eager and expectant of the next words he should let fall.

"Well," said the King, "we haven't got him here, and we must think for ourselves; but that must be right. The soup is too good for that," and he began to partake again. "Here, Denis, lad, on second thoughts it must mean that we are being recognised. The islanders know who I am, and that pleasant-faced woman wishes to give us warning. Saint Simon, my lad, fetch our sword and hang it by the belt upon the corner of the chair. Do the same by your own. I am not going to leave this soup, and if we are to fight for what is evidently intended for an excellent dinner, why, fight we will."

Saint Simon obeyed, and then at a sign from the King re-took his place and went on eating with such appetite as he could command.

"Shall I stand on guard by the door, sir, till you have dined?" said Denis.

"No, boy. Eat your soup and what else comes. We shall all three fight the better for a meal."

Chapter Nine
The scent of danger

It was hard to imagine that there was danger in the air, for in that comfortably furnished panelled room everything was suggestive of plenty and peace, and, noticing as he went on with his meal how impressed his two followers seemed to be, the King paused, spoon in hand, and cried with a laugh:

"Come, boys, where are your appetites? Are we to be scared with a scrap of paper, a Latin exercise, perhaps, written by our hostess's son?"

As he spoke there was a faint rasping sound as of wood passing over wood, making Denis turn sharply and put out his hand towards his sword, for it seemed to him that there was a tremulous motion in one of the panels of the wall behind where the King was seated.

"What's that?" cried the latter sharply, as with a bound the lad sprang past him to stand between him and the side of the room.

For answer Denis drew his sword and pointed to the panel.

"Well? Why don't you speak?"

"There is a door there, sir, and I saw it move."

"There is no door here," cried Saint Simon, as he felt about the panel, which was perfectly rigid; and just then the hostess entered, followed by the maids bearing fresh dishes, to look wonderingly from one to the other.

"Ah, mistress!" cried the King. "Is there a door there? Does one of those panels open?"

"Oh yes, my lord," she replied. "It is a hatch to pass dishes through into a smaller dining chamber." And she smilingly stepped to the wall, turned a carved rose at one corner of the panel, and pressed it sidewise, showing a square opening through which a similarly furnished room could be seen.

"Send away those women," said the King sternly.

The hostess started, spoke to the two girls, who stepped back with the dishes, and she closed the door after them.

"One of my followers saw that panel move," said the King sternly. "There is some one there."

"Oh no, my lord," she cried, "The room is empty. Look."

"But the panel moved," cried Denis, "and I heard a sound."

"Impossible, sir," said the woman.

"Then what does this mean?" said the King, taking up the scrap of paper.

The woman took it, looked at it blankly, and passed it back.

"I don't know," she said. "It is a foreign tongue."

"Humph!" ejaculated the King. "This is strange, madam. That paper lay beneath my plate, and some one must have been watching us at our meal."

"No, my lord," said the woman; "it is impossible. Nobody could have been there. If anyone has dared—" She said no more, but angrily thrust the panel back into its place and turned the oaken rose, which gave a snap as of a bolt shooting into its socket, and then, raising her hand to the diagonal corner, she turned a fellow ornament in the oaken carving, to produce another sound as of a second bolt being shot.

"There," she cried, "it is quite fast now. One minute, and I will return."

She hurried out of the room, and the next minute they heard the sounds of knuckles rapping the panel on the other side and directly after the loud closing and locking of a door.

A few moments later, as the party stood there waiting, the woman was back at their side, to lay a large key upon the table, looking flushed and angry.

"I am very sorry, my lord and gentlemen," she cried, "and angry too"—a fact which was plainly enough marked in her countenance. "But this is a public inn, and some insolent idler, moved by curiosity, has dared to watch. I never imagined anyone would venture; and now I beg you will resume your meal."

"But there is the paper," said the King.

"Yes, yes," she said, "the paper. I do not understand."

"Ah, well," said the King, "we will not spoil our dinner; but I do not like to have hungry dogs watching while I make my meal. Sit down, gentlemen, and let us finish."

Setting the example, he recommenced, but thrust the half-finished bowl away with an impatient "Bah! The soup is cold. Here, hostess! Call those women back. And I want some wine. What have you in the house?"

"Some of the best vintages of France, my lord," said the woman eagerly, and drawing a deep breath of relief in the feeling that the trouble was at an end, though there was a twitching now and then at the corners of her eyes suggesting that she was not quite at ease.

The fresh dishes were placed upon the table as soon as the soup was removed, and soon after the hostess herself bore in a couple of rush-covered flasks of wine.

"Burgundy—Malvoisey," she said, indicating each in turn.

"The Burgundy," said the King, and as the glasses were filled, and they were once more quite alone, he made as if to tear up the paper, but altering his mind folded it quickly, and thrust it in the pouch he carried at his belt.

"Come, gentlemen," he said: "that scrap of paper shall not spoil a pleasant meal. It is a mere molehill in our path. Here's success to our expedition.—Hah! better vine than my own."

A few minutes later the hostess returned, and smiled once more upon finding that her guests were hard at work evidently in the full enjoyment of their meal.

"Ah, madam!" cried the King, raising his glass and drinking again. "You keep good wine. I would not have wished for better; but tell me, what other guests have you in the house?"

"None, my lord," said the woman frankly. "There have been some of the country people at the market, but they have gone. There was an ordinary traveller too, earlier in the day. He came from somewhere in the south, I believe, but he has gone. You are the only guests I have, and I humbly hope that the meats are to your liking."

"Excellent, madam, excellent," said the King, looking at her fixedly. "Then we are quite alone?"

The woman met his eye without wincing, and bowed gravely.

"Yes, my lord; quite alone."

"Then we will have no one here while we stay, madam. I like to be undisturbed. Understand me, please. I take the whole place, and you can charge me what you please."

The woman made a grave courtesy, and retired to see to the next course she had prepared, wiping her brow as soon as she was outside.

"Some great French noble," she muttered, "travelling to London, to the Court perhaps. I wonder who he is. Yes," she said to herself excitedly, "and I wonder too who dared to enter that next room. It must have been that evil-looking traveller, that starveling. I believe he was a thief. It could not have been— Oh no, I know them all by sight."

Chapter Ten
How Leoni lost his eye

The meal was ended, and the King in the best of tempers, in that condition of mind which a good digestion produces, and ready to be friends with all the world.

"It is absurd," he said, "to let a scrap of paper which may mean nothing, and the curiosity of some country idiot who wanted to get a peep at me, interfere with our enjoying a comfortable rest in this excellent inn, and then going on fresh and well in the morning."

"Then you mean to stay here to-night, sir?" said Denis anxiously.

"Of course, boy."

Saint Simon shook his head as if in dissent, and the King glared at him.

"Did you hear me, sir?" he cried. "I said I mean to stay here to-night."

Saint Simon drew back respectfully, and the King, apparently mollified, continued:

"An excellent dinner. I suppose it was having such a bad night, and tossing about. It has made me feel quite drowsy." And as he spoke he settled himself down in a big chair and closed his eyes, while those of the two young men met in a wondering glance, and had they dared, as they thought of the night they too had spent, they would have burst into a roar of laughter.

But they contented themselves with just raising their brows, and then sat there for a time silent and thoughtful. They could not converse for fear of disturbing their lord and master, who now began to breathe rather heavily. And then a curious thing happened to each: Saint Simon began to think of the frightfully wearying night he had passed, and in an instant the wind was whistling and shrieking through the rigging, the sea rising with a heavy splash against the vessel's bows, to now and then deluge the deck, and the shivering horses in turn were straining their muzzles towards him in the darkness as if appealing to be relieved from their miserable state.

With Denis it was on this wise. He sat back in his chair watching the King for a few minutes, before fixing his eyes upon the wall just to his left. Then he too as if in a moment was down in the dark cabin with the dim lamp swinging to and fro, and the King sleeping heavily and giving forth that deep breathing sound, while a panel seemed to have formed itself in the bulkhead of the ship, where it began gliding sideways till there was room for a hand to appear, holding a tiny scrap of paper. This was passed through very slowly, to be followed by wrist, elbow, and then the whole of an arm so long that it stretched out like a spear-shaft, and the fingers reached the King's plate and thrust the paper underneath.

Then it gradually shrank back and grew shorter and shorter till it had all passed through the panel, which next closed of itself with a soft dull roar. Then Denis's eyes opened and he sat up with a start, realising the fact that he had been fast asleep and that the closing of the panel was only the King's deep snore.

"Having no sleep last night," the lad said to himself. "Enough to make anyone drowsy; that and the long ride. Why, Saint Simon's worse than I was. Nice pair of guards we make! Suppose instead of an arm a spear were thrust through that panel, an enemy might reach his heart."

Making an effort to shake off his lethargy, the boy stepped to where Saint Simon lay back sleeping soundly, and then, buckling on his sword the while, he bent over him, took his sword-belt from where it hung over a corner of the chair back, and thrust the cold hilt into the heavy sleeper's hand.

"Quiet, my boy," muttered Saint Simon, "and keep your nasty cold wet muzzle out of my hand. We shall get there some time," he added murmuringly, "and you are all right. I am not going away."

"Pst! Pst! Saint Simon! Rouse up, man! Don't go to sleep."

"Is it nearly morning, skipper?" grumbled the sleeper.

"No, and it isn't night," whispered Denis, with his lips close to the other's ear. "Quiet, or you'll wake the King."

"The King—the King! Vive le roi!" muttered Saint Simon.

"Stupid!" whispered Denis, laying one hand lightly over Saint Simon's lips and shaking him softly with the other. "Wake up. You're asleep."

"I kiss your Majesty's hand," babbled the sleeper softly.—"Eh? Asleep? Nonsense! Who's asleep?"

Then coming suddenly to himself, his hand closed tightly upon the hilt of his sword, and dashing away the fingers upon his lips he sprang fiercely to his feet, gazing wonderingly at his companion.

"Pst! The King!" whispered Denis.

"Eh? The King?" said Saint Simon, lowering his voice and glancing at the slumbering monarch. "I say, I haven't been asleep, have I?"

"Sound as a dormouse in December."

"Oh, horrible! Suppose he had woke up. But he would have found you on the watch."

"He wouldn't," said Denis, laughing silently, "for I went off as sound as you; and no wonder after such a night. What with that and the dinner, and this hot room, a weasel couldn't have kept awake. Here, let's go outside into the open air. I want to see if the horses have been well fed."

"Yes, of course. We ought to have thought of that before," whispered Saint Simon; and together they crossed softly to the door, passed out, and closed it behind them without a sound; and then, with a soft pleasant air greeting their cheeks, they passed along the open hall, caught sight of their hostess, who smiled a reply to their salute, and entered the great inn-yard, going to the far end and the big range of stables where they had left their steeds.

"Yes," said Saint Simon thoughtfully, in response to his own thoughts, "we must look after the horses, or else the chief will be wishing again that he had brought the old physic-monger. Nice time we should have of it if he were here! He always makes me uncomfortable with those eyes of his. I should like to catch him asleep some time."

"Why? What for?"

"To put it to the test. But you never catch a weasel asleep, and I believe old Leoni always snoozes with one eye open."

"I daresay; and I wonder which. But what do you mean about putting it to the test?"

"Whether he can see with that fixed eye of his."

"Whether he can see? Why shouldn't he?"

"Why, you know, of course?"

"Not I. Why, of course he can."

"Do you mean to say that you have been all this time at Court and don't know about that?"

"About what?"

"About that eye of his."

"I only know that it's precious ugly, and used to make me very uncomfortable, because I always felt as if I must look at it instead of at the other or at both at once."

"But don't you know what they say?"

"Who do you mean by 'they'?"

"Well, *on*; everybody. That he had the point of a sword jabbed into it once when he was fencing."

"Oh, I never heard that," cried Denis. "Then that accounts for its queer fixed look."

"Queer fixed look? It's horrible! I don't think that I am quite a coward; but old Leoni, when he fixes me with that eye of his, quite gives me the creeps."

"Well, he does look queer sometimes. But I say, this is refreshing after that hot room," said Denis. "There's a great garden yonder, and open fields. I should like to have a wander there for an hour or two."

"So should I," said Saint Simon; "but we must get back, in case his lordship wakes."

"Yes. It won't do for us to forget ourselves. Esquires ought never to want to sleep," said Denis; and then quickly, "nor grooms nor hostlers neither. Here, look at these two red-faced pigs."

He pointed on to the two men who had taken charge of and rubbed down their chargers upon their arrival, and who were now lying in a heap of straw, eyes shut, mouth open, and with their heavy faces looking swollen and red, breathing stertorously.

"Why, the brutes are drunk," said Saint Simon. "If their mistress knew, I fancy their stay here would be short, for she seems a thorough business soul."

"Sim!" cried Denis excitedly, gripping him by the shoulder.

"What's the matter, lad? Can you see a ghost or a nightmare in the dark corner there?"

"No, nor can I see our horses. They were haltered yonder. Where are they now?"

"Ah!" yelled Saint Simon, and snatching out his sword he made as if to prick the two sleeping grooms into wakefulness; but Denis flung his arm across his chest and cried angrily:

"Never mind them! The horses, man, the horses—the horses! They may be only in the field, led there to graze."

"You are mad!" cried Saint Simon angrily. "But yes; go on out through that farther door."

Denis was already making for an opening at the far end of the long low building, through which the afternoon sunshine streamed. Passing out, they found themselves in an inner yard, and beyond that there was a long open meadow, surrounded by a high hedge. But for the moment all was blank, and a feeling of despair made the young men's hearts sink as they mentally saw at a glance that their beautiful chargers had not excited attention for nothing—that they had been followed, horse-thieves had been at work, and that their noble steeds were gone.

"How shall we dare to face the King?" thought Denis, and the next instant he grasped the fact that there must be a lane beyond the distant hedge, for he just caught sight of the head of a man whose covering seemed familiar gliding along above the fencing, now seen, now disappearing, as if he were mounted on a walking-horse.

"Look! Not too late, Sim," he whispered. "They're over yonder. We must make for that lane. I'll go this way to cut that fellow off; you go to the left there, to meet him if I turn him back."

"Think the horses are there?" whispered Saint Simon hoarsely.

"Think!" cried Denis, in a low, harsh voice that he did not know as his own. "No: I am sure."

No further words passed, for, separating at once, Denis dashed off to the right to make for the far corner of the field, in the faint hope of reaching it and getting through into the lane in time, while Saint Simon ran swiftly to the left to get into the horse-track there and follow the marauders up.

Chapter Eleven
First blood

Denis was in no trim for running, but he ran.

"This would wak He began running at a gentle trot now, to husband his strength for what might come, when all at once his heart seemed to give a violent leap and then stand still; for coming round a bend he caught sight of the black, heavily maned head of the King's horse, and then of the soft, pointed cap of the horse-dealer whom he had credited with the theft.

He was not looking forward, but bending over to his right, evidently doing something to the rein of another horse he was leading—Denis's own—while, in the middle of the three abreast, he was mounted on Saint Simon's. The three horses were fully in sight some fifty yards away, just as the man sat up again and began to urge them on from their walk, when he suddenly caught sight of Denis in the act of drawing his sword in the middle of the lane to bar his way.

The effect was to make him pull up short, and then with a cry to the horses he swung them round and set off back at a canter, to disappear round the bend directly after, with Denis running far in his rear.

"Now," panted the lad, "if Saint Simon has only done his work we have him between us." And he tried to utter a prolonged whistle, which he hoped might reach his charger's ear; but he had not breath to give more than the faintest call.

"Oh, if I could only run ten times as fast!" he groaned. "I know what he'll do. He will get them into a gallop, and ride my poor comrade down. If I were only at his side! And I seem to crawl!"

But he was running pretty fast, though to his misery he heard the dull *thud, thud* of the cantering horses grow fainter and fainter till it seemed to die right away.

"Sim's let them pass him," he groaned piteously. "*No*! No! No!" he literally yelled. "They are coming back! Saint Simon's turned them, and it will be my chance after all."

For still invisible, after the thudding of the hoofs had quite died out, the sounds came again; then louder, louder, and louder still, coming nearer and nearer, till all at once the noble animals swept into sight again round the curving lane, galloping excited and snorting, Saint Simon's horse right in the centre being urged forward by the rider, while the other two hung away right and left to the full extent of their reins. While perfectly unconscious of his peril, thinking of nothing but checking the headlong gallop, the lad stood with extended blade right in the middle of the lane.

It seemed an act of madness. Certainly he was a well-built youth, accustomed to athletic exercises, but as a barrier to three fine chargers urged by the rider of the centre one forward at a hand gallop, and armed only with a long thin Andrea Ferrara blade, he seemed but a fragile reed to stem the charge. But the unexpected happens more often than the reverse, and it was so here. One minute the horses were tearing along as far apart as the reins would allow; the next they seemed to have passed over the brave youth, and went galloping down the lane at increasing speed, leaving Denis flat upon his back in the middle of the road and his sword-arm outstretched in a peculiar way above his head, with the keen blade pointing in the direction taken by the steeds.

He lay perfectly motionless for some moments as if dead, while the horses tore on with the rider bending forward over his mount's neck till they had gone about a couple of hundred yards, when the man suddenly began to sway in his saddle to right, then to left, recovered himself, to sit upright for a few moments, and then with a sudden lurch went headlong down, to fall with a thud in the grassy track, roll over once or twice, and then begin to crawl to the hedge on his left, creep painfully through a gap, and disappear; while the horse he had ridden stopped short, like the well-trained beast he was, and turned to follow his late rider towards the hedge, snuffling and snorting in alarm.

The others continued their gallop for some seventy or eighty yards before, missing the guidance and companionship of their fellow, they too stopped short, to utter a low whinnying neigh, which was answered from behind and drew them trotting back to the halted beast.

By this time the marauder had disappeared, and the three chargers seemed to hold a consultation, uttering low whinnying neighs, and then, as if moved by one impulse, they trotted back slowly to where Denis lay with his head towards them, apparently dead. As they stopped short the youth's charger lowered its muzzle to begin to snuff at his face, when all at once the lad made a sudden movement to jerk back his outstretched arm into a more natural position, making his bright rapier describe an arc in the air, giving forth a bright flash in the afternoon sunshine and making a whistling sound like the lash of a whip. The consequence was that all three chargers started violently, to move off for a short distance; but as the lad was motionless again they stopped short and began to return, led by their companion, which seemed drawn to its fallen master. But before it could reach him there was the sound of feet, and Saint Simon came panting up to the group.

"Hah!" he ejaculated breathlessly, as he dropped on one knee by Denis's side. "Don't say you are hurt, lad! Not wounded, are you? Ah! There's blood upon his sword! Denis, lad, where are you wounded? For Heaven's sake speak! Oh, my poor brave lad! He's dead—he's dead!"

The drops that started to his eyes were a brave man's tears, blinding him for the time being as they fell fast, while he eagerly felt Denis's breast and neck, ending by unfastening his doublet and thrusting his hand within to feel for the beatings of his heart.

Those hot blinding tears fell fast, several of them upon Denis's upturned face, and at the fourth the nerves therein twitched; at the fifth there was a quick motion; and when six and seven fell together the lad's left hand came up suddenly to give an irritable rub where he felt a tickling sensation; and he opened his eyes, stared hard and blankly for some moments in the countenance so near his own, and exclaimed angrily:

"What are you doing?"

"Ah!" ejaculated Saint Simon, with a cry of joy. "Then the horses were worth winning back, after all."

"Horses? Winning?" faltered Denis wonderingly; and then as his companion snatched a hand from his breast, he cried again impatiently, "Here, what are you doing to my face?"

Saint Simon dashed his hand hastily across his own, his already ruddy countenance glowing of a deeper red, as he stammered out confusedly:

"Drops—perspiration—I have been having such a run."

"Drops? Run? My head's all of a buzz. Who ran? What have you been doing to my neck?" continued the lad, passing his left hand across his throat. "Something seemed to jerk across me just here. Ah, how it hurts!"

He made an effort then to raise his sword-arm, but it fell back upon the grass.

"Here, my shoulder's bad too," he cried. "Just as if my arm was wrenched out of the socket." Then as his wandering eyes fell upon his horse, "Oh!" he cried, "I understand now. I have been thrown."

"Never mind now," cried Saint Simon, in a choking voice, as he mastered the hysterical emotion that had seized upon him. "You're alive, boy, and we have saved the horses, and our credit with the—with the—"

"Comte," said Denis faintly. "I am beginning to recollect now. Here, where's that ruffian who was galloping away?"

"You've killed him, I suppose," cried Saint Simon, "for there's blood upon your sword. How was it, boy?"

"I don't know," said Denis dreamily; and then in an excited voice, "Yes, I do!" he cried. "I remember it all now. He came galloping along on the centre horse, with the others on each side at the full extent of their reins. I stood there to stop them, and he came right at me to ride me down. But I started a little on one side and thrust at him, when my horse's tight rein caught me right below the chin, and at the same moment my right arm was jerked upwards, and— that's all. Where is he now?"

"Gone," said Saint Simon, "and with your mark upon him too. Why, you brave old fellow! You, a mere boy! I daren't have faced three galloping horses like that. But you are not wounded?"

"My right arm seems to be gone. Is it broken, Sim?"

The young man began to feel it gently from shoulder to wrist, raised it, and laid it down again, while the boy bore it for a time, flinching involuntarily though again and again, till he could bear no more.

"Oh!" he groaned at last. "Don't! It's horrible! How you do hurt! I suppose I shall have no arm. It's horrible, Sim. I wish he had killed me out of hand."

"What! Why, my dear brave old fellow, it's only a horrible wrench, and will soon come right."

"Not broken?" cried the boy wildly.

"Broken? No, or it wouldn't move like that. Why, Denis, lad, when you gave point you must have run him through, and as he tore on your arm must have been wrenched round while he dragged himself or was carried away—of course, as the horses galloped on."

"But where is he?" cried Denis.

"I don't know. He wasn't here when I came up. He must have taken flight—I mean, crawled away, for he must have been wounded badly."

"But the horses are all right?" said Denis faintly.

"Yes; the brave beasts were as you see them now, standing round you. Ah! Stop a moment. What does this mean?"

He had been looking from side to side as he spoke, and caught sight of the crushed-down herbage which grew densely at the foot of the hedge, nettle and towering dock and hemlock looking as if something had crawled through; and, rising quickly, he found somewhat of a gap through which a person might have passed.

And he found ruddy traces which made him go on a few paces to where the hedge seemed thinner, so that he could force his way through, to return on the other side to the gap and see traces again in the grass where some one had crawled. This track he followed for a few yards to a spot where the long grass was a good deal trampled, and beyond that there were regular footprints, as if some one had risen and walked light across the field.

"Gone," said Saint Simon to himself; and he hurried back to the lane, where Denis was lying very still with his eyes closed, and the three horses ready to raise their heads from where they were calmly cropping the thick herbage and ready to salute him with a friendly whinny before resuming their meal.

"Well, Denis, boy," he cried, "how is it now?"

"Oh, a bit sick and faint, but I'm better. Have you found that brute?"

"No; he has gone right away. But we don't want him, unless he comes back to take revenge on you, and then I should like to see you use your sword again."

"Oh!" groaned Denis. "With an arm like this! I feel as if I should not lift it again for months."

"Bah! Nonsense, man—boy, I mean," said Saint Simon, with a laugh. "But I say, you must have given it to him somewhere. He was bleeding like a pig. I followed his track to where he must have sat down on the grass to bind up his wound. And there he stopped it, to rise and walk off, making good strides for a dead man. You gave him his pay for horse-stealing, and I'll be bound to say he feels more sore than you, my hero. Now then, how do you feel about getting up?"

"I feel sick, and as if I want to lie."

"But the—ahem!—Comte? He must be awake by now."

"Ah! I forgot him. Here, give me your hand—Thanks—Ah!—It hurts horribly—my throat's better—but my arm feels as though it had been screwed out of the joint. Would you mind sheathing my sword? I can't."

"I ought to have done it before," said Saint Simon; "but I say, lad, let go. Why, your fingers are grasping it with quite a grip."

"Are they?" said the boy faintly. "I don't feel as if I had any. Everything is hot and numb."

"Yes, you have had a nasty wrench. But that will soon be right. We soldiers don't mind unless we are killed. That's better. Here, let's wipe the blade," and he picked a bunch of grass. "I am not going to soil my kerchief with the ruffian's blood. That's better," he continued, as he returned the long thin blade to its sheath. "I'll give it a polish for you when we get back to the inn. Now do you think you could mount?"

"No, not yet," said the boy. "Give me a little time."

"Hours, lad; and here, let me arrange your scarf. Stand still. That's the way. Over your right shoulder—tied in a knot—now opened out widely here so that your arm can rest in it, like that. Those are soldiers' knots for a wounded limb.—That feel easier?"

"Not much," said Denis. "Yes, that's better. It seems to take the weight, and I'm beginning to feel that I've got one now."

"Oh, yes, it will soon come round," cried Saint Simon joyfully. "Now, boys, it's time you left off sullying your bits with grass," he continued, to the horses, as he unbuckled their reins, so that in leading one he led all three; and offering his right arm to Denis, who gladly took it and leant upon it heavily, he led the way back along the lane to where they had parted, and from thence into the great stable-yard and through the long stable to where the two hostlers were still sleeping heavily, not in the slightest degree roused by the trampling of the chargers upon the stone-paved floor.

"Now then," said Saint Simon, "shall we tie up the horses here again?"

"No," cried Denis sharply. "Look—through the door yonder. There's the Comte!"

Chapter Twelve
A well-meant warning

Saint Simon glanced in the direction indicated, to see across the yard the King standing at the open doorway, talking, and evidently questioning their hostess, who was pointing towards the stable where the young men were.

"Now for a storm, Denis, boy, with plenty of royal thunder, and flashes of lightning from his kingly eyes. Bah! How hard it is to forget his rank! How are you now?"

"Oh, better. The sight of — the Comte seems to string me up."

"Come on, then, to make our excuses for the breach of duty, and take our three witnesses to back our words."

The young men led the chargers out through the low doorway into the yard and began crossing to where the King was drawing himself up with a stern look upon his countenance, his right hand upon his hip, his left upon his sword-hilt, which he kept on pressing down and elevating and lowering the long thin blade behind him, the afternoon sun throwing it out in a long dark streak from his shadow, giving him the effect of some monster wagging its wiry tail.

The hostess was still there, drawing back a little into the shadow of the comparatively dark doorway, a mingling of curiosity and sympathy detaining her to hear how her offending guests would fare.

She had not long to wait, for as the young men came up with the horses' hoofs clattering upon the paved way, "Now, gentlemen," was growled forth, "why am I left like this? And by whose orders have you brought forth those steeds?"

"What!" thundered the King fiercely, after hearing a brief narration of his followers' adventure; and turning to their hostess, who heard every word and stood loaning forward with agitated face and clasped hands, "And so, madam, you call this the safety of your inn! This, then, is the meaning of that warning paper which you have disavowed. Gentlemen, we seem to have settled in a nest of thieves. Have your valises placed at your saddles. I thank you for the way in which you have saved us from disaster at the beginning of our journey. We will ride on at once."

"Oh," ejaculated the hostess, "that it should come to this!" And ceasing to wring her hands she ran out past them and crossed the yard to the open stable-door, disappeared for just long enough to verify the young men's words by a sight of the sleeping grooms, and then came running back to where her guests were making preparations to continue their journey.

"Oh, my lord," she cried, "it is a disgrace and shame to my house that all this should have taken place. I pray your forgiveness."

"Indeed, madam!" said the King haughtily. "Tell my gentlemen there what there is to pay, and spare your words."

"But, my lord—"

"Silence, madam! I have spoken. Gentlemen—"

"But, my lord," she interrupted, "I will have trusty strong men to watch the stables and the house all night. This was the work of a stranger—some horse-thief from afar. It cannot occur again."

The King waved his hand, and turned to his followers.

"Gentlemen, you will not leave those horses a moment. Finish the preparations. Pay this woman, Saint Simon, and come and tell me when all is ready for the start."

Then turning his back upon the hostess, he strode into the house, fuming with rage and glowering fiercely at the group of servants whom he passed.

"Oh, woe is me!" sobbed the landlady, wringing her hands. "That this great misfortune should happen to such a noble lord as this! And this gallant boy too, hurt as he is! No, no, sir," she cried pettishly to Saint Simon, who approached her, purse in hand; "don't talk to me about money. I am thinking of the honour of my house. There, there," she cried, lowering her tone; and she caught Denis by the doublet and signed to his friend to come closer. "Your lord is angry," she said, "and he has just cause; but you two must speak to him and try to calm his wrath. I have made all preparations for his staying here to-night, and believe me, everything is safe. I will have trusty friends in, and not a soul here but you shall close an eye. You must sleep here to-night."

"Must, madam?" said Denis, forgetting his own sufferings in something like amusement at his hostess's pertinacity. "There is no must with our lord."

"Don't say that, my child," cried the woman anxiously. "He must give way to-night. I can see with a mother's eye that you are not fit to mount your horse. You are hurt, and need rest. Go to him and persuade him that he must stay."

"Madam, it is impossible," said Denis; "and leave me, please. You heard our lord's commands. We have our preparations to make."

As he spoke Denis glanced at Saint Simon, who had waved back a man who came to help, and was examining their horses' girths himself. Then, turning his eyes towards the doorway, he caught sight of the King returning, unnoticed by the landlady, who clutched at Denis's doublet again, and continued in a low, excited voice:

"You do not know, my child. Before long it will be dark."

"There will be a moon nearly at the full, madam," said Denis.

"Oh yes, yes, sir; if it is not clouded over; but the road from here towards London is through the forest and overhung with trees and—and," she added, in a whisper, "it is not safe."

"We have our swords, madam," said the youth; but he winced as he spoke, for his right arm seemed to give him a sudden warning twinge of his inability to use his weapon. "What do you mean about the road not being safe?"

The woman drew herself closer to him, and her ruddy buxom face became blotched with white.

"Bad men," she whispered. "Robbers and murderers have a stronghold in the forest, from which they come out to lay wait for rich travellers."

"Are they mounted men?" said Denis, as the King slowly drew nearer.

"Yes," she said, "with the best of horses."

"And do they steal horses too?"

"Oh yes," she whispered, with a shudder.

"Then that man who watched us here was one of them, was he not?" cried Denis excitedly.

The woman's jaw dropped, and the whiteness in her countenance increased.

"You saw that man, and you know!" cried Denis excitedly again.

The woman closed her lips and seemed to press them tightly together, as she said in a strange voice:

"You will be advised by me, and stay here, where you will be safe. I cannot—I will not—let you go."

"Indeed!" said the King fiercely, and the woman started as she realised that her guest had heard her words.

"Back into your own place, madam," continued the King. "I allow no one to tamper with my servants."

The woman shrank trembling back, for there was that in her guest's manner which she felt she must obey; and with her hands clasped to her breast as if to restrain her emotion, she went slowly into the house, the King watching her, till she turned her head, started on encountering his eyes, and then disappeared.

"There, it's plain enough, gentlemen. This woman is in league with a band of the rogues."

"I think not, sir," said Denis quickly. "I think she is honest, and her trouble real."

"Indeed?" said the King mockingly. "Wait till you have a few more years over your head, boy, before you attempt to give counsel to one who is used to judge mankind. Foolish boy! Can't you see that it is part of her work to trap travellers into staying at her house? Why, I believe if we rested here we should be plunged into a long deep sleep, and one from which we should never wake. Now, Saint Simon, you ought to have finished. I want to mount and go."

"The horses are ready, my lord," said the young man quickly.

"But you have not paid the woman."

"I offered her ample, sir, and she refused it."

"Bah! Leave that to me," said the King haughtily. "But what about you, Denis, boy? Don't tell me that you are too bad to mount, and force me to stay in this vile nest of thieves."

"No, sir. If Saint Simon will help me to mount, I'll manage to ride the long night through; but I fear if there is need that I could not fight."

The King hesitated, and stood striking his two stout riding gloves twisted together sharply in his left hand.

"Yes, you look hurt, boy. Perhaps it will be better that we should stay. We could hold one room, unless they burnt us out, and take turn and turn to watch."

"Oh no, sir; I am well enough to go," cried the lad. "Here, Saint Simon, give me a leg up. I am better now, and shall feel easier still when in the saddle."

"Keep back, Saint Simon!" said the King. "Let me be the judge of that. Here, your foot, boy? Do you hear me, sir? Quick!"

The lad raised his foot as the King impatiently clasped his hands stirrup fashion and raised the young horseman smartly, so that he flung his right leg over and dropped lightly into the saddle.

"Well," continued the King, as he watched his young esquire keenly, "can you sit there, or are you going to swoon?"

The boy smiled scornfully, and the King gave him an encouraging nod.

"You will do," he said, "and if you cannot use your arm you will be able to ride between us if we are attacked and charge the scoundrels when we make them run. Mount, Saint Simon. Have we left aught behind?"

"No, sir," replied the young man, and he hesitated a moment to let the King be first in the saddle; but an angry gesture made him spring into his seat, urge his charger forward, and hold the bridle till his master was mounted, pressed his horse's sides, and then reined up shortly in the great entry of the inn, level with the door at which the hostess was standing, pale and troubled, and backed up by the servants of the place.

"Here, woman," cried the King, drawing his hand from his pouch; "hold out your apron. Quick! Don't stand staring there."

The words were uttered in so imperious a tone that the woman involuntarily obeyed, and half-a-dozen gold pieces fell into her stiff white garment with a pleasant chink.

The next minute, in answer to a touch of the spur, the horses went clattering through the entry out into the main street, the noise they made arousing the two hostlers from their sleep to come yawning and staring to the open stable-door, while the hostess stepped out into the entry and hurried to the front with hand clasped in hand.

"Oh, that gallant boy," she muttered, with her face all drawn. "If I had only dared to tell them more plainly! But they would have marked me if I had, and it is as much as my life is worth to speak. Why does not our King put an end to these roving bands who keep us all in a state of terror and make us slaves?"

Chapter Thirteen
An unknown land

The ride out from the town was uneventful, save that the people hurried to their windows and doors to see them pass, and admire the beauty of their steeds. Then as the city gate was passed and they rode out into the open country, with the way before them seeming perfectly clear, the King cried cheerily:

"Hah! I can breathe freely now. I must tell my brother Henry that the road to his Court is a disgrace, and travellers' lives not safe. Now, in my kingdom of beautiful France every road to the capital from the seaports is— Why are you looking at me like that, Saint Simon?"

"Well, sir," said the young man bluntly, "I was thinking about two or three cases where people have been waylaid and plundered and—"

"Yes, yes, yes," said the King impatiently; "I think that there was a case or two, but surely we are better than this. Well, Denis, boy; how's the bad arm?"

"Very stiff, sir, and aches; but I don't mind now."

"Not you, boy! Too brave a soldier! Ha, ha, ha! I almost think that I can see it all. My faith! I would I had been there to have seen you, you stripling, standing sword in hand in that lane to meet that ruffian's charge with three horses abreast. And you wounded him too, and saved the beasts. I should like to see the young Englishman who would do a deed like that! Why, Saint Simon, you and I must look after our laurels. We ought to be proud of our companion, eh?"

"Oh, sir," shouted Denis, giving a cry of pain, for as he spoke the King had clapped him heartily upon the shoulder that was nearest to him— unfortunately the right.

"Tut, tut, tut!" cried the King, leaning towards him, for the lad turned ghastly white. "There, hold up, boy. I wanted to show you how pleased I was with the bravery of your deed, and I have only given pain."

"Not only, sir," said the lad quickly. "Your hand hurt me for the moment, but my K— lord's words of praise are thrilling still."

"Just saved yourself, boy," cried Francis; "for if you dare to say you know what till we are back again in my own fair France your punishment will be short and sharp." He gave Saint Simon a merry look as he spoke, and then rode gently on, sweeping the landscape with his eye and making comments from time to time. "Better and better," he said pleasantly. "My brother Henry has a goodly land. All this woodland landscape forms a pleasant place. Hah! but he should see my hills and forests about Rouen, with the silver river winding through the vale. But that is far away, and this is near, and it will pass if we do not meet the dangers that woman prophesied upon our road."

They rode on in silence for a time, just at a gentle amble, the King giving a shrewd look now and again at his young companion to see how he bore the motion of the horse.

It was a glorious evening, and they saw the sun sink like a huge orange globe; the soft, warm, summer evening glow seeming to rise and spread around them from the west.

There was a sweet delicious fragrance in the air, and the soft English landscape began gradually to darken from green to purple, and then to deeper shades, while as the glow in the west disappeared the eastern sky grew more pearly; but the indications of the rising moon were not as yet.

"Hah!" cried the King at last, speaking as if to two companions of his own rank enjoying with him a summer evening ride. "Here have I been so taken up with our late adventures that I have had no thought of what is to come. Our saddles are comfortable, and after that pleasant dinner and my nap I feel ready for anything. But there will come a time when we shall want to think of supper and of bed, for we can't go on riding all night even if we are undisturbed. Now then, Saint Simon, what have you to say?"

The young man slowly shook his head.

"Bah!" cried the King. "What a dumb dog you are! And I know nothing of the way. I begin to feel that we ought to have had old Leoni with us, after all. He has maps, and knowledge always ready in his brain; and he speaks these islanders' language better than they can themselves. But he would only have been in the way, and I wanted freedom. Here, Denis, boy, what have you to say? Where shall we sleep to-night?"

"I had scarcely time, sir, to mark down our course, and the only place I can recall is one called Hurstham."

"Ah!" cried the King. "What of that?"

"I know nothing, sir, except that there is a good road over hills and through forests, and that there is a castle there."

"Then that will do," cried the King. "Once within its walls we can laugh at thieves and murderers. There, boy, you have your task before you: lead us there."

"But I do not know the way, sir. Would it not be best to get a guide from the first village we ride through?"

"Excellent!" cried the King—"for him to lead us straight into the den of the forest outlaws."

"It would be his last journey, sir," said Saint Simon grimly, as he significantly touched the hilt of his sword.

"And what good would that do us," said the King, "if we never saw tomorrow's sun? Here, I must lead. Look out sharp, both of you, for the next guide-post or stone. I will warrant that those old Romans planted some of them beside the road, telling the way to London."

"Yes, sir," said Denis drily, "but it will soon be dark."

"Ah, well, we must chance everything. I don't believe that we shall find the road unsafe; but even if it is we must keep to it all the same. It will lead us somewhere, and—hah! here comes the moon!"

It was a welcome light for the travellers, who rode slowly on to ease their steeds, for as the King said, they had all the night before them, and sooner or later, even if they did not reach the castle, they were sure to pass upon this direct road to London some good town where they might venture to stay. But the miles seemed to grow longer, the country more hilly, wild and strange, and, in spite of all endeavours to keep bravely to their task, the two young men had the weight of the past night's watch upon their brains. The consequence was that just after crossing what seemed to be an open furzy down, and when the road, looking white in the moonlight, had turned gloomy and black, save where it was splashed by the silvery light on the trees of the forest patch into which they had passed, they began to nod upon their horses, and the King's voice grew as he talked into an incoherent drone.

Then they were wide awake again, for just in the darkest part, where the trees met together across the road, a shrill clear whistle rang out, which made all draw rein and listen to the sound of horses' hoofs clattering upon the hard road they had just traversed.

Chapter Fourteen
The war-cry

The whistle in front and the sound of following horsemen had but one meaning for Denis, and that was danger; and there was a movement common to nearly everyone in bygone days when danger was afoot, and that was to throw the right hand across the body in search of the hilt of the sword with which every traveller was armed.

It was involuntary then that, upon hearing the whistle and the trampling hoofs, Denis tried to draw his sword, but only uttered a faint cry of pain, for nerve and muscle had during the past few hours stiffened and made him more helpless than before, so that his arm sank back into its sling, but with the hand sufficiently free to receive the reins, which he passed across, thus leaving his left hand at liberty for his dagger.

"Hah!" said the King. "They are not fools. They have chosen a likely place for their trap, and we have walked right in. Well, gentlemen, we don't surrender. Which is it to be—retreat or advance?"

"Advance!" cried the young men, in one breath, excitedly, and it sounded like one voice.

"Draw, then, and forward," cried the King. "You, Saint Simon, guard Denis on the left; I shall have the honour of forming his right flank. But no desultory fighting. We advance and keep together as one man with one aim—to pass through the enemy, however many they may be. Forward!"

Denis writhed at his helplessness, as in obedience to a touch of the spur the three horses sprang forward, kept in the centre of the dark road, and broke at once into a hand gallop; and for some fifty yards the way seemed perfectly clear.

Then all at once the route was barred by a number of men who sprang from each side, yelling and shouting, while from behind the trampling of horses came nearer, and the advance was checked; for apparently with reckless bravery men rushed out of the darkness to seize the horsemen's reins, with the result that the King struck at the nearest a downward blow with the hilt of his sword, which took effect full in the man's face, so that he sank with a groan, while, drawing back his arm, the King's second movement was to give point, running the next man through the shoulder, and he fell back.

Saint Simon's actions were much the same, but in reverse, for he thrust first, and equally successfully; while Denis sat supine, the feeling upon him strong that he was a helpless heavy log to his companions, and in their way.

So successful was the resistance to the attack that for the moment the way seemed open, and the boy's breast began to throb with excitement as he felt that they had won. But they had only dealt with four, and as they were urging on their horses once again at least a dozen were ready to stay their progress, while with a loud shout of triumph four mounted men came up in their rear to hem the trio in.

"Give point! Give point!" roared the King, setting the example, and every thrust seemed to tell; but where one enemy went down there seemed to be three or four more to take his place, and in the darkness there was a *mêlée* of writhing, struggling men hanging on to the panting, snorting horses and regardless of the keen steel, striving to drag the wielders down.

"It's all over with us," thought Denis, and a chill of despair seemed to clutch his heart, as he rose in his stirrups and, dagger in hand, strove, but in vain, to give some aid to his two defenders, who were growing breathless with their exertions and hampered and overpowered by their foes.

The horses, too, were becoming frantic, and reared and plunged, greatly to the riders' disadvantage, but advantage too, for more than one of the assailants fell back from the blows struck by their hoofs, to be trampled the next moment under foot; and then amidst yells, threats, and savage cries, there was a fresh shout of triumph, for on either side the defenders' arms were held, and but for the way in which the well-trained horses pressed together, both the King and Saint Simon would have been pulled from their saddles.

Just at this crucial moment, in the midst of the lull which followed the triumphal yell, there was the loud trampling of hoofs upon the hard road in front, the shouting of a war-cry—"France! France!"—seemed to cut through the darkness, and with a rush a single horseman looking like a dark shadow dashed down upon the group, scattering, so to speak, with wondrous rapidity a perfect shower of thrusts, making those who pinioned King and courtier fall back, some in surprise and dread, others in agony or in death, leaving their prisoners at liberty to assume the offensive once again and aid their new supporter in his gallant efforts upon their behalf.

"Right!" he shouted, in a strange shrill voice. "About at once! Now, all together, charge!" And, taking advantage of the temporary astonishment of the enemy, the new-comer ranged himself by the King's side, and all setting spurs to their horses, the brave beasts shook themselves free from those who grasped their reins, and together broke into a gallop, trampling down and driving to the right and left those who, half-hearted now, held fast and strove to stop their way.

The attempt was vain, and away the little party went along the dim, shadowy road for about a hundred yards, when the stranger's voice rose above the trampling hoofs in the order to halt and turn, followed by a louder command to charge back once more.

They needed no urging on the part of the riders, for the horses, excited now to the fullest extent, recognised the orders, and broke into a gallop once again, dashing back over the ground they had just traversed towards where men were gathering together in obedience to excited voices and preparing to once more stop their way. For the danger was not yet over; the first charge had driven the horsemen, who had so far not been seen but heard, into a headlong flight; but at the halt they had rallied again, and as the gallant little band of four had turned for their second charge were coming on in full pursuit.

"Gallop!" yelled their new ally, and even in the wild excitement of those few moments, while he seemed borne here and there like the prisoner of his friends, the only help given being by the weight of his horse, Denis fell to wondering who the gallant Englishman could be that had come so opportunely to their aid; for there was a something not familiar in the tones which, trumpet-like, gave forth their orders, but somehow strange in the way in which they seemed to raise echoes in his brain.

"Gallop!" he yelled again. "France! France!" And like a flash the question darted through the boy's brain, why should he use the battle-cry of France?

Momentary all this as, before reaching the little, dimly seen crowd that once more barred the way, the chargers attained their fullest speed; and then there were a few slight shocks as man after man went down in their half-hearted resistance, and the rest were scattered, the little line of horsemen passing through them, driving them here and there, and charging on in their headlong gallop forward beneath the overhanging trees which suddenly ceased to darken their way, for the gallant band had passed out into the full bright moonlight once again, and the sound of pursuit by the enemy's mounted men had died away.

Chapter Fifteen
The friend in need

They must have gone a mile at full gallop before the King cried "Halt!"

As the beat of their horses' hoofs ceased he sat with raised hand as if commanding silence, listening; but the heavy breathing of the four steeds was the only sound that broke the silence of the glorious night.

"Forward slowly now," said the King quietly. "The danger is past for the moment, and we shall have good warning if they come on again, for it is not likely that they have thrown out a second detachment to take us if we escaped the first. Now, just one word—who is hurt? Denis, my brave lad, how is it with you?"

"You took too much care of me, my lord. I am only hot."

"Well done!" cried the King. "And you, Saint Simon?"

"A bit battered with blows, sir," replied the young man; "and I expect when the day dawns I can show some rags."

"No wounds?" cried the King.

"Not a scratch, sir."

"But what of you, sir?" cried Denis eagerly, "I am afraid you must have suffered badly."

"I have," said the King shortly. "I feel as if my beauty is spoiled by a blow one ruffian struck at my face. But he was the one who suffered," he added, with a low hiss suggestive of satisfaction. "But no more selfishness. Though I have left him to the last, it is not that I do not want to thank our gallant English preserver, who has given us the best of proofs that he is ready to welcome strangers to his shores. I don't know by what means you knew, sir, of our peril, or why you should think it worth your while to play the brave knight, and fight against such odds to rescue us from the spoilers, and perhaps from death. Pray give me your name, sir, that we three strangers may bury it deeply in our hearts as one of the most gallant islanders we shall ever meet."

"My name, your Majesty?" said the stranger quietly.

"What!" cried the King. "You know who I am?"

"As well as your Majesty knows his faithful servant," came now in familiar tones.

"Master Leoni!" cried all three, in a breath, the King's voice sounding loudest of all.

"Yes, Sire," said the owner of the name quietly, as if there were no such thing as excitement left in his composition, and instead of being a fighting man he was the most peaceable of souls. "Your Majesty, in the fullness of your confidence, thought you would not need your follower's services, but I feared that you would, and hence I came. You see, you did."

"But how—and mounted! How came you here? You bade us farewell at Fontainebleau a week ago."

"Yes, Sire; a week gave me plenty of time, as you travelled slowly, to get to the port two days earlier than you. I have been well before you all the time."

"Then that paper!" cried Denis excitedly. "It was you who placed that beneath the King's trencher at the inn?"

"I did, Master Denis," said Leoni quietly, "and I think the warning was needed. It would have been safer if his Majesty had taken it to heart, though I feared in his reckless bravery he would laugh at my warning, and so I kept watch and came on in advance."

"Then you knew that the road was haunted by folk like these?" said the King.

"Yes, Sire; I found that in a forest not far from here they have a gathering place, and are always on the look-out for rich travellers on the way to London. They have spies at the port and at the principal towns to give them warning, and I wonder that you escaped so far without the loss of your horses."

"Humph!" ejaculated the King sourly. "We should have lost them but for the brave action of young Denis here; but look you, Master Leoni," he continued sternly, "I gave you my commands to keep watch and ward over my goods and chattels at my palace of Fontainebleau until my return."

"Your Majesty did," said Leoni humbly.

"And disobedience to my commands is treason, sir, and the punishment of that is death."

"Yes, Sire; but your royal life is the greatest of your possessions, and I felt that might be in danger. You gave me a free hand to do what was best in your service, and even if I have offended I deemed it my duty to save my sovereign's life even at the cost of my own. Your Majesty, I have no further defence to make."

"Hah!" said the King. "He has disarmed me, boys, and I as his master almost feel that I cannot order him to execution for such a crime as this. What say you, Denis, lad?"

"I say, sir," said the boy, laughing softly, "that this is England, sir, and that you are not King, but my Lord the Comte de la Seine, who has no power to inflict such a punishment as this."

"Hah!" said the King, chuckling. "And you, silent Wisehead Saint Simon, what is your judgement?"

"Oh, sir, I think Denis is quite right; but I should like to add one thing."

"Hah!" cried the King. "This fight has made you find your tongue, my lad. Now then, let's have what you think about Master Leoni's offence."

"I think, sir, that we had better get on a little faster, for I don't want another fight to-night."

"Neither do I," said the King, laughing softly, "for I am sore all over, and I should be miserable if it were not for the thought that this ruffian gang must have suffered far more than we. Why, Master Leoni, the point of your sword I could well believe must have been everywhere at once."

"A trick of fence, sir, merely a trick of fence," said Leoni quietly. "Your lordship knows how for years I have studied every Italian trick, and it comes easy and useful at a time like this."

"My faith, yes!" said the King, drawing a deep breath. "There, Master Leoni, I must forgive you this time; but don't offend again. Now then, before we drop into a canter, I believe you know the English roads by heart: can you act as our guide to-night?"

"I have studied them a little, sir, and been along here three times before."

"Then you can take us to a place of safety?"

"Yes, sir, I can; and you will pardon me when I tell you that four days ago I sent forward a trusty messenger to an old town some ten miles from here where there is a fine old manor-house, the home of a studious English nobleman of whom I asked for hospitality for the noble Comte de la Seine should he by any possibility on his journey to the English Court appeal to him on his way. I and Sir John Carrbroke have often corresponded upon matters of scientific lore, and you will be made welcome as my patron, you may be sure."

"Hah!" cried the King. "There seems to be no end to you, Leoni. You know everything, and are always ready at a pinch. Well, I must let you serve me this time, but to-morrow morning, mind, I shall be sore and stiff, and savage as a Compiegne wild boar, so you had better keep beyond the reach of my tusks when I order you back to France."

"I take your warning, sir," said Master Leoni, rising in his stirrups and placing his hand to his ear.

"Hah!" cried the King. "Are they coming on again?"

"No, sir; all is quiet, but we have many good English miles to ride, and it would be wise to keep our horses at a steady pace to get well beyond the outlaws' grasp, for you do not want to reach my old friend's manor and rouse his people up with a following of outlaws at our heels."

"There, I give up," said the King, "and I must give you your due, Leoni. You are the wisest man I know, and I am afraid that you possess a very ungrateful master. Forward, gentlemen, and let's get there, for I am beginning to grow boar-like and to long to stretch my sore and weary limbs in a good bed, if I can, or merely on a heap of straw. Here, Leoni, I suppose you have not brought any of that healing salve with which you have treated me more than once when I came to misfortune in the hunt?"

"By rights, sir, I am a *chirurgien*, or leech," said Leoni gravely. "On my travels a few simples and my little case are things I never leave behind."

These were almost the last words spoken during the ten-mile ride, the latter part being intensely silent, until Leoni drew rein upon the slope of a wooded hill and pointed across a little valley, where a silver streamlet flashed before their eyes, to the gables of a long low English manor-house whose diamond-shaped casements glittered like the facets of so many gems in a setting of ivy, full in the light of the unclouded moon.

Chapter Sixteen
The next morning

"Yes! Hallo! What is it?"

Denis started up upon his left elbow, gazing in a confused way at a glistening oaken door.

He was in a well-furnished room with tall narrow window through which the sun shone brightly, lighting up the furniture, and streaming across the bed in which he lay; but for some moments it did not light up his intellect, which was still oppressed with the impressions of a confused dream, half real, half imaginary, of chasing horses, being ridden down, fighting for life, and then galloping on and on all through the night, while as he stared at the door he was conscious of a heavy, dull, aching pain extending from his right hand right up his shoulder, and giving him sharp twinges every time he breathed.

"Some one called," he thought to himself, and as the idea passed through his brain a pleasant-sounding voice said in English:

"Breakfast directly. May I come in?" Then the door was thrown open, and a handsome, frank-looking English youth of about his own age came quickly forward into the sunshine, to stand gazing at the guest from the foot of the bed.

"I hope you slept well?" he said eagerly.

Denis looked at him admiringly, for there was something about the lad's face which attracted him.

"Oh yes," he said—"Oh no. It has been all a troubled dream. I got hurt yesterday, and my arm throbs horribly."

"Ah!" cried the new-comer. "I am very sorry. You are wounded?"

"No; I was in a bit of a fight with a man on horseback."

"You were? I wish I had been there!" cried the new-comer eagerly. "Well? did you beat him?"

"I think so. He ran away. But I had my arm nearly wrenched out of the socket."

"That's bad. You have had it seen to by a doctor, of course?"

"Oh no. It will get well. But who are you?"

"Oh, I'm Sir John Carrbroke's son Edward; but he always calls me Ned. I was so tired last night and slept so soundly that I didn't hear you and your friends come. Father woke me a little while ago and told me to come and see you and welcome you to the Pines. Glad to see you. You've just come from France, haven't you? But I needn't ask," continued the boy, smiling. "Anyone would know you were French."

Denis flushed a little.

"Of course I can't talk English like you," he said pettishly. "But you said something about breakfast."

"Yes. It will be all waiting by the time you are dressed."

"Then would you mind going—and—"

"Oh yes, of course; I'll go. Only I wanted to see our new visitor, and—but you said your arm was all wrenched."

"Yes. I have only a misty notion about how I managed to undress."

"Of course. It must have been very hard. Here, I'll stop and help you."

Denis protested, but the frank outspoken lad would not hear a word.

"Nonsense," he said. "I shall help you. I know how. I am a sort of gentleman in waiting at the Court."

"Indeed!" cried Denis, looking at him wonderingly.

"Oh yes. I haven't been there long. My father used to be just the same with the late King, and that made him able to get me there. It's only the other day that I left the great school—a year ago, though; and now," he added, laughing, "I am going to be somebody big—King Harry's esquire—the youngest one there. I say, isn't it a nuisance to be only a boy?"

"Oh no," said Denis, laughing, and quite taken by the friendly chatter of his new acquaintance. "One wants to grow up, of course; but I don't know that I ever felt like that."

"Perhaps not," said his companion, busily helping him with his garments; "but then you see you're not at Court where there are a lot of fellows who have been there for a bit, ready to look down upon you just because you're new, and glare at you and seem ready to pick a quarrel and to fight if ever the King gives you a friendly nod or a smile.—No, no: I'll tie those points. Don't hurt your arm—but wait a bit.—I am young and inexperienced yet, and they're too much for me, but I am hard at it."

He ceased speaking, but stood with his mouth pursed up, frowning, as he tied the points in question.

"I see you are," said Denis, "playing servant to me; and it's very good of you, for my arm does feel very bad."

"Good! Nonsense!" cried the lad merrily. "You'd do the same for me if I were visiting at your father's house, and crippled."

"That couldn't be," said Denis sadly. "I have no father's house—he's dead."

"Oh, I am sorry!"

"He was a soldier, and died fighting for the King."

"Hah!" said the other softly. "That's very pitiful; but," he added, with more animation, "it is very grand as well.—No, no, no: be quiet! I'm here, and what's the good of making your arm worse? You're a visitor; and you wouldn't like me to go away and send one of our fellows. I shall be a knight some day, I hope; and it's a knight's duty to fight, of course, but he ought to be able to help a wounded man. Now you're a wounded man and I'm going to help you, wash you and all, and I say, you want it too. You look as if you had been down in the dust. And what's this? Why, there's clay matted in the back of your neck!"

"Well," said Denis, smiling, "I am such a cripple I can't help myself, and so I must submit."

"Of course you must. I'll feed you too, if you like, by-and-by."

"But what did you mean," said Denis, to change the conversation, as he smilingly yielded himself to the busy helpful hands of his new friend.

"What did I mean? Why, to help you."

"No, no; I meant about those fellows riding roughshod over you and wanting to pick quarrels."

"Oh, I see. I meant, I'm waiting my time. Can you fence—use a sword well?"

"Not very, but I'm practising hard."

"Are you? So am I. We've got a French *maître d'armes* at Court, and he's helping me and teaching me all he knows. He's splendid! He likes me because I work so hand, and pats me on the back, and calls me 'grand garçon' and dear pupil. Ah, he's a wonder. Only he makes me feel so stupid. He's like one of those magician fellows when you cross swords with him. Yes, it's just like magic; for when he likes he can make his long thin blade twist and twine about yours as if it were a snake and all alive; and before you know where you are it tightens round, and then *twit, twang*, yours is snatched out of your hand and gone flying across the room, making you feel as helpless as a child. Ah, you don't know what it is to feel like that. I say, hold still. How am I to wipe you? That's better."

"But I do know what it is to feel like that," cried Denis, as soon as he could get his face free from the white linen cloth his new friend was handling with great dexterity.

"You do?" cried the latter. "What, have you got a *maître d'armes* over where you came from?"

"Yes, and he's here in this house now. You should have seen him in a desperate fight we had last night against about a score—"

"Of the road outlaws coming through the forest?"

"Yes, and they attacked us."

"And you got away."

Denis nodded.

"My word! You were lucky!"

"It was through my fencing master," said Denis warmly, as his dressing was hurried on. "He can do all you say when he's teaching; and when he fights as he did last night—"

"Oh, I do wish that I had been there!"

"—his point seems everywhere at once."

"That's the sort of man I love," cried the English lad excitedly, and he gave his visitor so hearty a slap on the shoulder that Denis changed colour and reeled.

"Oh, what have I done!" cried the lad, catching him in his arms and hurriedly lowering him into a settee, before fetching him water in a silver cup and holding it to his lips.—"Feel better now?" he said.

"Oh yes, it's nothing. Don't laugh at me, please. I turned faint like a great silly girl. You touched the tenderest place, where my arm was hurt, and—"

"Denis, boy! May I come in?"

"Yes, yes," said the lad faintly. "Come in. Carrbroke, this is Master Leoni, the gentleman who handles his sword so well."

"I am glad to know you, sir," said the youth, drawing himself up and welcoming with courtly grace the slight, keen-looking, elderly man whose strange, penetrating eyes seemed to be searching him through and through. "I am so sorry that I was asleep when you came last night. I was helping my father's visitor just now, and I am afraid I have hurt him a great deal. His shoulder is hurt, and he tells me that it has not been treated by a leech."

"Hurt?" cried Leoni, speaking quickly. "I did not know of this. Why did you not tell me last night?"

"Oh, I didn't think," said Denis. "I had enough to do to sit my horse and manage to get here; and," added the lad lightly, "I thought that it would be better."

"Ah," said Master Leoni quietly, "let me see." And he looked at the boy fixedly with that curious hard stare of the left eye which Denis never could explain.

"Oh no; I'm nearly dressed now, and breakfast is waiting."

"How did this happen?" said Leoni, paying no heed to the lad's words. "Sit still, boy, and tell me everything at once."

Denis gave a hurried narrative of his encounter, and his listeners eagerly grasped every word.

"I see," said Leoni gravely. "Your blade must have passed through the ruffian, and been held long enough by the muscles for you to receive a horrible wrench. There, set your teeth, and if I hurt you try and bear it. I will be as gentle as I can."

A rapid examination followed, and then the carefully educated fingers ceased their task, and Leoni spoke again as he drew a white kerchief from his pouch and gently wiped his patient's moistened brow.

"There is nothing wrong," he said, "but a bad strain at the tendons, and of course the slightest touch gives great suffering. I will return directly. I am only going to my room for something that will lull that pain, and nature will do the rest."

He nodded gravely to both the lads, and passed quickly from the room, while as the door closed the young Englishman said eagerly:

"I like him. He seems to know a deal. But you said that he was a *maître d'armes*."

"He's everything," said Denis with a faint laugh—"*chirurgien*, statesman—oh, I can't tell you all. Oh, how he hurt me, though! If you hadn't been here I believe I should have shrieked."

"Not you," cried the other. "I was watching, and I saw how you set your teeth. Why, if he had pulled your arm off you wouldn't have said a word. I say, I wish you were English."

"Why?" said Denis wonderingly.

"Oh, I don't know," said the other rather confusedly, "only I seem to like a fellow who can act like that."

"Then because I am French you feel as if you couldn't like me?"

"That I don't!" replied the lad bluffly. "Because I do like you, and I'm glad you've come. I say, can you shake hands?"

"Like the English?" said Denis. "Of course."

"Oh, I did not mean that," said the other. "Of course I know that you fellows embrace; but I meant about your arm. Can you shake hands without its hurting? Because we always do it with our right."

"Try," said Denis, smiling, as, passing his left hand under his wrist, he softly raised the injured limb, and the next moment the two lads seemed to seal the beginning of a long friendship in a warm, firm pressure, which had not ended when they became conscious that the door had softly opened and Master Leoni was standing there, a dark, peculiar-looking, living picture in an oaken frame, an inscrutable-looking smile upon his lips and his eyes half closed.

The blood flushed to the cheeks of both the lads, as the young Englishman tightened his grip and stood firm, while without appearing to have noticed the lads' action, Leoni came forward, and they saw that he had a little silver *flacon* in his hand.

"Feel faint now, Denis?" he said.

"Oh no," was the reply. "That passed away at once. Is that what you have been to fetch?"

"Yes," said Leoni, smiling, "and you need not think that I am going to give you drops in water such as will make you shudder. I am only going to moisten this linen pad and lay it beneath your waistcoat. I believe it will quite dull the pain. There," he said, a few minutes later, after carefully securing the moistened linen so that it should not slip, and fastening the lad's doublet to his throat, "it feels better now, does it not?"

"Better?" said Denis with a low hiss, and speaking through his teeth. "Why, it's as if a red-hot point was boring through my shoulder."

"Yes," said Leoni, smiling; "and that's a good sign. In another minute you will not feel the same. Come, Master Carrbroke, let us both finish dressing our patient and get him to his breakfast."

"Oh, I couldn't have believed it," cried Denis, five minutes later. "Master Carrbroke —"

"Ned," said the young man correctively. "Ned always to my friends."

"Ned, then," said Denis warmly; "once more, this is Master Leoni, and you ought to make him one, for you never before met such a man as he."

Chapter Seventeen
A few bars' rest

A short time later, the dull aching pain seemed to have passed completely out of the injured shoulder, and after a few words evincing his gratitude, which Leoni received with a rather cynical smile, they passed together, led by their new young friend, into the long low dining-hall of the house, where the King, in company with Saint Simon, both apparently none the worse for the previous night's experience, was impatiently waiting, and conversing with his host, a tall grey-bearded man of sixty, whose aspect told at once that he was father to the youth who ushered in the injured lad.

"Let me introduce my son, my lord," said Sir John. "Ned, my boy, this is Comte de la Seine, a French nobleman about to visit your royal master's Court. My lord, my fighting days have long been over, and I only serve my King now with my counsel; but he has honoured me by accepting the service of my only son for his father's sake, and has made him, young as he is, one of the King's esquires."

"And a brave one too, I'll warrant," said Francis, holding out his hand, quite forgetful of his new character as a travelling nobleman, for his host's heir to kiss.

He winced slightly, his face twitched, and an ejaculation nearly passed his lips, while the sinister look on Master Leoni's countenance deepened as he half closed his eyes, at heart enjoying the scene; for the youth advanced with the frank, manly courtesy of a young Englishman, and instead of bending over and kissing, courtier-like, the extended hand, he took it and shook it with a hearty grip.

"I am glad to know my father's guest, my lord," he said. "It was not from want of respect that I was not here before. I have been with your esquire.—He was badly hurt yesterday, father; he mustn't go on. You must keep him here for days, till we have set him right."

"Gladly, my boy," cried Sir John, "if his lordship will honour my poor home with his presence."

"Oh no, no," said the King shortly. "Why, Denis, boy, you are not so bad as that. Here, Master Leoni, what have you to say?"

"That he must rest two or three days at least, sir. His arm is badly wrenched, and he is not fit to sit a horse."

"But he sat one bravely enough last night," cried the King.—"But, Sir John, are all your roads like this? If the people we passed last night could have had their way you would have no guests to throw themselves upon your kindness, for we should have been lying somewhere in the forest to feed the English crows. But there, we have kept you waiting long enough," and he made a gesture towards the well-spread board.

Sir John raised his eyebrows slightly, for his visitor's imperious, authoritative way impressed him unfavourably. But no suspicion of his status occurred to him then, and directly after he was busily employed doing the honours of his table, the good things spread thereon soon having a mollifying influence upon his guest, whose autocratic ways became less prominent under the influence of a most enjoyable meal.

Thoroughly softened then by his meal as far as temper was concerned, the King now began to find out that he was exceedingly stiff, and questioned Saint Simon a good deal about his sensations, to learn that he too was in the same condition.

"Ah, well," he said, "riding will soon take that off. Here, let's go and have a look at the horses."

Sir John accompanied his guest into the great stable-yard, followed by Saint Simon and the two young esquires.

The chargers had been carefully tended by Sir John's men, who did not fail to point out that they were not taking their corn happily; and it was perfectly evident to everyone that their hard day's work, following so closely upon much riding down to the port and the stormy crossing, had made them in a very unsatisfactory condition.

"Humph!" grunted the King. "They don't look as I should like."

"Splendid beasts," said Sir John; "but they want eight and forty hours' rest. You will not think of continuing your journey to-day?"

"Indeed but I shall," said the King,—"er—that is—how do you think they look, Saint Simon?"

"Bough," said the young man laconically.

The King grunted and frowned.

"I fear you think that you will not be welcome, my lord," said Sir John, "and I beg that you will dismiss all such thoughts. Make up your mind, pray, to stay for the next eight and forty hours. I beg you will. Then we shall see how the poor beasts are. Besides, we have to think of our young friend."

The result was that the King consented to stop for the aforesaid forty-eight hours, at the end of which time, feeling himself very comfortable and enjoying his host's company, he needed very little pressure to prolong his stay, especially as Leoni announced that, though Denis was mending fast, riding might have a bad effect and delay his recovery.

Chapter Eighteen
The Doctor is busy

But the King could not conceal his anxiety to be once more in the saddle *en route* for Windsor; and although Sir John Carrbroke urged him to remain so far as the dictates of hospitality required, yet he forbore when he saw the impatience of his guest to be once more on his way, and at dinner the night before the departure he spoke only of the journey to be undertaken on the following day.

"You will find the roads safe enough from here onward, sir," he said courteously, and the King bowed gravely.

"I trust so," he said; "I trust so. England had been represented to me as a land where everyone was safe."

Sir John leaned forward.

"I doubt not," he said, "that when you represent to his Majesty the peril you encountered the south will be cleared of that roving band."

The King laughed.

"Well, we did something towards ridding the country of the robbers, eh, Leoni? I—" He stopped speaking, for at that minute there was the sound of a horse cantering into the courtyard, and a minute later Sir John's own serving-man entered the apartment.

"It is a message, Sir John," he said, "for my young master." And he handed a document to Ned Carrbroke, who hastily unfastened it and read.

"Lord Hurst orders me to return at once," he said to his father.

"Ah," said Sir John. "You see, sir," he exclaimed with a smile, looking at the King, "how important an individual the boy there is becoming. But," he went on, "you were expecting this summons, my lad, and now as it happens you will be able to act as additional escort to our guest—that is, if he will permit."

"Permit!" cried the King. "I shall be glad to have our young friend's company—glad indeed." And as he spoke Sir John gazed musingly at the sparkling ring which his guest wore, one which flashed in the light of the candles as Francis made a gesture with his hand.

A few minutes later Ned Carrbroke glanced at his father, and then rose from his chair, making a sign to Denis as he did so.

"Come," he said quietly, as the two lads moved to the door and passed out. "It was in my mind before, and now it has happened just as I would have wished. I shall come with you."

"Yes," answered Denis. "I am glad."

"I shall be able to show you much," the other went on. "You have never seen a Court; I shall be able to introduce you to that of our King."

"Well," said Denis hesitatingly, "I have been to Fontainebleau."

"Fontainebleau? Where's that?"

"The Court of the King of France."

"Ah! You have seen King Francis?"

"Yes."

"What is he like?"

"Brave, handsome, noble!"

"So is my King too. You will have to stop with me in England and serve King Henry."

While Denis accompanied his new-found friend the talk went on in the big wainscotted dining-room, and the King, who was leaning back in his chair, had finished a long story of the chase, when his host half rose.

"If you will excuse me, my lord, for a few minutes," he said, "I have to give an order as to your departure to-morrow?"

Francis made an inclination of assent.

"When you visit France," he said, "I trust, sir, that I shall be able to make you some return for your kindness to me and to my followers here." And then a minute later, left alone with his two companions, the King yawned. "Gentlemen," he exclaimed, "do not let me detain you." And Leoni and Saint Simon rose, the doctor hesitating a moment at the door.

"You do not, sir," he began, "see any disadvantage in—"

"In what?" said the King sharply.

"Why, sir, in our taking this English stripling along with us on the morrow?"

"By my sword, no!" said the King. "Why should I?"

"He is keen and clever."

"And what of that?"

"Simply this, sir: he might divine the truth. A word, a look—"

"Leoni, have I not acted my part well till now?"

"Yes, sir."

"Then—"

"With your permission, sir; you are a King, and those who are chosen by Heaven to reign cannot assume the guise of other men."

"But my disguise, Leoni—my disguise!"

"Has been admirable, sir."

"Then trust me for the future," was the reply.

And as the door closed and a puff of air caused the lights on the table to dance, the King leaned back in his chair and just then caught his own reflection in a tall glass at the further end of the chamber.

"Ah," he mused, "Leoni doubts of my address. Let him be quite assured. And this Henry who has ambitions on my land of France! Shortly I shall meet him, and my strength will be greater than his since I shall know who he is, and he—he will be ignorant as to who I am.

> "Never in France
> Shall England reign!"

he hummed.

"To-morrow I shall meet him, and then that stone—for Leoni must be right—that jewel will be mine, and the last link which binds us to the old invasion will be snapped."

The King rose and took a turn up and down the apartment.

"I must speak again with Leoni," he said. "Where has he gone?" And he lifted a *portière* and walked out of the apartment, entering a long corridor where a coloured lamp hung from the ceiling. "Our host is well lodged," he continued musingly, as he passed on, stopping at a door through which a stream of light issued forth.

The King pushed the door, which swung back noiselessly on its hinges, and gazed inside, to see Leoni sitting at a table, studiously intent upon some work—lost in the depths. He called softly:

"Leoni!"

The doctor did not turn his head.

"Leoni!" said the King once more, raising his voice; and the man of learning leaped to his feet and came towards his master.

"My lord!" he ejaculated.

The King stepped into the room, and the door closed behind him.

"Busily engaged, Master Leoni?" he said bluffly.

The doctor bowed.

"In your service, sir," he replied humbly.

Chapter Nineteen
The glittering stone

"You are satisfied, I trust, doctor, with our programme?" said the King, in a slightly ironical tone, as he passed to the window, humming an old hunting song as he tapped the panes, while Leoni remained standing near the table at which he had been busily engaged writing.

"Sir—" he began.

"Sit down, Master Leoni; sit down. You can respect my disguise better, and also more thoroughly please me. I was saying, you are satisfied?"

"Everything, sir, that you order is the best. Of that I am convinced; and yet, sir, I am anxious about the Majesty of France. I am common clay, sir. I am nothing; I can die; whereas you—"

"No, no, Leoni; not here, not here. We have left that in France. Do you not understand? Just at present we are travelling companions, and I look to you and to your great learning for assistance, just as I received it in the forest that night; and then it was timely indeed."

"You are too indulgent, my lord, to any poor attainments that your servant may possess. Such as they are, they will always be at my lord's service," replied Leoni, and he slowly resumed his seat in the high-backed chair, in obedience to a commanding gesture from the King.

Francis laughed lightly.

"The best swordsman," he said, "in all my fair kingdom of France—cut, parry, and point; the greatest savant; and, by my sword, the best of patrists.—No, no, Leoni, old friend, I am not too indulgent," and he gave his follower a keen glance. "But as to the route; is it good to start to-morrow?"

Leoni bowed.

"Yes, sir, it is good," he said, and he blew some few grains of sand off the paper at which he had been engaged.

"Ah!" said the King. "'Tis well."

"And then, sir—"

"Then—I do not understand."

Leoni leaned forward, and with his elbows on the table joined the tips of his fingers, and then clasped his hands and, with the weird strange look in his eyes, said:

"What does my lord propose to do?"

"To do? Why, to go to the Court of our quick-tempered brother Henry at this palace of his at Windsor."

"Ah!" said Leoni.

"You are doubtful?"

"I think, sir, that there may be difficulties in the way." And the speaker glanced at the document before him.

"Difficulties for me! You are mad."

"No, sir, only cautious. When you are in France, at Fontainebleau, at Compiegne, in Paris, no matter where, does his Majesty the King receive any errant English nobleman who may be abroad to study the world? I think not. Your minister would inquire into the traveller's papers, and ask whence he came, and why."

The King turned thoughtful in a moment, and the haughty look died away on his lips.

"By Saint Louis, I never thought of that! Leoni, you are wiser than I."

Leoni gazed intently at the King, who winced; and Francis ended by putting his hand before his own eyes, as if the peculiar fixed stare annoyed him.

"I was arguing by analogy, sir. Is it likely that this English monarch will act differently from the first King in Christendom? I think not. Henry apes your Majesty. It is you, Sire, who lead, and whom other kings follow. Go in your proper person, and there is not a door in all this land, or in any other, which can be thrown open wide enough to admit you; but—"

"Leoni," interrupted the King, "what are you writing?"

"A suggestion, sir, to offer you."

The King crossed the chamber, and, leaning over Leoni's shoulder, read out the words:

"To our well-beloved Cousin, Henry, King of England.

"Dear Cousin and King,—

"The bearer of this our letter, the noble Comte Reginald Herault de la Seine of Angomar and Villay, is our good friend. We ask you to receive him as such, and to permit him to see your Court, of which all the world speaks, and your kingdom of England, whose power is so beneficent and so mighty an agent of Heaven's will on this earth."

"Will it serve, sir?" asked Leoni.

"Of course!" cried the King; and snatching the pen from the doctor's hand, he took the letter to the other side of the table and clumsily scribbled down a signature. "There," he cried, tossing the letter back; "will that do?"

Leoni fixed him with his eyes and shrugged his shoulders slightly, and his peculiar cynical smile played about his lips.

"I wish, Leoni, you wouldn't stare at me like that," cried the King petulantly. "Yes. I know; it is bad—not like your regular writing. I don't pass my time handling a pen."

"I was not thinking of the writing, sir, but of the signature."

"Oh, I see," cried the King; "I am not used to it. I shall write it better by-and-by. Well, won't that one do?"

"Your lordship had not thought before you put pen to paper."

"Yes, I did; I thought that the sooner I got it over the better. Well, what do you want now?"

"I was wondering," said Leoni, with a mocking smile, "what King Henry would think of a Comte de la Seine who writes a letter in the King's name to introduce himself."

"Bah!" cried the King angrily. "What an idiot! No; it was my honest nature rebelling against deceit. Here, Leoni, what's to be done?"

"I'll write the letter over again, sir, and you will sign it this time as the King."

"Good!" murmured Francis.

The letter was rewritten, and the King signed.

"With this passport, sir, King Henry's Court at Windsor will be free to you and to yours."

"Excellent," said the King, and he glanced at the document endorsed with the royal signature—"François, R."—at which he smiled with self-satisfaction. "Now nothing more remains to be done."

The King looked fixedly at his servant, and then laid his hand on the latter's arm.

"It is good," he said. "What you have done is well done. Leoni, with mind and sword you have served me well, and that France which we both love with loyalty and faith. And now—now that we are nearing our journey's end, you hold it still to be the truth that Henry guards jealously in his possession this jewel, which in his hands is an agent for the downfall of France?"

"I hold it to be true, sir," said Leoni solemnly, and he laid his hand on a little golden crucifix which lay on the table before him. "I hold it to be true, and that the old ambition which brought the English hordes to our country is kept alive by the influence of that jewel. He will serve France well who reclaims it and restores it to its rightful place—your crown, Sire." And the speaker dropped on one knee, but the King motioned him to rise.

"Not now," he said; "not now." And then, as his royal master appeared to be lost in thought, Leoni went on; "Never, sir, would I have brought this matter to your notice, deeply though it concerns the welfare of France, had I not been convinced."

"And why so?"

"Because, sir, I knew your nature—reckless, valiant, ready to risk all, ay, even your life, when the interests of your country are involved."

"And rightly so. It is as a Valois should act, as a Valois will act to the end."

"Yes, sir; and yet I dreaded at first to speak, for I foresaw something of what would happen, since to those who study deeply a vision of the future is vouchsafed at times, and I realised even then what might be your resolve—namely, to undertake the perilous quest yourself."

"It was for France."

"Yes, sir—"

And then the King, in a softened voice, said slowly:

"You blame me, Leoni?"

"It is not for such as I to blame. All that you have done, sir, is good; but there is the future. Of that we will take thought. You are in a strange land, sir, amidst people who to-morrow may be foes. You are far from the army which would follow you to death, and to meet the dangers which may come into your path there are but three swords, three loyal hearts."

"And they will be enough," said the King. "Leoni, old friend, you must have no fear."

"I have none, sir."

"Well," said the King, "between ourselves, Leoni, I have. This thing begins to look more awkward now we are getting so near. King Henry is always very civil to me in his letters, and no doubt he will give the Comte de la Loire—"

"Seine, sir—Seine."

"Bah! Yes, of course. I knew it was some river. I say: I mustn't make such a mistake as that again, or he will find me out. Here, hadn't we better change the name to something else? Seine—Seine—it's rather a stupid name."

"Too late, sir," said Leoni earnestly. "You must hold to it now. But you were about to say something, my lord."

"Yes, of course," cried the King hastily. "Suppose Henry does find me out, and has got me there. Why, by my sword, Leoni, he'll hold me to ransom, and instead of my getting back that one jewel he'll make me give up my whole crown."

"No, sir; no, sir," cried Leoni earnestly. "Have more faith in yourself, and go forward. You cannot turn back now. You will soon get used to the part you assume, and it will be easy."

"I don't know so much about that," said the King. "I am a bad actor. Why, you can't keep it up yourself. If I hadn't stopped you just now you'd have been down upon your knees to kiss my hand."

"That was only my reverence and duty to my King."

"Yes, I know," said Francis angrily; "but just recollect that you have no king now, and let's have no reverence, for if you get me regularly into trouble over this, good a servant as you have been to me, your friends will have to prepare your tomb, a short one too, for you will lose your head."

"In the service of my country and my lord, sir," said Leoni calmly. "I shall have done my duty. But we shall not fail."

Chapter Twenty
The King's bullies

It was towards evening that the little cavalcade came within sight of the town where was situated the famous castle which was so much to the liking of Henry; and at this point there was a separation, for young Carrbroke took leave.

"We shall soon meet again," he said to Denis, as the two lads bade each other farewell. "When does your master go to the Court?"

Denis shook his head.

"I do not know. Ask him."

"I dare not."

"It will be soon," exclaimed Denis, "for I believe that my lord will not remain in England long."

The King took dinner that night at the hostelry by the side of the ferry and ford they had crossed that day, having previously despatched Denis with the letter which was to bring him face to face with the King of England, the lad shortly returning, having intrusted the missive to a captain of the Royal Guards, by whom it was to be handed to the chamberlain on duty.

But the meal was not concluded when Francis was asked to receive a messenger from the castle.

"Bid him enter," said the King, and he rose and stood by the wide hearth, as the emissary of the English King entered and bowed low.

"His Majesty," he said, "wishes to welcome the noble Count de la Seine, and tells me to assure you, sir, that had he known of your coming he would gladly have provided an escort from the coast. He begs that you will honour him this evening with your presence at his Court."

"Tell his Majesty," said Francis gravely, "that I am very sensible of his kindness, and that it is my most urgent wish to wait upon him."

The royal messenger was bowed out, and Francis turned sharply to Leoni.

"Well, Leoni, we are outside the lion's den at present. Are we to go in?—Don't!" cried the King angrily.

"My lord!"

"Don't stare at me like that. I know what you are thinking—that I am afraid."

"Heaven forbid that I should think such a thing of—"

The King made a gesture, and in a hoarse whisper:

"You were going to say 'King.' One might think from your visage that in walking into his palace I was stepping into a lion's den.—What now, boy? What were you thinking?" he cried, turning sharply to Denis, who had been listening impatiently to his companion's words.

"Only, sir, that if it be a lion's den the Comte de la Seine has his sword."

"To be sure," said the King.

"And three followers who carry theirs, and—"

The boy stopped short, for as he uttered his boastful words he was interrupted by a hoarse, mocking laugh which came through the partly open door, rousing the boy's ire so that he clapped his hand to his weapon, the others turning also in the direction from which the sound had come.

"What!" came in a loud, bullying tone. "The room engaged? Nonsense! Who are they! What are they doing here?"

"French gentlemen, Sir Robert."

"French dancing masters, I suppose, come to teach the Court lads minuets; and are they to keep English gentlemen waiting outside because, forsooth, they have engaged the public room? Come in, boys. Here, landlord; a stoup of wine. I'm thirsty. Frenchmen! Why, we can make them dance!"

There was a thump struck upon the panel of the door, which flew open, and a big, soldierly-looking man in horseman's boots covered with dust swaggered in, followed by a couple more, who looked, like their leader, hot and dusty, and, judging by their accoutrements, appeared to have just dismounted.

Francis started and frowned as he met the English officer's insulting gaze—insulting, for the stranger gave a contemptuous look around at the assembled party, swaggered forward, unbuckling his belt and throwing it and his sword upon the table with a bang, before dragging forward a chair over the polished floor, raising it a little, and then bringing it heavily down, to throw himself into its seat and then cry:

"Come, boys; the chairs are not all occupied. How long is that fellow going to be with the wine?"

Francis turned pale; Leoni bit his lip, drew closer to him, and whispered softly:

"Pay no heed, M. le Comte;" while Denis and Saint Simon, after gazing fiercely at the new-comers, turned to look at the King as if to signify their readiness, and mutely ask his consent to drive these intruders from the room.

The result of this was that the painful silence was broken by the officer addressed as Sir Robert bursting into another loud insulting laugh. He looked at first one and then at the other of his companions, before doubling his great gloved fist and beginning to make his sword dance upon the table by thumping hard and shouting loudly:

"Now, landlord! Wine—wine—wine!"

"Pay no heed, sir," said Leoni softly. "They are trying to provoke a quarrel, and you cannot stoop."

"What's that, Frenchman? Can't you speak English? None of your miserable monsieuring here! Do you know where you are? In the shadow of the Court of the great King Hal. Here, youngster, what are you doing with that hilt? It isn't a fiddlestick. I didn't know dancing masters carried swords.—Ah, here's the wine. Pour out landlord; and here," he continued, as the host nervously filled the cups he had brought. "Bah! Fool! Into the cups, not all over the table. Your wine is always bad, but sack is too good to polish English oak. Now, boys, here's to—Stop! Let's make this French springald drink King Harry's health. There, boy. Take up that cup."

Leoni stretched out his hand to catch Denis by the arm, but he was too late, for, with his eyes flashing, the boy stepped quickly forward to the table, caught up the cup, and raised it towards his lips.

"Montjoie Saint Denis! God save the King of France!" he cried, and was about to drain the cup, while Leoni uttered an impatient hiss, when the vessel was brutally struck from his hand by the English officer, the wine being scattered about the room, and bringing the King to his feet.

"Insolent!" cried Sir Robert, with his face now crimson, as he too sprang to his feet, and catching up another of the filled cups. "But he shall drink it, boys, or I'll slit his miserable ears. Do you understand plain English, you minuet-dancing puppy?"

"Yes," panted Denis, between his teeth, and never taking his eyes from the Englishman; "every word."

"Ah! That's good. Then take this cup, and down upon your knees and drink King Harry's health, or 'fore Heaven you shall go back to your miserable country marked by an English blade."

There was a momentary pause in the room, every eye being centred upon the boy, fascinated as all were and self-forgetful, as they watched for the outcome of the incident.

They were not kept waiting long, for the fierce look upon the boy's countenance gave place to a pleasant smile which the Englishman did not read as meant mockingly. He stretched out and took the cup, and the bully returned the smile as he gave his companions a quick nod of the head.

"You see, boys," he cried, in his loud bullying voice, "this is the way to teach French monkeys! Now, my mincing young skipjack, God save King Harry!—Malediction!" he roared, as he snatched up his sword, for with a quick motion the boy had emptied the wine-cup full in his face.

Chapter Twenty One
Trapped

At the English captain's action his two companions sprang from their chairs and drew their weapons, for Denis had stepped back with his own blade leaping from its scabbard—a movement followed at once by his three companions, who stood on their defence.

"Now, boys," raged out Sir Robert. "Hah! The window is open. Ready?"

"Yes," came fiercely.

"No deep wounds; but prick and make them dance till they reach the window and leap out. I'll tackle this boy."

The next moment there was the harsh, grating, rasping, hissing sound of steel edge against steel.

"Back, boy!" raged out Francis. "Let me punish this English *canaille*."

"No, sir," whispered Leoni sharply. "They are three. Let your servants finish this."

"Here's for you!" shouted one of Sir Robert's companions, and they made for the King and his two followers; but they were hindered from crossing swords by Sir Robert, who, stepping back to avoid a sharp thrust delivered by Denis, felt his foot slip upon the wine-moistened polished oaken boards, and in saving himself he came in contact with the table, driving it heavily in his comrades' way, so that the two parties were separated, the centre of the room being taken up by Denis and his adversary.

"The unlucky boy!" muttered the King angrily. "Leoni, he is no match for that English bull."

"No, sir," said the doctor coolly, as he stood watchful with his blade advanced; "but he can fence a little. Give me place, and I'll see that he does not come to harm."

Seeing that their adversaries were disposed to hold their hands until the couple engaged had finished their encounter, Sir Robert's two companions stood waiting for their turn till the unequal match was finished; for unequal it was, Denis being pressed hard in the fierce onslaught made by the strong-armed bully, who kept on thrusting and driving the boy sideways as, lithe and agile, he avoided or parried every thrust. At last his fate seemed sealed, for his arm was growing weak and his defence being beaten down, when with a quick movement and just in the nick of time Leoni made a sudden dart forward and turned aside a very awkward thrust.

"Ah! Coward!" roared the English officer. "Two to one! Here, boys, come on!"

The command was unnecessary, for Leoni's action was imitated at once by Sir Robert's followers, who sprang forward, to have their blades engaged at once by Saint Simon and the King.

Then in a general *mêlée* the swords gritted and twined and seemed like flashing serpents in deadly fray, while those who grasped them came in contact with and were hindered by the furniture of the by no means extensive room.

The floor was made slippery by the wine which bedewed the boards, but before the encounter had lasted a minute there were other drops which added to the peril; for Denis's thin blade had passed along the fleshiest part of the English captain's ribs, and raging now with passion and pain as he felt the sting, he fought furiously, forcing Leoni to do more than guard the boy, whose strength was utterly failing; and interposing now, he literally took the Englishman's blade to his own, beat upon it heavily, and the next moment sent it flying through the open window, out of which he was to have been made to jump.

Uttering a yell of fury, Sir Robert snatched the dagger from his waist, and regardless of the danger, sprang with a yell at Denis, when the door was suddenly flung open and an officer of halberdiers stepped in, backed up by about a dozen followers, whose approach had been unheard, while about a score more could be seen forming up through the window, their great steal spears with their battle-axe blades glittering in the ruddy evening sun.

As if moved by one impulse, everyone within the room lowered his blade, while the King, taking in his position at a glance, and placing his own interpretation thereon, ejaculated angrily the one word:

"Trapped!"

Chapter Twenty Two
What Denis thought

"Sir Robert! Gentlemen!" cried the officer in command of the halberdiers. "What does this mean?"

"Can't you see?" growled Sir Robert angrily. "Fighting. Chastising a pack of insolent musicians, dancing masters, or whatever they are, who insulted us."

"It is not true!" cried Denis angrily; and as he spoke Carrbroke, who had received warning from one of the inn servants of the fight that was going on, shouldered his way in through the halberdiers. "These men, whoever they are—they cannot be gentlemen—"

"What!" roared Sir Robert.

"—insulted my master and these members of his suite," continued Denis, gazing defiantly at the English captain. "We were standing on our defence."

"The boy lies," cried Sir Robert.

"No: Sir Robert lies," cried Carrbroke hotly. "Captain Bowman, these gentlemen were my father's guests last night—yes, Sir Robert, my father's guests, and you must have insulted them, or they would not have drawn."

"This is insufferable," cried Sir Robert.

"Yes," said the captain of the escort coldly; "quite; and I am afraid, Sir Robert, that when his Majesty hears of the treatment which his guests, whom I have been ordered to escort into the palace, have received, I shall have another duty to perform."

"What do you mean?" cried Sir Robert insolently.

"Your arrest, sir, and that of your friends. I am afraid his Majesty is getting tired of your brawling and overbearing ways."

"What!" cried Sir Robert fiercely, as he clapped his hand again to the dagger he had sheathed.

"I see you have lost your sword," said the officer contemptuously, "and spared me the trouble of disarming you for drawing within the precincts of the Court. Take my advice, sir—not that of a friend, but of one who has his duty to do towards keeping order here. Take your friends away and consult with them as to what steps you should take before his Majesty hears of this outrage. Monsieur le Comte," he continued, turning to Francis, "in his Majesty's name, let me apologise for what must have been a grievous mistake on the part of one of the King's officers. I am commanded to escort you and your followers into the palace, where his Majesty will receive you at once."

Francis bowed, and the halberdiers formed up ready for the visitors to pass between their ranks, while Leoni, who looked calm and saturnine as ever, bent forward and whispered a word or two to the King.

"My faith, yes!" he cried, and he turned to the Captain of the Guard. "But, as you see, we are travel-stained and hot with this encounter; we ought to have some minutes to prepare."

"His Majesty knows that you have been travelling, sir, and will not notice that you have been making some passes in your defence. My master, sir, is impatient, and as he expects you, if I might advise I would say, let me lead you there at once."

The King bowed and stepped forward directly, closely followed by his suite, and passed out to the front of the hostelry, where a little crowd had gathered, attracted by the exciting incident that had taken place.

The next minute, with about a dozen of the halberdiers to clear the way, the rest behind, the order was loudly given, and the little procession moved towards the great gate of the castle on the hill, the Captain of the Guard marching with drawn sword respectfully by the travellers' side.

Rather breathless still, the King remained silent, while Denis could not refrain from glancing back, to see his late adversary standing at the inn-door in the act of taking a wine-cup from the hands of the host.

The next moment the figures of the halberdiers shut him from sight, while the boy heard his royal master's next words, uttered in a low tone to Leoni.

"It's wonderfully like being prisoners, doctor," he whispered; "and mind this, if we do not get free again you'll have to pay the forfeit. Ah, there you are, my young esquire! I'd half forgotten you. Well and bravely fought. Yesterday, as it were, I looked upon you as a page; you are now my esquire indeed. By my sword, the fighting we have had already on this English soil has made quite a fire-eater of you. Why, Leoni, I feel as ready as can be now to enter into the lion's den. Not get out again! Tchah! With followers like these, who's going to stand against us? *Vive la France!*"

"*Vive la France, Monsieur le Comte*," said Leoni, in a low meaning tone. "If I might say so, I should think his Majesty King Francis would feel proud of the bearer of his letter, if he could know how bravely one of his nobles kept up the credit of his court of braves."

"I hope he would, Leoni," said the King, laughing to himself, and he looked sharply upward as the halberdiers' footsteps echoed from the grey stone walls of the arched entrance to the courtyard. "A noble-looking castle. May I ask, monsieur the captain, what building that is to our left—the chapel of the palace?"

"Yes, sir, and the great hall," replied the Captain of the Guard.

Then uttering a sharp order, the advance-guard bore off to the left.

"His Majesty awaits you, sir, in the ante-chamber. We turn in here for your reception in the hall."

"Hah!" said Francis, and he looked at Denis as he spoke. "Well, boy," he said, in a low tone, "are you wondering what Henry of England will think when he sees the Comte?"

"No, sir," replied the boy sharply.

"What then?"

"Will the Comte excuse me saying?" said the boy, turning furiously red.

"No, he will not," said the King sharply. "Out with it at once! What were you thinking?"

The boy hesitated, but the King's eyes were fixed upon him fiercely, and with a desperate effort he blurted out:

"I thought you were playing a very dangerous game."

Chapter Twenty Three
A Royal welcome

There was plenty of colour and brightness in the group awaiting the coming of Francis and his travel-stained followers. Courtiers stood around with their gay, picturesque garments rendered more striking by the sunset glow, vivified by passing through a stained-glass window which shone down upon the central figure of the group, a big, bluff, rather heavy-faced, typically English yeoman in expression, upon whom Francis fixed his eyes and kept them there as upon the principal picture, all the rest being merely frame.

Irrespective of his position, the visitor would have known him at once from the descriptions he had heard from ambassadors to the English Court of what the English King was like; and forgetful of everything else, all courtly custom, his secret mission, and his assumed character, Francis made a slight obeisance and stepped forward eagerly to greet his brother King.

On the other hand King Henry gazed curiously at his visitor who bore such worthy credentials, and he put out his hand as he stood drawing himself up proudly, expecting to see the Comte sink upon one knee and press it to his lips; but, to his utter astonishment, Francis came close up, apparently not in the slightest degree dazzled or abashed by his magnificence, to stop short when within easy reach, and, instead of sinking down, exclaimed, "Aha! The brave, soldierly King Hal!" clapped both hands upon his brother monarch's shoulders, let them glide quickly onward till they joined behind the King's neck, and the next moment the embrace tightened as he kissed the plump cheeks that were beginning to flame smartly in turn.

"This," he cried, "is a great joy that pays me for my long journey here."

The English King drew back in astonishment, and glanced quickly to right and left of his assembled courtiers, as if asking the meaning of this outrage, this strange conduct so completely in opposition to all Court etiquette.

He was completely stunned for the moment, and his inclination was to exclaim, "Is this man mad?" But as he looked round it was to see face after face expanded or contracted by the mirthful feeling within his followers' breasts, and then rendered grotesque by their owners' efforts to turn solemn and serious once more.

A change came over the King's countenance. It was as a reflection of the smiles upon his courtiers' lips.

"He is a Frenchman," he said to himself, "and does not understand our ways, though I should have thought—" he continued to himself, and then broke off, to follow the example set him by his visitor, and clumsily and with ill grace returned the salute, before bidding him welcome in English, which Francis understood fairly well, turning occasionally to Leoni, who stood close behind him, ready to interpret whenever his master was at fault.

The interview went off very well, for Henry took at once to the bright, vivacious French monarch, finding in him one ready to talk eagerly about his pursuits, the pair being well in accord as to their tastes; and the meeting was nearly brought to an end by the King telling his visitor that the letter from his brother Francis was sufficient to make one of his favourite nobles quite welcome to the hospitality of the English Court.

"Believe me, I am glad to welcome my royal brother's favourite. A suite of apartments will be prepared for you, sir, by my people, and a place on my right hand at my table. Rest assured that your stay shall be made pleasant here."

Francis bowed and smiled, and seemed as if about to supplement his embrace; but the King went on speaking.

"But what is this I hear about an insult offered to one who occupies the position of an ambassador, and whose person should be sacred? I hear, Comte, that you were attacked by one of my officers and his companions, here, close to my palace gates. Is it true?"

Francis shrugged his shoulders nearly to his ears with a half contemptuous smile upon his lips.

"Oh, a mere nothing," he said; "a little sword-play."

"A mere nothing!" cried Henry fiercely. "An insult to one of my guests a mere nothing!"

"Oh, don't speak of it," replied Francis, laughing. "I was not surprised."

"You amaze me, sir!" cried the King.

"Indeed, Sire? Why, we always knew in France that there is nothing an Englishman loves better than to fight. I came to your gates unannounced, and two or three of your bluff soldiers—officers, you say—exclaimed amongst themselves, 'What does this Frenchman here, trying to enter our master's court?' As your defenders, they drew, to try and drive us away. But we would not be driven. Then your gallant escort arrived. They found out the mistake, and it was all at an end. I congratulate you, my—" Francis coughed, as if to get rid of an impediment in his speech, or as if he were suffering from some forgetfulness of the English words he ought to use— "my noble English sovereign, upon having such brave defenders at your gates."

"I thank you, sir," cried Henry. "But this is too much! These soldiery assume more than is their right. I have heard before of this man's brawls. He is a fighter out of employment now, for we are at peace, and I will not have him insult my guests."

"But you will pardon him, Sire?" said Francis. "We were not hurt. Next time we meet, your brave officer will doubtless make amends."

"He must! He shall!" cried Henry hotly. "And—"

"Sire," interrupted Francis, smiling, "I am your visitor. Grant me the first favour that I ask."

"Anything," cried the King, smiling in his turn.

"Then you will forgive this brave man?"

The King bowed.

"I wish you to be perfectly welcome at my Court, Comte; and now you would like to retire to your rooms to rid yourselves of your travel-stains. Later on I look to meet you at my board."

Francis bowed in turn, and drew back, seeing that the audience was at an end, and half turning saw that Denis had approached.

"Yes, boy?" he said.

"The horses, Comte," whispered Denis.

"Ah, to be sure! They must not be left there." And he turned, to catch the King's eye fixed on him searchingly.

"Yes, Comte," he said; "you were about to speak?"

"It is nothing, Sire," replied Francis. "My esquire reminded me that our steeds were at the hostelry, and—"

"Ah, you love horses!" cried the King. "So do I, and the hunt as well. My stables are at your service, and my Master of the Horse will see that they are well bestowed. Once more, sir, the favourite of my brother Francis is welcome here. I look to see you again to-night."

Chapter Twenty Four
Denis is sleepy

His Majesty of England was in high good humour that night, since the preparations for the grand reception he had ordered in honour of the ambassador-like visitor from France had been carried out quite to his satisfaction.

There was show, there was music, and there was dancing going on, as he entered the *salon* from his private rooms and looked round searchingly before turning to speak to his stately chamberlain.

"Our visitor?" he said laconically.

"Fatigued, perhaps, with the journey, Sire. He has not yet arrived."

The King frowned, and his chamberlain raised his eyebrows a little, half expecting to be taken to task for not having the visitor there.

"See that everything is done, Hurst, so that he may go back to my brother of France full of admiration of my Court. We must make him envious," added the King, with a laugh.

At that moment there was a flourish of trumpets, and, escorted by two noblemen of the English Court, Francis, followed by his three gentleman attendants, advanced to meet the King.

Leoni watched his master narrowly as he followed his progress through the brilliant throng of courtiers towards the spot where Henry stood awaiting his coming, and there was but one thought animating his brain—the thought of whether Francis with his impetuous nature would not commit some act in this strangest of all episodes—King meeting King, and one ignorant of the other's real identity—which would enlighten Henry and maybe bring disaster on them all.

"But Henry has never seen our King," he murmured softly to himself. "Why should there be this presagement of harm? He cannot be recognised here, or if any of these gentlemen who have travelled do imagine a resemblance, they will laugh it on one side."

He felt reassured again as he saw Henry advance a step to meet his guest and take his hand with a few words of welcome, ere he pointed to a seat near at hand.

"Our brother of France is indeed fortunate," he said, "to be represented by yourself, Comte." And then followed words which Leoni did not hear, for a gentleman approached the group formed by himself, Saint Simon, and Denis, and with a bow said courteously:

"May I present you gentlemen to his Majesty?"

A minute later Leoni heard Francis say:

"Your Majesty will permit me to present to your notice Master René Leoni, the most learned of doctors, and at the same time one of the most tyrannical. But to those who understand well the subtle art of medicine, we must forgive all."

"True," said Henry, and he leaned forward with a gracious inclination. "We can read in your countenance, sir, the deep learning of the south. Would to Heaven that there were more of it here! I trust that the stay you make at our Court will not be displeasing to you, for that it will be productive to us I make no doubt."

Leoni bowed low before the two Kings.

"My master has exaggerated my poor abilities, your Majesty," he said, and then he drew back to allow of the introduction of his two companions, to each of whom Henry addressed words of encouragement and welcome.

Later, as the music struck up, the English King turned to his visitor and asked more questions concerning Francis.

"He is at Fontainebleau?" he asked.

"Not at present, Sire," said Francis drily, and with a glance at Leoni.

"Ah!" and Henry seemed to relapse into thought.

"I would that he were here, Sire, in order that he might see how well you treat his envoys."

But Henry waved the compliment aside.

"Tell me about France," he said; "tell me about France." And he looked fixedly at the messenger from the kingdom of the fleur-de-lys, while Leoni would have given anything to draw nearer, to gather up if it were only scraps of the conversation that ensued; but he was bound to imitate the action of those around and draw back, full of anxiety about his pupil, but fain to content himself with looking around at the gay throng, before sinking into a chair where he could think about his mission, his searching eyes always busy looking about, especially at the jewels that were flashing on every side, as he hungrily sought for some thread which might form a clue to lead him ultimately to the object of his quest.

Meanwhile Denis and Saint Simon, looking as courtly as the most brightly dressed among whom they stood, were invited by one of the dignified functionaries to join in the dance, but declined on the score of fatigue; and the former had sauntered away from the throng, to stand near a curtained window a moment, when he heard his name spoken, and a hand was laid on his arm. He turned sharply, to find himself face to face with Carrbroke.

"Found you," he said. "Well, it did not require my services to show you the Court. What do you think of it? Better than Fontainebleau, is it not?"

It was not necessary for Denis to reply, because his companion went on quickly to speak of other things.

"We shall be able to see a great deal of each other, I hope," he said.

"I hope so," responded Denis readily.

"I am sure. There is a great banquet to-morrow. You will be there."

"Would they ask me?"

"Why, of course; but—here, come this way," and Carrbroke touched the other's arm. "You are not going to dance, so let us talk—out here in the garden."

Denis accompanied his friend out on to a wide terrace where there came to the ear the sound of the music still, and where there were the thousand scents of the flowers on that soft June night.

"The King sometimes walks here," said the lad; "but he will not come to-night. I like this place. Yonder is the river. You have not a river like that?"

"Oh, we have the Seine."

Carrbroke made a movement of dissent.

"They laugh at me here," he said, "because I fish. Lord Hurst would have one always wearing one's best and acting the courtier; but the King loves sport, and so do I. Let's go this way, and enter the palace by another door. There will be supper soon, and one must eat."

A moment before, Denis was beginning to think that the place was not so attractive after all, but the word supper seemed to accord well with his sensations.

He was weary with the excitement of the day, and he suddenly felt that some of his distaste was due to hunger, which he was ready enough to appease, being well looked after by his new friend; while the rest of the evening was filled up by faintly heard sounds of music and conversation which seemed to be buzzing around him, as he sat back in one of the many chairs of the grand *salon,* completely overcome by an invincible sense of drowsiness which seemed dark and cloudy, while out of it came a familiar voice, saying:

"Why, Denis, boy, I have been seeking you everywhere. Saint Simon was looking for you too, and said you must have gone off to bed."

"Bed—bed?" the boy remembered saying, and then all was confused again till Master Leoni's voice whispered in his ear:

"Come, wake up."

"Where's Carrbroke?" he said drowsily.

"Gone away in attendance on the King, who will soon be leaving the *salon.* Come, we must be in attendance too."

The next thing that occurred was the sudden starting up of the boy in his bed, with the bright morning sun shining in through the window.

"Where am I?" he muttered. "How did I come here?" And then by degrees he began to have some faint recollection of Leoni helping him to his room.

"Why, I must have disgraced myself in some way," he muttered. "What could I have done? Gone to sleep in the middle of that *fête*? I don't know; everything seems a blank."

Chapter Twenty Five
Carrbroke tells secrets

The days passed quickly, with the Kings the best of friends, for Francis proved himself a boon companion, a good horseman, and quite after the King's own heart.

He made himself a favourite too, and the most courtly at the Court, ready if he had been present to have brought a sneering smile to the lips of Sir Robert Garstang, who, when the minstrels were busy in their gallery, might have seen some justification of the bullying captain's sneer respecting dancing masters, for Francis was ever ready and eager to lead some Court lady through the mazes of the dance.

For revels were plentiful at Windsor then, and Denis in the companionship of Carrbroke found the time pass pleasantly enough, on the terraces, in the park, and along the banks of the silver Thames; but he was quite forgetful for the most part of the special mission upon which he had crossed the sea.

For Ned Carrbroke had always something fresh to propose in the way of horsemanship, and often enough invited his French companion to swordplay, which was readily accepted; and to Carrbroke's wonder and delight Leoni would come to look on, and at Denis's request advise them upon questions dealing with offence and defence, and proper conduct of the rapier both in French and Italian schools.

"Why, he's splendid," cried Carrbroke one day, "only I don't like him. He puts me out of heart. I used to think that I was a good fencer, but when I cross swords with him I feel quite a baby. You are lucky to have some one like that to give you lessons. Why, you must be splendid yourself."

Denis laughed merrily.

"Why," he said, "I always feel worse than you. Master Leoni, when I fence with him and he gives me a lesson, makes me feel as if there were magic in his blade which sends a strange aching pain all up the muscles of my arm."

"Yes," cried Carrbroke, "that's something like what I feel. I say, he's your friend, isn't he?"

"Well, hardly a friend. I feel more afraid of him than anything."

"Yes," said Carrbroke eagerly, "that's how I feel—well, not afraid," he continued hastily, and flushing up; "but you won't mind my speaking out? You and I seem to have so taken to one another."

"Well, yes," said Denis, "we do seem to like one another a bit."

"Then you won't mind my speaking out quite plainly?" continued Carrbroke.

"Not I. What is it?"

"Only this. Do you think that there is something queer in his blade?"

"Only that it is best Italian steel."

"Yes, of course," said Carrbroke impatiently. "But I mean what they call magic—that there is something curious in it? You see, it turns so, and seems so strong."

"Yes, that is strange," said Denis. "It is no matter how you parry; the point always seems as if it could enter your breast if it liked. I always feel that Master Leoni could kill anyone just as he pleased."

"Of course you believe in magic?" said Carrbroke.

"I don't know. I suppose I do," replied Denis.

"I do," said Carrbroke; "and your friend seems so different from other men. Look at his eye."

"Oh, I never do if I can help it," said Denis. "You've noticed it, then?"

"Noticed it?" cried Carrbroke. "Who could help it? When he fixes it on me, as he always does, it makes me shiver; although he is always very kind, there is something about him I can't understand, and if he were my enemy I should be ready to give everything up and go away. There, what a bad job! I was just going to say, let's go for a long ride, or else make some of the King's rowers take us up the river, and then float down, and it's going to rain, and I don't want to get wet. It spoils one's doublet so. Here, I know; I'll take you all through the castle, if I can, into all the King's private rooms. They'll be with the ladies at this time of day. I can show you everything that there is to see."

"Can you?" said Denis, whose thoughts suddenly turned to his mission there.

"Oh yes; I am allowed to go where I like, as the King's youngest esquire." And then half pettishly: "They consider me only a boy. But come along."

Carrbroke was quite right, for the rain began streaming down; and a few minutes afterwards the two lads were in the royal apartments, which were quite deserted, and Carrbroke was proudly showing the different pictures, King Henry's armour, and choice collections of weapons of war. At last he stopped in front of a beautiful Italian cabinet which differed from ordinary pieces of furniture, being made to stand four-square in the centre of the apartment, each side being richly ornamented with carving and delicate inlaid work which covered the doors and drawers.

"I wish I had the keys of that," said Carrbroke.

"Why? What's inside?"

"I hardly know; but my father told me once to take notice of it, for he believed that it was full of gems and curious jewels that had been presented to the King. I never saw it open yet, but there must be many curiosities there, swords and petronels, as well as jewels."

"Indeed!" said Denis, colouring slightly.

"Oh yes; some of those curious gems that they say have magic properties—charms, don't they call them? Magic crystals that confer singular powers upon those who own them, bring good luck, and influence the fate of people. I say, do you believe in such things as that?"

"Ye–es, I think I do," said Denis, and the colour on his cheeks grew a little deeper, and then deeper still, and he winced a little as if he felt that Carrbroke's searching eyes were reading his inmost thoughts; and then he started and felt worse, for it seemed to him that his companion suspected his reasons for being there, so that he was ready to utter a sigh of relief when Carrbroke said:

"Well, you needn't look like that. You needn't be ashamed to believe in such things. I do, for there's a lot one doesn't understand. I was told once that different precious stones have very curious qualities; some will protect anyone from magic, some from enemies. There was a ring I once heard of which if a person wore would guard him from poison. It was an Italian ring, I suppose, for I believe that they try to poison people there."

"Yes, I have heard so," said Denis drily, as he stood with his eyes fixed upon the cabinet, wondering whether the treasure Leoni sought could be there. "But it seems nonsense. I don't see how a diamond or a ruby could do such things."

"No," said Carrbroke; "no more do I, unless you swallowed it to keep the poison from doing harm. Perhaps it's all nonsense. But the King believes it, I suppose."

"Why do you say so?" asked Denis.

"Because he's got a lot of such things in here. I say, don't you feel as if you'd like to smuggle some of them?"

"What!" cried Denis, flushing scarlet and gazing wildly in his companion's eyes.

"Don't look like that," cried Carrbroke, laughing. "I said smuggle; I didn't say steal. I thought you might feel as if you'd like to have one of these charms which hold such magic power."

"I am not afraid of being poisoned," said Denis huskily. "Here, come away from this; show me something else."

"Oh, haven't you seen enough? But I say, is this better or worse than Fontainebleau?"

"Oh, I don't know," said Denis hastily, for he felt mentally disturbed. "They are both beautiful places. Where does that corridor lead?"

"All along one side of the King's apartments."

"Well, let's go down there."

"But there's nothing to show you but furniture and walls covered with arras and—oh yes, there is: I know. I say, you haven't got any secret passages at Fontainebleau?"

"We have all kinds of places hidden in the walls. Have you got any here?"

Carrbroke nodded.

"I say, we are friends, aren't we?"

"Of course; the best of friends."

"Then I'll show you something; only it's a secret. Not that it matters about you knowing it, as you are not going to live here. It's something I found out myself. I was on duty here—as page in attendance on the King— one evening, just at dusk, and the candles weren't lit. There had been a grand banquet the night before, with music and dancing, and I'd been up all night, and just as it began to grow dark I turned so sleepy I couldn't keep my eyes open. I tried ever so hard, but it was of no use, and I sank down in a chair close up to the hangings in a dark corner, and was asleep in a moment. I don't think it could have been long before I woke up again with a start. I suppose some noise must have woke me, and I sat there staring and wondering where I was, for I felt quite stupid, when all at once the arras that covered the wall just opposite to me seemed to open, and something dark came out, to stand still for a few moments as if listening. Then there was a rustling of hangings, and the dark figure came straight towards me, making me turn cold; for I felt then that I had been asleep, and I thought it was some one come to punish me. But the figure did not come close up to where I sat, but suddenly turned off towards a light which appeared at the end of the corridor and came nearer, while directly after I made out that some of the servants were bringing in candles, and directly after, though I only saw his back, I knew it was the King."

"Then he didn't see you?" said Denis.

"No, fortunately for me."

"Then he must have come out of some secret passage."

"That was it, and of course you know what I did afterwards—not then, but the first day that I had the chance?"

"Searched for the secret door, of course. I should."

"Yes, and I found it; and that's what I'm going to show you. We are not likely to be disturbed now."

Before many minutes had elapsed the two youths were standing in front of a huge needlework picture representing a classic scene, covered with warriors and triumphal cars.

"There, you wouldn't think there was a door behind there, would you?"

"No, that I shouldn't," replied Denis.

"But there is. You see that warrior's shield with the boss on it that stands out as if it were real?"

"Yes," said Denis; "it is very cleverly done."

"Yes, but it is real," said Carrbroke, and he glanced to right and left to see if they were observed. "We are quite alone. Now you touch that boss."

"Yes: it's hard and round," said Denis.

"Now give it a twist."

Denis did as he was told, and there was a faint click like the lifting of a latch.

"Now push," continued Carrbroke.

Denis again obeyed, and something gave way as if he had pushed a door which opened from him.

"Now then," said Carrbroke, "what do you think of that?"

"That if I lifted the arras I could pass into another room."

"Not quite right; not into another room, but into a dark passage made in the wall. I went in one day when the King was out hunting and I felt grumpy because I had been left behind, and I thought I should like to see what there was there."

"Yes, and you went?" said Denis eagerly. "Yes, all along a dark passage for ever so far. Then I came to another door, which opened easily, and there was a flight of stairs; at the bottom of that there was another door and another long passage, twice as long as the first, and then another door."

"Did you open that?"

"Yes; and where do you think I was?"

"I don't know. In the cellars perhaps."

"No; in a dark part of the terrace all amongst the trees. Then I wasn't satisfied, for it was all new to me, and I felt curious to see where the dark winding walk that was before me went to."

"Yes," said Denis eagerly; "and where did it lead?"

"Right away down and down to some stone steps close to a little pavilion on the banks of the river, where there was a boat fastened to a post. That was the King's private way, of course."

"Yes," said Denis; "but what did he want it for?"

"Oh, I don't know; and I didn't want to know, for anyone who meddled with the King's secrets might come in for the loss of his head, and I didn't want to lose mine. I came back as fast as I could. There, you can have a look through into the dark passage if you like. Kneel down and lift up the hangings. There, what can you see?" continued the lad, as Denis obeyed, finding the abundant folds give way easily, so that he could peer right beyond.

"Nothing at all; it is quite dark."

"Come away," said Carrbroke quickly. "That's right," he continued, and then quickly taking Denis's place he quite disappeared.

"Am I to follow?" said Denis wonderingly; but he had hardly finished speaking before Carrbroke reappeared, laughing.

"Only shutting the door," he said. "Has anyone seen us?"

"No," said Denis, after a glance in both directions.

"That's right," said Carrbroke. "I say, though, it is interesting, isn't it? But now I've told you I can't help wondering why I did. But there, you won't go and tell King Hal that I told you his secrets, will you?"

"Not very likely, is it?" said Denis, smiling, but troubled the while by an uncomfortable sensation which made him feel as if he regretted his knowledge, though at the same time he knew that he had acquired information that might be of extreme value if their masquerading were discovered, perhaps mean the saving of his King.

His musings were suddenly broken off by the voice of companion.

"There," he said, "let's go out of doors in the sunshine. I feel as if I had got dark passage on the brain."

Chapter Twenty Six
So does Denis

It was the very next day that Denis, after his attendance upon Francis, who had gone to join Henry, was alone in the King's apartments, standing in the deep recess of a casement window, which he had flung open, and was leaning out gazing at the landscape stretching far and wide before him, and giving him a silvery glimpse here and there of the bright glittering river.

He was so lost in admiration of the scene that he did not hear the door open, and was only made conscious of some one being in the room behind him by hearing a low muttering voice say:

"A blind search! A blind search! What shall I do next to bring it to an end?"

Denis made a sharp movement, catching the sleeve of his doublet against the copper fastening which held open the casement; and as he turned a nervous hand suddenly seized him by the shoulder in a painful grasp, for it was as if fingers of steel were pressing into his flesh.

"You, Master Leoni!" he cried, as the clutch was relaxed as quickly as it came. "Yes, my boy," said the doctor; and the lad shivered slightly as the fierce fire in one of Leoni's eyes died into a pleasant smile, though the cold fixed stare in the other remained the same as of old.

"I thought I was alone."

"Well, boy; do you like your life here in the castle?"

"Oh yes," cried Denis; "but when are we to have, Carrbroke and I, another fencing lesson?"

"At any time when the King does not require my services," said Leoni, smiling. "Why, you will soon be a better swordsman than I."

"Oh, sir!" cried Denis deprecatingly.

"Well, say as good, my dear boy, when you know all that I can teach you."

"And you will teach me all, sir?"

"Of course, of course," said the doctor, laying his hand caressingly on the boy's shoulder. "You are a pupil of whom I feel proud. But tell me," he continued, as he passed his hand softly along the muscles of the lad's arm, "what about the stiffness and pain?"

"All gone, sir. That salve you applied seemed to make it pass entirely away."

"That is good," said the doctor, nodding his head. "But tell me, boy, was I speaking aloud when I came into the room?"

"Not aloud, sir, but just so that I could hear what you said."

"Ah, a bad habit! And what did I say?"

"It was something about a blind search."

"Ah, yes; and you guessed at once what I meant?"

"Why, yes, sir. I immediately thought that you meant the—"

With a quick movement, accompanied by a smile, Leoni's long, thin, brown fingers were laid upon Denis's lips.

"Hist, boy! We are in King Henry's palace, where walls may have ears. Speak it not. We understand one another, and know what in our master's service we have come to seek. Denis, you are a boy in years, but I find you in many things a man at heart, and there should be no half confidences between us two. I like you, my boy, and always have, stern and cold and severe as I may have seemed. My face may have been hard, but there are moments when my heart is soft. Denis, my son, we are working for the King and for France, and so far I am at fault. I thought my task would be so easy that, once here, that which we seek would be within my grasp; and so far it seems beyond me, while the golden hours glide swiftly away, and before many days have passed our visit with all its risks must have an end. I shiver sometimes, boy, as I stand close by and listen to our master's careless, light-hearted speech. Again and again he has been within an ace of betraying who he is, and at any moment some of the sharper-witted of the courtiers by whom we are surrounded may grasp the truth, and then, Denis, as Francis has said, we are in the lion's den and the risk is great."

"Yes, sir; I see all that," said Denis, in a low earnest whisper. "Then you have no idea where the jewel of France is kept?"

"Not the slightest, boy, and I want you to use your eyes and ears to help me all you can. There is that young English esquire. You are great friends; perhaps he might know. I don't like asking you to play the spy and betray your friend, but the English are our natural enemies. We are here upon a sacred mission, and we must quiet our consciences with the recollection that what we seek was torn by conquest from the Valois diadem."

"Yes, I know, sir," whispered Denis eagerly, influenced as he was by the masterful spirit and words of his tutor.

"Then try, boy; try your best to help me, while we have time. You promise me this?"

"Of course, sir. But what," cried Denis, with his eyes flashing, "if I already know?"

"Boy!" cried Leoni excitedly; and he caught his young companion by the shoulders, but checked himself, instantly drew back, walked slowly across the room to the door, opened it and looked out, and then came back and signed to Denis to close the window, while he softly moved here and there; and the boy noticed how, as if to examine the beauty of the silken hangings, he touched them again and again, as if to make sure that no listener was concealed behind.

Leoni ended by joining his young companions in the deep embrasure of the window, taking him by the arm, and pressing him towards the diamond panes of the casement as if to draw his attention to something out beyond the terrace and the steep slope below.

"Now," he said, in a quick whisper, "speak beneath your breath. You know where?"

"In the tall, square-turreted cabinet three parts of the way down the long corridor by the King's private apartments."

"Ah, I have not been there, and dared not raise suspicion by asking permission to go. Are you sure?"

"Carrbroke has as good as told me it was there. He spoke of a charm with fateful powers of its own, and that the King held gems as sacred relics."

"Ah!" ejaculated Leoni softly. "Boy, you make me begin to live."

"Shall I tell you something more, sir?"

"There can be nothing more that I wish to hear," whispered Leoni. "Boy, you have filled an empty void. But speak; tell me what more you have to say."

"The King has a secret passage whose door is in the arras two chambers down the long corridor farther on."

"Young Carrbroke told you so?"

"Yes."

"Bah! But it would be a secret way known only to himself, of no avail to us. It could not be found. Once the relic is in our hands, a silken rope and some window must be our way."

"But I know the secret of the passage, sir, how to open the door, and where the passage leads."

"Where, boy, where?" cried Leoni excitedly.

"Down to the grounds, and then by a long winding alley through the private gardens to the riverside."

"Hist!" whispered Leoni. "No more, boy, for your words have seemed to burn. Ah, it is strange! The workings too of fate. What I have striven for in vain has come to you without seeking, without thought. It is fate, boy, fate. The spirit of our great nation is working on our behalf, and has made you the chosen instrument of our success. We must, we shall succeed, and through you. Now silence; not another word but these. I say silence, Denis. It is for our master's sake and for *la France*."

Chapter Twenty Seven
The Chamberlain has suspicions

Several days passed at the Court in a succession of gaieties including hunting, an excursion on the river, and at night banquet and dance. Henry was charmed with the pleasant sprightliness of his guest, whose lively French manner attracted him more and more. He distinguished himself in the field and in the chivalrous sports in the Castle Yard.

There were moments when the King looked grim and slightly disposed to be jealous of the applause given to the Comte, and more than once Lord Hurst saw his master frown heavily upon seeing how great a favourite Francis had made himself with the courtiers, who were delighted with the change the gay Frenchman made in the monotony of their daily life. But Leoni felt that the luxurious seats he occupied at Windsor were stuffed with thorns, and that they were placed close to the edge of a mine that might at any moment explode.

Still the time wore on and the danger seemed as far off as ever, for in obedience to Leoni's prompting Francis, though often sailing very near the wind, dexterously gave a turn to the rudder just at the right time, and the doctor breathed freely once again, while he waited for the moment when he could put into action one or other of the plans he had thought out, to get possession of the fateful jewel whose resting-place he felt he knew, lying as it did, though still distant, almost within his grasp. For short of gaining entrance to the private corridor where it lay, and boldly breaking open the cabinet some night, to carry off the prize, he could not yet see his way.

"That must be the last resource," he said to Denis. "The Comte and I must exercise subtlety. The knowledge came from you, boy—given to you by fate; and we must wait longer, even if it be for days. Who knows but, as she has favoured us so far, fate may place in our hands the fruit that is ripe to pluck?"

"I wish they'd pluck it or leave it alone," said Denis to himself. "I hate the whole business. It is very pleasant being here, and Carrbroke makes himself quite like a brother, though I can't help laughing at him sometimes when he speaks such bad French; but that doesn't matter. He laughs at my bad English just the same, and it's all capital sport when we are together, if I didn't feel so treacherous. There are times when I should like to tell him all, and why we are here; but I can't, for that would be behaving treacherously to my King."

The lad ended his musings rather gloomily, as he felt sure that before long they would be found out and the daring business be all come to an end.

Similar thoughts kept Leoni awake the greater part of each night in his luxurious chamber, spoiling his rest, and making him attend his master the next morning terribly troubled in mind, but only to brighten up on finding how well in favour the Comte seemed with the King, who was always seeking his visitor out for some new pursuit in courtly pleasure or excursion.

But the cloud was gathering all the same, and the discovery very near at hand.

One morning Lord Hurst was in attendance upon Henry, making his customary daily reports and taking his orders for various preparations to carry out something fresh in the way of entertainment, when the King waved his hand impatiently.

"There, there," he cried, "no more of this!" Then, good-humouredly, "Well, Hurst, what do you think of our ambassador?"

"Think of him, Sire?" replied the courtier.

"Yes, yes," cried the King testily. "Do I not speak plainly? Why do you look at me like that? Do you not think he is a most worthy representative of his master?"

"Undoubtedly, Sire, but—"

"Hurst," cried the King furiously, "have I not made you my trusted adviser?"

"Yes, Sire, and I am your faithful servant, always ready to advise."

"Then why do you not speak out? I know you of old. You are keeping something back. What does this mean? Have you some suspicion about this man? Hah! I have it! You believe him to be a spy sent by Francis to learn all he can about my Court—about my realm! Man, man, you do not believe that this French King is plotting something to rob me farther of the possessions gained by my ancestors in the past?"

"No, Sire, no; but I am troubled in my mind," said Hurst, speaking in a low anxious tone.

"Out with it, then! What is your suspicion? What is it you know?"

"I know nothing, Sire," replied Hurst; "but I am troubled, in my grave anxiety for my master's weal, as to the real motives of this Comte's visit."

"Hah!"

"And I doubt, Sire, as to his being the Comte de la Seine."

"What!" cried the King. "Some impostor! Hurst! This is an insult to my guest, as noble and accomplished a gentleman as ever entered our Court—one whom I already look upon as my friend. Speak, man! What is it you think—that he is some cheat?"

"Cheat, Sire? No; but I believe him to be far higher in station than he says."

"Hah! Higher? How could he be higher?"

"Some prince, Sire, of royal blood."

"Bah!" cried the King contemptuously. "Fool! Dreamer! And at a time like this, when the horses are waiting and my guest doubtless ready, waiting till I join him! Always like this, Hurst, thinking out some wild diplomatic folly to cast like a stumbling-block in my way when I am upon pleasure bent. It is but little rest I get from cares of state, and you grudge me even that. Bah! I will hear no more.—Stop!" cried the King, after turning away. "See that there is a better banquet to-night, something more done to honour my French brother's emissary; more music and dancing, too. There, that is enough." And, hot and fuming, the King strode from the chamber, leaving his chamberlain standing alone, thoughtful and heavy.

Shortly afterwards there came through the open window the trampling of horses, eager voices, dominating all the loud, bluff, hearty voice of the King, followed by the sharper, rather metallic tones of the Comte, and then the merry laughter and ejaculations of the ladies who had joined the cavalcade. Then silence once again.

"Perhaps I am wrong," said the chamberlain thoughtfully; "and too much zeal may prove my ruin, for mine is a dangerous post and I fear that I have gone too far. I don't know, though. The suspicion seems to grow. We shall see, though; we shall see."

Chapter Twenty Eight
And opens the King's eyes

The chamberlain had worthily carried out his master's orders, and the scene in connection with the supper that night was brighter than ever; but the King did not seem satisfied. His heavy face looked gloomy, and Francis banteringly asked him if he was too much wearied by the hunt that day, receiving a grave nod in reply.

Later on Francis, who was excited and annoyed by the dullness of his host, made an excuse to leave him and join the dance, but only to find his progress stayed by Leoni, who led him aside to make some communication — one which made his master frown and whisper back angrily. But Leoni spoke again, and Denis, who was near, saw the King make a deprecating gesture with his hands, and then hurry off to enter the *salon* where the dancing was going on.

Denis stood watching Leoni, who stood looking thoughtfully after his master.

"I thought so," said the boy to himself, for as he watched Leoni he saw the doctor turn slowly and with his peculiar fixed look sweep the well-filled room till his eye rested upon the young esquire.

The next moment he had raised his finger to his lips, gazing at him fixedly for some moments, before turning and moving towards the door, when Denis heaved a deep sigh and looked round in vain in search of Saint Simon; but he was nowhere near, and the boy slowly followed Leoni, whom he found waiting for him just outside the door.

Meanwhile Hurst, upon seeing the Comte's departure, drew near to where Henry sat moody and alone, the various gentlemen in attendance, knowing their master's ways, having drawn back a little, to enter into a forced conversation, waiting for the King's next move.

They had not long to wait, for he suddenly looked round till his eyes rested upon the chamberlain, when he rose, to lay his hand upon his counsellor's shoulder and walk out with him towards the now deserted corridor, into which the strains of music from the ballroom floated again and again.

"There, Hurst," he cried, as soon as they were alone, and they paced together slowly towards the end, "what am I to say to you?"

"Sire?"

"If I were not in a good humour I should be disposed to punish you by the loss of my favour for spoiling what ought to have been a joyous day."

"Sire, I am deeply grieved. You must credit me with anxiety in my duty towards your Majesty."

"Yes, yes, I do," cried the King impatiently. "But your suspicions have been absurd, and have made me behave almost rudely to my brother's ambassador, as noble a gentleman as I ever met. Zounds, man! Is a king's life always to be made bitter by his people's dreams of plots? Your suspicions are all folly. He a prince of France! Absurd!"

The chamberlain walked on in silence, and stopped short where the corridor opened out into a well-lit chamber whose walls were hung with portraits.

"Well," said the King, "what now?"

"Would your Majesty step here into this alcove?" said the chamberlain, after a quick glance around to see that they were alone.

"What now?" cried the King angrily.

The chamberlain made no reply, but still stepped forward to the far side of the chamber, where he took a candle from one of the sconces on the wall to hold it up above his head in front of a large full-length canvas, the work of some great master, whose brush had so vividly delineated the features of his subject that the portrait seemed to gaze fixedly down at the King, while a faint smile just flickered upon its lips.

"Does your Majesty know those features?" said the chamberlain. "Who is that?"

"What!" cried the King, in startled tones. "Philippe de Valois."

"Yes, Sire; and my suspicion grows stronger every hour."

"Hah!" cried the King. "But no: impossible! And yet the same eyes; that same careless, half mocking smile. Hurst, there is something in this. The features are similar."

"Yes, Sire. It is a strong family resemblance."

"But who could it be, and why should he come here? To play the spy; for it could mean nothing else. What sinister plots and plans can there be behind all this? But you were thinking. You know something more?"

"I know no more than your Majesty. I only suspect."

"Suspect! Suspicion! I hate the very sounds of the words, and all the black clouds that hang around them. A family resemblance? Then who could this man be?"

The chamberlain was silent.

"Man," whispered the King hoarsely, "you are my servant. Don't thwart me now. If you value your place here—more, your life—speak out!"

The chamberlain returned the candle to the sconce, and then said slowly:

"Your servant's life is at your service, Sire. I am not sure, but I tell you honestly that which I believe. This gentleman is wearing a disguise, and comes here under an assumed name, and from my soul I believe he is—"

"Who?" whispered the King, grasping him fiercely by the arm.

"Francis, King of France."

"Hah!" ejaculated the King hoarsely, and with his face taking a fierce expression mingled with anger, surprise, and triumph. "And what has brought him here? If you are right. Hurst—mind, I say, if you are right—But you had never seen this man before, and it may be only a resemblance."

"It may, your Majesty, but—"

"If it is," whispered the King, with his face looking purple in the dim light, "the fox has come unbidden into the lion's den, and if the lion should raise his paw, where would be the fox?"

He looked fiercely and meaningly in his follower's eyes.

"France," continued the King, in a hoarse whisper. "France, how much of those fair domains won by my predecessors with the sword have been wrested from the English crown bit by bit—the noble domains over which these Valois now rule as usurpers. Hurst, what if the sceptre of England should be held again swaying our ancient lands of France. Supposing, I say, there were no Valois, or he perforce had been called upon to render back all that had been stolen from our crown. I am the King, and as my father used his gallant sword to gain one kingdom, why should not I by a diplomatic move win back another?"

"Your Majesty is King," said the chamberlain slowly and meaningly.

"Yes," said the King, in a hoarse whisper; "and when I am moved to act my will is strong."

There was silence for a few moments, and then Henry continued angrily:

"A ruse—a trick, put upon me for some strange scheming of his own, a gin, a trap to capture me, but for the setter to be caught himself. Francis, King of France!" he continued hoarsely; and then a peculiar smile, mocking, bitter, and almost savage, came upon his, lips as he gazed piercingly at his companion.

"No, Hurst," he said meaningly, "I know no King of France. He would not dare to beard me in my own home like this. This man, this mock ambassador, this Comte de la Seine, is the only one with whom we have to do—an impostor who shall meet with the trickster's fate."

"But your Majesty—" said the chamberlain eagerly.

"My Majesty, Hurst, is going to work his own will, and as he will."

"But, Sire, you will be just?"

"Yes, Hurst, as I always am. I grant that you may still be wrong, and we will clear this up."

"Your Majesty is going to—"

"Straight to the ballroom," replied the King, "to see this Comte de la Seine and have the truth."

"Now, Sire?"

"Yes, now at once."

The King turned abruptly, and, closely followed by the chamberlain, made for the ballroom, where the dancing was in full progress; but the Comte was not leading one of the brightest ladies of the Court through the mazes of gavotte or minuet, and as the King turned angrily to his chamberlain it was to find him in close converse with one of the gentlemen in attendance.

"The Comte made the excuse of a bad headache, Sire, some few minutes back, and retired to his apartments with his suite," whispered Hurst.

"Then I am afraid we shall make it worse," said the King bitterly. "This way, Hurst; I must have the truth of this before I sleep." And he strode from the room, closely followed by his companion, to whom in his excitement as he followed the angry lion the movements of the dancers seemed mocking, and the music sounded strange.

Chapter Twenty Nine
Dark work

More than one of the Court ladies thought the gallant Comte strange in his manner, as they waited, fully expecting that he would come up and offer his hand to lead them through the next dance; but it soon became evident that nothing was farther from his intentions, and after looking on for a short time he slowly left the great apartment, and began to make his way towards his own rooms. "I don't like it; I don't like it," he muttered. "It is vile and degrading. I feel as if only to think of it were lowering myself to the level of some cutpurse. I would I had never come. No," he added sharply; "the time has passed too gaily for me to say that; and the good, bluff, hot-tempered, cheery Henri! I like the brave Englishman, and my faith, I have made him like me, traitor as I am.—No, it is not I. It is the spirit of that cunning, subtle Leoni, with his horrible fixed eye. I cannot tell why, but he masters me— King as I am. He turns me round his finger and forces me to obey even against my better feelings; for I think I have some. Can it be that he is more than man, that he possesses some strange power over one's brain, as he does over the body when one is ill? Well, I'll be master now. I will not do this thing. By my sword, is this cunning Italian to force his master to become a thief? No! He shall learn to-night that I'll have none of it. Conceal who I am! Play the part of a masquerading spy! No! to-morrow I'll tell my brother Harry the whole truth."

He started violently as he came to this conclusion, for a dark figure suddenly glided from behind one of the statues in the long passage he was following. "You, Leoni?" he said, in a hoarse whisper. "M. le Comte! Yes, it is I. You have been long."

"Long?" said Francis haughtily. "How—" He stopped short, for Leoni placed his lips close to his ear. "France is anxious, Sire, and the time has come."

"The time!" said the King sharply. "Not for that?"

"Yes, M. le Comte, for that. I have been waiting for the fateful moment to arrive for the great opportunity, and it has come."

"But," cried Francis, "I have been thinking—my position here—my good friend the King. Leoni, all this must end; I cannot, I will not do this thing."

"Sire!" whispered Leoni.

"No, no, man. It is the Comte de la Seine you speak to, and who tells you he will let you lead him no more through these devious ways. Who are you that you should dare to force me onward into such a crime?"

"Your servant, sir, but at the same time he to whom it is given to lead you aright towards making your country the greatest in the world."

"Through crime?" said the King hotly.

"The acts of kings, sir, are outside crime. You are the anointed, and can do no wrong."

"Of my own will, no; but this:—"

"Sir, the spirit of your country calls upon you to act. The fateful jewel we came to seek is ready to pass into your possession, and the time has come—"

"Leoni, I will not hear you. I swear I will not sully mine honour with such an act. This deed shall never be done by me."

"Deed—deed, sir—act! You speak as if it were a crime," whispered Leoni.

"It is a crime," cried the King angrily. "Dare not to speak to me of this deed again. Now, enough. The King expects me back, and to-morrow I will place myself outside temptation, and leave this place. Whatever happens, my visit here is at an end."

"Your visit ends to-night, sir," said Leoni, in a low, harsh whisper; and as he spoke he leaned forward, passed his hands quickly before the King's face, and then caught him by the wrist.

"Leoni!" said Francis quickly. "What means this?"

"I have told you, sir. It is too late to attempt to shrink back now that the fateful moment has arrived. Quick, sir, and in an hour's time we shall be on our way to the coast. Silence, sir," he whispered sharply, as Francis essayed to speak, looking half dazed the while in his companion's eye, as Leoni leaned towards him with his hot breath passing over the monarch's face. "This way, sir—quick!"

"Where? Where?" faltered the King. "What does this mean, Leoni?" he whispered. "Have you been tricking me with one of your accursed drugs?"

"Silence, sir! I am calling you back to your duty," whispered the doctor, as he guided Francis quickly along the passage, still holding him tightly by the wrist, "for once more I pray you to prove yourself our country's greatest son."

Francis made no reply, no sign, but, yielding helplessly, allowed himself to be led to the door of his ante-chamber, where the door opened without being touched, and, once inside, closed behind them, Saint Simon having been waiting, while Denis, who looked pale and excited by the light of the two candles that illumined the room, rose up from where he had been kneeling, securing the straps of a valise.

No one spoke a word, for Leoni raised his hand as if commanding silence, as he still held the wrist of Francis, who gazed vacantly from one to the other as if he were in a dream.

"Is the Comte ill?" said Denis anxiously.

"A little over-excited," said Leoni quickly. "A cup of water, boy." And as he spoke, without leaving his grasp of the King's wrist, Leoni thrust the hand at liberty into his breast and drew forth a little golden *flacon*, which glistened in the light.

"Set down the cup," said Leoni quickly, as Denis returned from the bedchamber with the water. "Now, boy, unscrew the top of this, and hold it in your hand."

Leoni held out the little glistening flask, retaining it tightly, while Denis twisted off the tiny, cup-like top.

"Not that way, boy; turn it up so that I can fill it to the brim. Now," he whispered, "empty it into the water, and screw on the top once more."

This was quickly done, and the *flacon* replaced.

"Now," continued Leoni, "hand the cup to the Comte. The ballroom was overheated, and the wine he has drunk to-night has affected him.— Drink, sir; you will be better then."

The King started slightly, looked wildly in the eyes that seemed to master him, and with a slight shiver took the handed cup, drained it, and uttered a low, deep sigh.

"Ah," said Leoni, smiling in a peculiar way. "Now, gentlemen, the time has come for action. You, Saint Simon, be silent, and alert. There must be no bloodshed unless it is to save the Comte. You will come with us, and I shall depend upon your sword for our protection if there is peril in the way. You, Denis, boy," he continued, turning to the young esquire, who stood looking on now with his lips apart and a strange feeling of misery and despair oppressing him, "you have your duty to perform."

"Not to—" began Denis; but he was checked by the angry gesture the doctor made.

"Silence, sir! Your master's work. Follow us outside, and remain there on guard. The Comte's valise is ready. Never mind our own. Here, quick! Where is the cloak?"

Denis darted to a *garde-robe* and drew out the monarch's cloak.

"That's right. Throw it down there. You will now allow no one to pass in here, but stand on guard till we return. If we are not back here by the time the castle clock has chimed twice you will take the cloak and valise, go down the long corridor, if possible unseen, and make for the stables, where you will have the horses saddled at once."

"But—"

"But!" snapped out Leoni. "They must be saddled. Quick! Slip off my pouch and gird it on. There is gold enough within, and if that will not move the people there you have your sword."

Denis uttered a sigh of relief as he hastily unclasped the doctor's belt, for this was work he felt that he could do.

The next minute he was following his companions across the ante-chamber, ready to close the door behind them and place himself on guard in a gloomy angle of the corridor, from whence as he watched them he saw their figures seem to glide along the lighted portion, the Comte yielding entirely to his leader's every motion, till they passed quickly out of the sentry's ken.

Chapter Thirty
Bearding a lion

The King walked swiftly on in the direction of that portion of the castle where he had lodged his guest, the polished oak boards of the floor resounding beneath his heavy tread, while the chamberlain heard him keep muttering to himself as he went, till he reached a portion where a couple of officers stood on duty by a heavy door, ready to challenge them; but seeing in the half darkness who their visitors were, they drew back saluting, and opened the doors to allow them to pass.

"Your Majesty," said the chamberlain, in a low tone, as they began passing down an inner passage, and Henry read in his voice a protest against the action he was taking.

"Have done with your scruples," he said. "I am not going to assassinate Francis, or even do him ill, only to make sure." And he proceeded on his way, motioning to another officer, who came forward and saluted, to resume his post.

Turning at right angles, and going some distance further on, the King stopped again.

"It should be here," he said quietly, and he moved towards a wide arched door, but drew back suddenly, for a figure emerged from the shadow into the full light, naked sword in hand.

"You cannot pass," said the sentry.

"Who are you?" said Henry.

"A follower of the noble Comte de la Seine," was the reply.

"And he mounts guards at his chamber door?" said the King haughtily.

"Yes; but by what right do you come here and question me?"

Henry advanced into the light of a lamp overhead, and threw back his robe.

"I have the right," he said.

Denis drew back, but only a step.

"The King!" he murmured. "The King!"

Henry nodded quickly.

"You know me? Good. I have another word I wish to say to your master to-night."

"Sire," said Denis, dropping on one knee, "it is impossible."

"Impossible!" thundered the King.

"Impossible, Sire."

"Impossible! To me! In to your master at once, and tell him I have words to say to him to-night. By Heaven, it is an honour I do him, I think!"

"But, Sire—" cried Denis, who still barred the way.

"You heard me, boy?"

"Yes, Sire."

"Then—obey!"

"I regret to repeat to your Majesty that I cannot."

"Cannot!"

"No, Sire."

The King burst into a harsh laugh, and turning to the chamberlain, pointed angrily at the boy, before facing him again frowningly.

"Stand back, boy, and let me pass."

"I regret, your Majesty. Order me to do something else far more difficult—I would cheerfully obey your commands."

"But I have nothing else which I wish you to do—only this. Let me pass."

"No, Sire."

"Boy, it is the first time in my recollection that I have been refused obedience. Why do you stay me?"

"My master, Sire, has ordered me to keep strict guard here."

"Hurst, what am I to do to this obstinate fool?"

The chamberlain stepped forward.

"Boy," he said, "it is from sheer ignorance that you place yourself in such a position of danger. Sheathe your sword at once, sir, and let his

Majesty pass. Do you not know that there are guards here at every turn? My royal master's guests will be well protected without your aid."

Denis stood motionless, and made no attempt to stir.

"Do you hear, sirrah!" roared the King. "I am in no humour to wait longer. Stand back."

This was too much for the determination of the young esquire. It was a king who spoke, and drawing back slightly, he yielded to circumstances, feeling that his puny efforts were in vain, and guarding the door no longer, he thrust his sword back into its scabbard and stood aside.

"Ah!" cried the King, growing mollified upon seeing himself obeyed, and looking admiringly at the lad. "Not bad, Hurst, for a mere boy," he said. "May I always be as well served by followers of mine. There," he continued, stepping forward towards the door, and looking back at Denis, "you can follow me, and I will make your peace with your lord, for I am master here."

He tapped sharply at the panel of the door with the hilt of his sword, and Denis heard him breathing heavily as if after some great exertion; but there was no reply, and he tapped again, with the same negative result. Then with an angry snort he said mockingly:

"Our young esquire seems to have reason on his side, and the Comte must be asleep. Am I to leave him to his slumbers, Hurst? But maybe he will sleep the better after awakening and hearing all I have to say. Open the door, Hurst. Bah! I need no help for this." And, brushing by the chamberlain, he noisily raised the latch, thrust open the door, and entered the room.

It was the ante-chamber, with the couple of candles burning on the mantel. The richly embroidered cloak lay upon the couch where it had been hurriedly thrown, and the valise lay ready packed and strapped.

The King's eyes flashed as the valise caught his eye, and crossing the room quickly he made for the door of the sleeping chamber, which was ajar.

There was no pause to ask for entrance here, for now fully roused, the King thrust open the door, with the light from behind him falling fall upon the unpressed bed.

"Hah! What I expected," cried the King angrily. "This way, Hurst. There is mystery and trickery here."

As he was speaking the clock from one of the turrets was chiming loudly, the sounds of the bells seeming to quiver in the still air and mingle with the faint strains from the room where the dancing was still going on.

The chamberlain rushed forward, looked sharply round, and made for the casement; but it was closed and fastened inside.

"The boy on guard, Sire, and no one here!" cried the chamberlain. "I do not understand."

"Nor I," cried the King; "but we will, and that right soon." Then making for the door, which had fallen back as the chamberlain entered, he dragged it open, crying angrily, "Boy, your master is not sleeping here. Where is he? What have you to say? Ha!" he roared, like the angry lion he had described himself to be. "Quick, Hurst! Our guards! The boy has gone!"

Chapter Thirty One
Leoni's weapon

But as Hurst made a step forward to summon the guard the King caught him by the wrist.

"By my faith," he ejaculated, "there is black treachery here! Am I in my own palace or in a tavern? These fellows come and go as if the place were their own. A mystery too. But by the crown I swear I'll solve it!" And for a few moments he stood fuming. "Here, Hurst," he said hoarsely, "your brains have been sharper than mine, and I'm beginning to think you are right about that portrait. Ambassador—poet—brilliant conversationalist—one who has won himself into favour with us all. Hah!" he went on. "He can be no Comte de la Seine! Can you ever trust a Frenchman? But come on!" And he led the way back into the long gallery. "I've got ears like a cat to-night," he said; "but unfortunately not the eyes of one. Surely those were footsteps down yonder?"

"Yes, Sire," said Hurst. "Beneath that window—a white doublet!"

"Yes," cried the King. "Come on!"

"But the guard, Sire? Shall I gammon them?"

"No, no," cried the King impatiently. "This is exciting. We will be our own guard, and find out the truth ourselves."

The King and the chamberlain had not gone many yards along the gallery when they they came to a halt, for a figure barred the way.

"Who goes there?" came from out of the gloom.

"Pst!" said the King. "Young Carrbroke.—England!" he cried.

The figure came nearer, into the light of a window—a slim figure in a white doublet; and the radiance of the moon flashed on a bared and shining sword.

"Your Majesty!" he exclaimed, and he dropped on one knee.

"Rise," said Henry. "You are on duty here?"

"Yes, Sire."

"Has anyone passed?"

"No, Sire."

"You are certain?"

"Quite certain, Sire."

"Good. Come, Hurst!" And the two proceeded on their way, turning the corner of the long gallery, passing from gloom to silvery light, and again into the dusk, as they walked beneath the windows, while at the angle the lustrous splendour was shed through red glass, falling brilliantly on the King's plumed hat, his sword and royal star, as the pair disappeared.

Carrbroke turned and looked after the retreating figures.

"I wish," he murmured, "that his Majesty had ordered me to follow him." And he stood gazing in the direction the King and chamberlain had taken, till growing weary, he stepped aside into the shadow, where he could half seat himself, half lean against the end of a great settee. "How I do hate this guard work of a night! Yes, and there's the music still going on. I just heard one strain. All bright and gay yonder, and here all dark and dull. But it's an honour, I suppose, to be on the watch over the ways to his Majesty's private apartments, and have him come and find me here. It means promotion some day, such private service as this. I wonder where French Denis is? Dancing with the prettiest girl he can find, I'll be bound. Oh dear, how dreary it is! And I feel as if I could lie down and go to sleep."

Then with a start he was fully on the alert, ready to step out into such light as was shed through the window near.

"His Majesty coming back," he muttered, for quick steps were heard approaching, and a few moments later he stepped quickly out to bar the way as he did a short time before, and with a feeling upon him that he would show his master how well he was on the alert.

He challenged, fully believing that it was Henry and the chamberlain, and started violently on finding out his mistake, for it was Francis, who cried angrily:

"Who are you?"

"Carrbroke, M. le Comte. This is the way to his Majesty's private apartments. You cannot pass here."

In an instant Leoni had glided alongside, to lay his hand softly on the youth's arm.

"My dear young friend," he said, "you do not recognise who it is speaking. It is the King's friend, the Comte de la Seine. The ballroom was hot, and these corridors calm, cool, and refreshing. The Comte is only going round this way to reach his apartment. We can reach it down this passage, can we not?"

"No, sir," said Carrbroke quietly. "I am sorry to have to turn you back, but you must seek some other way. I am on guard here, and it is his Majesty's commands that no one shall pass this private corridor by night—and no wonder," thought the lad, as he recalled his discovery of the private doorway not far from where they stood.

Francis uttered an impatient growl.

"Tell him," he said angrily in French, to Leoni—"tell him I object to being treated like a prisoner"—words which Leoni translated, in the belief that they were not understood.

"The Comte de la Seine says, Monsieur Carrbroke, that surely his Majesty would make an exception in favour of his friend."

"I regret it much," was the reply, "but unless the King gives me such orders in contradiction of those which I have received, I cannot let you pass. Once more, gentlemen, it is impossible, and you must return. Did you hear me, M. Saint Simon? Ah, sir, you—" He said no more, for Saint Simon had passed onward, as if to go on in spite of all that had been said, but only to turn quickly and seize his arms from behind, while at the same moment his speech was cut short by Leoni's hand—the subtle Franco-Italian having literally glided at him to clap a strongly smelling hand, moist with some pungent fluid, across his mouth.

The action seemed to the lad as instantaneous as its effect. He made a bold brave struggle, uttering a groaning half-stifled sound, and he vainly strove to free himself from the pinioning hands of Saint Simon; while, as if through a misty dream, he saw with starting eyes the dim figure of his master's guest straight before him, and pointing a stiletto at his throat.

The next minute Saint Simon, in obedience to the whispered orders of Leoni, had raised the helpless lad in his arms.

"Is there to be no end to this black night's work?" muttered Francis angrily. "I don't know how it is. I don't think I took too much of my brother Henry's wine, for I wanted to dance; but my head is all confused and strange."

"It was the heat of the room, perhaps, sir," said Leoni.

"Perhaps so. The place was hot and stifling," said Francis. "There are moments when my brain seems to whirl, and things go round. Did I go to sleep?"

"Yes, sir; you were certainly insensible to all that passed for a time."

"Of course I was," said the King angrily, "if I was asleep; but why don't you say so? Here, I don't know what's the matter with me. I must have dreamed that you took me by the wrist and led me along one of these dark galleries, to stop and lean against some great piece of furniture while something was going on. Then all was dark and strange again, and I seemed to be going for ever along dark passages, till I felt the fresh air coming in through an open window looking out upon the terrace. Well, come, Saint Simon; that was not dreaming."

"No, sir," said the young courtier drily.

"You were suffering from excitement, sir," said Leoni quietly. "A touch of vertigo. You have been doing too much of late. But you feel better now?"

"Oh yes, better now—and worse, for I am not certain but what this rough dealing with that boy is not part of another dream."

"That is no dream, sir," said Leoni meaningly; "but be silent and let me guide. We are on our way to make our escape."

"Escape!" whispered back the King excitedly. "Then—then—oh, it's coming back quite clearly. You have tried and failed?"

"Hist! Silence, Comte!" whispered Leoni, in a commanding tone, as he turned upon the speaker, but without taking his hand from Carrbroke's lips. "Our task is nearly at an end, sir, and I will answer to you later on.—Now, Saint Simon, lay the boy quickly on that couch."

"Have you killed him?" whispered Francis.

"No, sir; only plunged him into a deep sleep.—That's right, Saint Simon." And then in a mocking tone, "I am afraid that the faithful sentinel will be in trouble when they find him here asleep. I didn't think to find him here. Now, quick, before we are interrupted again." And he moved a few steps down the gallery, passing his hand along the hangings which veiled the panelled wall. "Somewhere here," he muttered; "somewhere here. I seem to know the place so well."

"Leoni," growled the King, "this night will end in our disgrace, and if it does—"

"Hist, sir! there is a way out here," whispered Leoni. "You hinder and confuse me, and at a time like this, when everything points to success, you—ah, here it is!" For his hand had at last come in contact with the boss, which he turned quickly, pressed hard, making the concealed door swing back, and then stooped in the gloom to raise the arras. "Now, sir; through here—quick!"

"What!" said Francis sharply. "Go through there into what may be a trap?"

Leoni made no reply, but turned to Saint Simon.

"Through with you," he whispered, with a contemptuous ring in his voice. "I would lead, but I must come last to close the way, for they must not know the route we have taken in our flight."

The young officer passed through without a word, and, half ashamed of his hesitation, Francis followed, to have his hand seized in the darkness by Saint Simon, who led him for a few yards along the dark passage, where they stopped listening, to hear Leoni close the door with a faint, half-smothered click.

Leoni joined them the next moment, "Let me pass now and go first," he whispered. "The passage is very narrow, and dark as dark. Thanks, Saint Simon," he continued, as he squeezed by him; and then, as if to himself, but loud enough for Francis to hear, "and then if there is any trap or pitfall in the way I shall be the sufferer, and they will hear me and escape. Ah," he continued to himself, "the way seems easy, and what did the lad say?—that it led after several turns to some stairs which descended to the ground floor, and finally to a door which opened upon a bosky portion of the terrace, and from there led on through various alleys to the river, a flight of steps, and a boat. Ah, a good way to escape; but we must have our horses, and trust to them. Well, once within the grounds—I have not been here all these days for nothing—and it will go hard if I do not find my way to the stabling, where Denis should be waiting with the ready saddled steeds, if he has done his duty as I bade."

As he thought this over to himself, breaking it up, as it were, into sentences between which were whispered words of encouragement to those who followed, bidding them come on, telling them that all was clear, and to beware of "this angle," and the like, he passed on and on with outstretched hands in front, his fingers gliding on either side over smooth stone walls, till at last he was suddenly checked by a blank.

"Ah!" he muttered, as he felt about cautiously. "This should be the top of the steps." And so it proved; for, proceeding carefully from the angle along to his left, his advanced foot, as he glided it over the floor, rested on an edge.

"The topmost stair," he muttered.

Making certain that it was, Leoni uttered fresh warnings, and then began to descend, followed slowly by his companions. At the bottom they proceeded for a while upon the level, when he was brought up short by his fingers encountering on one side the great iron pintle of a hinge, while the other touched the edge of a stone rebate, into which a heavy door was sunk.

"Hah!" he uttered, with a sigh of relief. "Here is the way out of this kingly fox-burrow." And his hand glided down the edge of the door till it came in contact with a huge lock, about which for a few moments his fingers played, while a chill ran through him, filling him with despair, for the truth had come upon him like a flash: there was no key in the lock; the door was fast; and just in this hour of triumph they were as much prisoners as if they were in a cell.

"Well, Leoni," whispered Francis, "why are you stopping? This place makes me feel as if I could not breathe."

"I am not stopping, sir," said the doctor bitterly; "I have been stopped."

Chapter Thirty Two
Check!—query, mate?

Feeling that the crisis had come, no sooner did Denis hear the first strokes of the second chiming of the clock, which came so opportunely upon the King's discovery, than the lad dashed off along the passage leading towards the staircase that he would have to descend to gain the inner court and the stabling.

But he had not proceeded many yards before he stopped short, startled by the thought that if he continued by this corridor he would come right upon some gentleman of the household, whose nightly duty it was to be on guard at the angle of the gallery which led towards the King's apartments.

"Oh," he muttered beneath his breath, "I had forgotten. Carrbroke told me he would be there to-night."

There was nothing for it but to retrace his steps, pass right round two-thirds of one of the lesser courts, and get back to the corridor again beyond the range of apartments sacred to the King.

Then reaching the end of the gallery, he began to hurry once more to make up for lost time, when feeling that, much as he desired to act, such hurried procedure would attract the attention of the first officer who was on guard, the lad checked his headlong steps, thrust his hands into his trunk hose, and began to walk carelessly along, catching up and humming the air which came softly from where the musicians were still playing.

It was well he did, for as he turned the next corner he came upon a couple of the King's guards upon the landing at the head of a staircase.

His face was familiar to the men as one of the King's guests, and it being right away from the royal apartments, they gave way for him to pass, and making a tremendous effort over himself, he descended very slowly and carelessly, the hardest part of all being to stop once or twice as if listening to the music, and then go on humming the air.

He breathed more freely as he passed out into the courtyard and crossed it, fully expecting to encounter a guard at the archway which gave upon the next court.

As he expected, there were a couple of armed men here ready to challenge him; but before they could speak he stopped short to ask whether he would find men in attendance at the stables, adding carelessly in very fair English:

"I want to see how our horses are getting on."

It was so likely a mission that the principal of the two guards volunteered the information at once that some of the grooms would be sure to be there at that time for a final look round before closing for the night.

"You know your way, sir?" added the man respectfully.

"Oh yes, thank you," said Denis carelessly; "I know my way." And he walked on, panting heavily now, in spite of his slow pace. "This is the hardest work of all," he muttered, "for I want to run—I want to run. But oh, how I do hate it all! They must be stealing the jewel now, for I can call it nothing else but a theft. How glad I am that they have sent me away, and I am not obliged to degrade myself with such a task. But yet I am helping, and seem as bad as they—but no, not *as* bad. Leoni says it is right, and—yes, it was stolen from us, and it is but to restore it to France—to France."

"Now for it," he muttered, as he neared the entrance to the great stables, where to his delight he could see by the light within that the door was open and a shadow passing the lit-up entry showed him that at all events part of his task would be easy. "Now no more thinking. I am but doing my duty, and it is time to act."

Increasing his pace now, he stepped boldly into a broad shelter from which a long, dimly seen vista of horse-stalls opened out to right and left, and he was confronted at once by two of a group of men, three of whom bore lanterns, and who were coming towards him as if about to leave the place.

"Here," he cried authoritatively, as he recognised one of the grooms as being he who had their steeds in charge, "I want our horses saddled at once."

"To-night, sir?" said the man, glancing at the lad's courtly costume in search of his boots and spurs, and seeking in vain, his eyes being only met by glistening silk and rosetted shoon.

"Yes," replied Denis haughtily; "to-night"; and then half laughingly, "It is fresh and cool and pleasant, is it not?"

"Yes, sir," said the man, "but—"

"The rooms are hot and stifling to-night, and the Comte my master wishes to ride forth. You will be well rewarded for the extra trouble and—

ah, here," he continued, thrusting his hand into Leoni's pouch, "I forgot; you will of course sit up till we return. Here is something to pay for wine."

He held out a couple of gold pieces, which, as they were taken, acted like magic, and a busy little scene of emulation ensued, every man being eager to assist in bridling and saddling the beautiful chargers that had been standing haltered in their stalls.

It was hard work for Denis, whose pulses were throbbing with impatience; but he carried out his part well, patting and stroking first one and then another of the noble beasts, and talking to them the while.

"It seems rather hard," he said, speaking in the same haughty tone to the man he had before addressed; "but a good canter round the park will do them good, and their work is very easy nowadays."

The groom agreed to everything he said, for the glint of the gold placed in his hand was still before his eyes; and in a very short space of time, long as it seemed to the impatient lad, the last strap and buckle were fastened, and with a man giving final touches to glistening coat and mane, the horses were about to be led forth.

"We are to take them round to the great entrance, sir?" said the chief groom.

"Oh no," replied Denis carelessly. "Just lead them into the entry; the Comte and his gentlemen are going to join me here. It is just for a quiet night ride, and—ah," he added, with a faint gasp of relief, "here they come!" For heavy footsteps approaching hastily could be heard outside—footsteps of only one, but which the lad in his wild excitement easily magnified into those of all his friends, as he walked far more swiftly than he intended to meet the three fugitives, ready to mount and in full career leave the hospitable place behind.

The words were on his lips to greet them and say, "All is ready; you can mount in here." But they were frozen on his lips, for the light from within fell full upon a big burly form, that of an enemy who, like a flash, the lad felt, could only have come upon a mission of evil; and he stood as if turned to stone, as a familiar voice exclaimed:

"Hallo, my French friend! I saw you cross the Court and come in here, and so I watched. What's your business, pray, at this time of the night? Have you come to steal his Majesty's steeds?"

Chapter Thirty Three
Leoni's pupil

"How dare you!" cried Denis.

"Oh, I'll soon show you how I dare, my lad," cried Sir Robert Garstang. "Here, you fellow, who gave you orders to get those horses ready?"

"This gentleman, sir," said the groom.

"What, this Comte de la Seine's page, or whatever he is? And what right has he to instruct you to get horses out at this time of night?"

"I don't know, Sir Robert. We were told to get them ready," said the man humbly.

"Ah, but this must be inquired into. There's something wrong here, I feel sure."

"Take no notice of this man," cried Denis, forgetting in his excitement that he must speak in English, however bad, if he wished the grooms to understand, and addressing them excitedly in French.

"Bah!" cried Sir Robert, in his most bullying tones. "Take no notice of the fellow's jabber. I order you not to let these horses go without the permission of the chamberlain or the King's Master of the Horse."

"But they are the gentlemen's own horses, Sir Robert," said the man quietly, "and not the King's."

"I don't care," cried the officer. "The rules are, as I know well, that no horses shall leave here without special orders after dark."

Denis grasped every word that was said, and stood literally trembling with excitement, anticipating as he did that at any moment his friends might arrive, when there would be a discovery of the attempted flight, and all would be over.

In his desperation, just as his heart seemed sinking to the lowest ebb, Leoni's words recurred to him. He had used the gold, while now, as the doctor had told him, he had his sword; and at this thought he drew in his breath through his teeth with a sharp low hiss.

"You hear!" cried Sir Robert sharply. "These horses are not to leave the stable till I return with some one in authority who shall decide what is to be done. You understand me? On your lives, obey!"

He swung round to stride out of the building, and then started with surprise, for the young esquire's rapier flashed out sharply in the dull light of the lanterns, as he drew and cried sternly:

"On your life, sir, stand back, and cease to interfere! I have the highest of commands for what I do."

"What!" cried Sir Robert. "Why, I have been waiting for this, to pay you back the smart you gave me—insolent French puppy that you are! Give up your sword, sir. Do you know that it is a crime to draw in the precincts of the castle? This you have done, and it is my duty as one of his Majesty's officers to arrest you on the spot. Give up your sword, sir, at once. You are my prisoner."

"Take my sword," cried Denis sharply, "and make me your prisoner, insolent boor, if you dare or can."

"On your head be it then," cried Sir Robert, loosening his cloak, twisting it quickly round his left arm, and drawing his sword, while the chief groom, startled by the danger in which the young esquire stood, whispered quickly to a couple of his underlings to hurry for the guard.

"Stop!" cried Sir Robert fiercely. "Let no man stir if he value his skin. I know what you would do, and that I'll do myself when I have corrected this springald here.—Now, boy," he roared, "your sword!"

"Now, Master Leoni," whispered the boy between his teeth, as he rapidly placed himself on guard and made a feint at the burly captain's chest. "Take it, insolent bully!" he said sharply; and the officer in his astonishment at the suddenness of the attack, fell back a pace; but recovering himself on the instant, he crossed swords with his young adversary. Then, to the excitement and delight of the grooms, who raised their lanterns to the full extent of their arms that the combatants might see, the triangular-bladed weapons began to give forth that peculiar harsh gritting sound of two steel edges rasping together.

The encounter was but short, for, relying upon the superior strength of his arm, and determined to punish his slight young adversary in revenge for the past, the captain pressed hard upon him, lunging rapidly with all the vigour he could command, his intention being to drive his antagonist backward against one or other of the walls and pin him there. But he had reckoned without his host, for though Denis was no long-practised swordsman, Leoni's lessons had not been without their effect, and as thrust after thrust was lightly turned aside, the young esquire firmly stood his ground, merely stepping sideways and letting his adversary's baffled blade glide by his slight form, while refraining from thrusting again and again when the burly captain had laid himself so open that he was quite at the lad's mercy.

"Oh," growled the captain at the end of a couple of minutes' encounter, and he drew back to rest. "That is your play, is it? You refuse to be disarmed when I have mercifully shown myself disposed to let you off without a scratch."

"Your tongue is sharper than your sword, sir," said the boy scornfully; "and it is worse. It is poisoned, for every word you have spoken is a lie."

"What!" cried the captain, enraged by the low murmur uttered by the grooms as if endorsing the young esquire's words. "More insolent than ever! Give up your sword, or, by Heaven, I'll send you back to the castle upon a litter."

"Send me, then," said the lad contemptuously, "or be prepared to go yourself."

"Bah! No more words. Come on," cried the captain; and he prepared to attack once more.

"My turn now," whispered the boy to himself, "and it is time;" for in his excitement he fancied that he could hear steps approaching. But there was not a sound save the gritting of the rapiers and the captain's hoarse panting breath as he uttered a loud expiration at every thrust.

For in his turn, in spite of his determination to make this second encounter an attack, and force his young adversary to remain entirely on his guard, the retort had begun, and before a minute had elapsed he uttered a sharp ejaculation as he felt the sharp pain caused by the lad's keen point ripping open his muscular right arm. Stung now with rage, hatred, and the determination to have revenge, he literally rushed at the lad, to force him down, with the natural result that he threw himself open to the point of his more skilful enemy, who chose his moment, and made one quick thrust which darted like lightning through the captain's bull-like neck, making him utter a low, deep growl as his sword flew from his hand, and he staggered backwards into the arms of a couple of the grooms, who lowered him to the ground.

"Hah!" ejaculated Denis, whose heart was beating fast, and stepping forward he stooped over his fallen adversary, raised a portion of his cloak and drew his blade through it twice over. "Stop!" he cried quickly. "What are you going to do?" His loud question was addressed to the chief groom.

"No," cried the boy sternly; "lift him in yonder," and he pointed with his blade towards the saddle-room. "Lay him there; tear strips off his cloak, and bind up his arm and neck. The greatest help you can give him now is to stop the bleeding."

There was a tone of command in the boy's uttered words which had the natural effect, and the men busied themselves at once with their task, taking with them their lanterns and doing at once as they had been told, while they were so intent upon their task that they did not notice that Denis had followed them, to draw to the door and slip the two bolts with which it was furnished into their sockets.

Then sheathing his sword, he turned quickly to the stable, where the four chargers stood untethered, and caught his own by the bridle, to begin leading it to the door.

He trusted to the nature of the horses for the result, old stable companions as they were, and it was as he expected, for the intelligent animals followed their leader quietly enough, to stand together in the entry waiting, like their master, for what might come.

Chapter Thirty Four
A dash for liberty

"Oh!" groaned Denis to himself, as he stood in the darkness watching the shape of the saddle-room door, marked-out as it was in lines of light from the lanterns within, listening to the low muttering of voices, and shuddering once as his wounded adversary uttered a low deep groan, which was followed directly after by an angry ejaculation as if he were enraged by the clumsy surgery of the men.

"Is all this going to be in vain?" muttered the boy. "It is as if the whole business is accursed and is bound to fail."

He stood listening, and the talking went on, to be interrupted by another fierce ejaculation from the captain, who gave some order; but what it was Denis could not grasp, and he literally groaned again.

"They do not come! They do not come!" he said. "It is all useless. They must have failed."

He had hardly spoken the words when he fancied he heard steps; but all was still, and then he started violently and clapped his hand to his sword, for some one tried to open the saddle-room door, then shook it, and the words of whoever it was came plainly to the lad's ears:

"I can't, Sir Robert. He has shut us in."

"What!" came hoarsely; and at the same moment Denis's heart leaped, for there was no mistake this time. Footsteps were rapidly approaching, whether friends' or foes' it was impossible to tell, and taking a step outside the door with his bridle over his arm, his horse followed him, setting in motion the other three, which, well-trained as they were, ranged up alongside upon the cobble stones before the double doors.

There was no doubt now, for three figures, plainly seen by the light which shone out of the saddle-room window, came breathlessly up, and the first to speak cried in familiar tones:

"My horse! Is it ready? Quick!"

"Yes, Sire," whispered Denis, and Francis uttered a quick low "Hah!" as he gathered up the reins and prepared to mount, his two companions following his example, just as the lit-up window was dashed out by some heavy blow, the glass coming tinkling down upon the stones outside, and a hoarse voice that Denis knew only too well roared out:

"Guard, here! Guard! Help! In the King's name! Guard!"

As the last words came hoarsely forth on to the night air, *clang, clang, clang*, burst out the tocsin of the alarm bell, silencing the music in the ballroom and sending an electric thrill through every listener within the precincts of the castle; but ere the great bell had sent forth a score of vibrating notes which came quivering through the darkness and echoing from every wall, the clattering of hoofs began in obedience to the whispered commands of his Majesty of France:

"Draw, draw, and all together to the gates. Then lead, Leoni, and ride hard—straight away, man, for the south."

The horses had not made a dozen strides before their sharp hoof clatterings upon the paved court gave place to the dull *thud, thud*, returned from gravel, while before a hundred yards had been passed over, a couple of lanterns began to dance here and there right before them, their dull yellow rays being reflected from the broad blades of halberds borne by men who were evidently forming up in obedience to a shouted order, before making for the castle.

The horsemen needed no command. They knew what they had to do—to charge right through the night watch assembling from the guard-room; and this they did.

There were shouts, commands to stop in the King's name, the impact of horse and man, and the clatter and jangle of steel against steel, as the fugitives rode their opponents down, kept together, and dashed on for another hundred yards or so, and then were brought up short by that which had not entered into their calculations, for they simultaneously drew rein as Saint Simon, fully excited now, roared in a voice of thunder; "The gates are shut!"

The King uttered a low gasp, and it was Leoni who said sharply:

"Only the great gates. The doorway—is it right or left?"

"Here," cried Denis; "this way, Sire!" And he made a snatch at the rein of the monarch's horse and drew back his own for him to pass, closely followed by Leoni, who was just in time to rise in his stirrups and make a thrust at a tall halberdier who had suddenly stepped forward to seize the rein of Francis's horse.

The man uttered no cry, only dropped his halberd and staggered back as Leoni passed on into the darkness, his horse running side by side with that of the King.

Meanwhile—it was almost momentary—Saint Simon, who was the next to pass through the narrow pier-bound way, cried out excitedly to his young friend:

"Come on, boy! It will be a ride for life."

Denis knew it, as he sat there motionless as a statue upon his horse, with his sword pointed towards the advancing enemy, a full score of them dimly seen in the gloom, who, recovering from the terrible shock they had received, came running with their clumsy partisans levelled for their charge, to take revenge upon and capture the daring unknown party which had made this desperate attack.

There were men among them who were suffering from blows and from trampling hoofs, and other injuries they had received; but as they ran they recovered their well-trained formation, and with their leader dashed two and two through the narrow postern gate and along the darkened road for full a couple of hundred yards, before the stern command rang out for them to halt.

As the trampling of their feet ceased to beat upon the road they stood in the silence listening to the tramp of hoofs, which grew fainter and fainter, till the last sound died away and the silence was broken by a deep groan uttered by one of the men, who now dropped out and sank upon his knees.

"Who's that?" cried the leader sharply.

"Staines Dick," was the reply.

"Humph!" grunted the sergeant who had led the pursuit. "That's two of us gone down. I saw the sentry had it as we passed out. Is there anyone among you as would like to be sergeant instead of me?"

"No," said another voice. "Why?"

"Because I am Sergeant of the Guard, my lads, and I shall have to go back and meet the King."

There was a peculiar sound from the little body of men, caused by their simultaneously sharply drawing in their breath, and then silence once again, as they listened to make sure that the beating of hoofs had passed beyond their ken. Then once more the sergeant spoke out.

"Halberds here," he said sharply, "and make a litter for this poor chap. That's right; lift him gently. Have you got it badly, lad?"

"No, sergeant; only my left arm broke. It was the hoof of a horse as he galloped over me and struck me aside."

"Hah!" said the sergeant, as he marched beside the improvised litter and went on talking to his injured man. "It's bad, my lad, bad; but it don't mean funeral march, and between ourselves, Staines Dick. I wish I was you."

Chapter Thirty Five
Bluff Hal rages

"I don't understand this, Hurst. I don't understand it a bit. One moment I feel that he is no Comte, at another that there may be something in what you say. But just now I can think of nothing but de la Seine not being in his room. Bah! He cannot have taken to flight, thinking that I have discovered who he is; but we must find out that."

At this moment the King was passing along the centre of the gallery devoted to the priceless treasures of his collection, to which Carrbroke had so proudly directed the young French visitor's attention, when his foot came suddenly in contact with something which he sent flying along the polished oaken boards, the object making a musical metallic sound.

"What's that?" cried the King sharply; and the chamberlain started forward into the gloom close beneath one of the windows, to pick up after a moment's search what proved on being held up to the light to be a beautiful little golden cup covered with such *repoussé* work as would most likely have been placed there by some Italian artist of the Benvenuto Cellini type.

A faint cry of wonder escaped the chamberlain's lips.

"A golden cup!" exclaimed the King, as he leaned over to gaze at the little object. "How comes that there? Why, Hurst, that little *tazza* should be in the big cabinet yonder, where the French jewel lies. Quick! Here."

The King turned sharply and hurried back to the centre of the gallery where the great cabinet stood, to find it on the two sides he examined perfectly intact; but the other two sides of the big ornamental piece of furniture fell to the chamberlain's examination, and he was so startled by the discovery he made that he remained silent and stood there with his lips compressed.

"Nothing here, Hurst," cried the King, in less excited tones. "It must have been my fancy; it cannot be the cup I mean. You see nothing?"

"Will your Majesty look here?" said the chamberlain gravely.

"Hah!" cried the King, and he joined his follower on the other side, to utter an ejaculation full of the rage he felt, for dim as the gallery was, light enough came through the window opposite to which the cabinet stood to show that one of the doors had been wrenched open; some of the drawers within were half unclosed, while several little objects that had evidently been dropped in haste were upon the floor.

"Robbery! Pillage!" cried the King angrily. "They must have been disturbed in their act of plunder, whoever it was, and—and—hah!" he raged out, as he snatched up a case that was lying open. "Look here, Hurst; this tells the tale. Do you know it?"

"No, Sire."

"You see it is empty."

"Yes, Sire."

"I could gage my life that within the last hour it held that fateful gem won by the Kings of England, the jewel from the French crown. Now, man, who is the robber? Speak!"

"Ah!" half whispered the chamberlain. "Your Majesty is right. This disappearance is accounted for at once. It must have been—"

"The Comte de la Seine!" raged out the King. "Stolen not only from my own palace, but out of my own private apartments, where I am supposed to be guarded night and day. Hurst," he continued grimly. "I am afraid some one is going to die on account of this. But the robbers cannot have gone far. They must be somewhere about."

"Yes, Sire. There are guards everywhere, and the gates are closed. They must be in the castle still."

"Then this be my task," cried the King, "to hunt the cunning schemers down. This way first. There should be two guards at the head of the south staircase—if they are not asleep."

In his excitement the King drew his sword and led the way to where the two officers were on duty, ready to challenge and answer frankly that only one person had passed there, and that the young esquire in the Comte de la Seine's suite.

"Bah! We are on the wrong track," said the King angrily. "They would not come this way. That boy was probably sent to take the guards' attention while the deed was done. Come back, Hurst; this way. You men arrest anybody who tries to pass you, no matter who it may be. Now, Hurst, quick, for the game is afoot and we must run it down."

He hurriedly led the way back along the gallery, past the broken cabinet without giving it a moment's concern, and when nearing the private corridor the King stopped short, to clutch his follower by the breast with his left hand.

"Hurst," he whispered hoarsely, the deep tones of his voice betraying the rage burning in his breast—"Hurst, have we been betrayed?"

"Surely not, your Majesty. Your people are too loyal for that."

"But the French are very cunning, man, and gold, even if it is foreign, will sometimes work its way."

"Your Majesty speaks in riddles," said the chamberlain nervously, for his master still clutched him by the breast, and the sword was trembling in his hand as if he were about to use it upon a prisoner he had taken himself.

"Riddles!" cried the King. "When we are searching for that vile culprit whom I believed to be still in the place, and who has not passed the guards at either end of these galleries? That boy Carrbroke: he told us that no one had passed by him."

"Yes, your Majesty; but still I do not understand your drift."

"Man, have you no brains to think? Is there not another way from here?"

"Hah!" cried the chamberlain in a hoarse whisper. "The secret passage!"

"Yes," said the King, in a low, deep voice. "Some one—if they have not watched and discovered for themselves—must have betrayed its existence, known only to me and you. But maybe it has acted like a trap—the outer door is locked, and a stranger would not be likely to find the key."

"Oh," whispered the chamberlain, "it is possible, Sire. I will call the guard."

"No," said the King, with an angry hiss in his voice. "You can use your sword, Hurst?"

"In your Majesty's service at any time," replied the chamberlain.

"And I am not a child with mine," said the King. "Hurst, man, your suspicions are right. This French visitor is no paltry Comte. There is the look of the Valois in his countenance. What if the great object of his visit here was to steal that gem taken from his land by conquest? Hurst, I should like to take this man redhanded myself. We are two, and possibly he is alone, for he would not trust such a task as this to other hands. We heard just now that his page, esquire, or whatever he is, had been sent away."

"Yes, Sire. But he will be desperate. Your Majesty's safety must not be risked. I implore you, let me call the guard."

"Well, as you will," said the King.—"No, it would only be to reveal that secret place to the common herd. No one shall know it but ourselves. But stop; there is some one close at hand whom I dare trust. Old Sir John Carrbroke's son. He will be trusty as his father was to me, and to my father in his time. Fetch him here."

The chamberlain hurried off, while the King followed slowly, sword in hand, till he was opposite to the concealed door, where he stood fast to wait; but an ejaculation uttered by Lord Hurst took him to the latter's side.

"Traitor!" cried the King angrily. "No, sleeper." And in his rage he drew back his arm as if to thrust at the youth who was lying upon the heavy couch.

"No sleeper, your Majesty," cried the chamberlain, bending over Carrbroke, to raise his eyelids one by one. "Pah!" he ejaculated. "The odour is quite strong. The poor lad has been drugged by some pungent medicament." And then as he drew back his hand he took a kerchief from his pouch to wipe his hands. "The noisome poison is still wet upon his face."

"Thank Heaven!" said the King. "It was a mercy I did not strike and slay a faithful soul. Come, then, Hurst; but draw and defend me if there is need. Now then, back to the arras, and let us see."

"The passage is all black darkness, Sire," whispered the chamberlain; and the King pointed with his sword to the nearest sconce.

"Bring a light," he said laconically.

The next minute they were opposite the secret door, which the King unfastened, and was about to raise the arras when the chamberlain pressed forward.

"I will go first, your Majesty," he said.

"After your King, sir. Yours the task to light me on the way."

A word of opposition was upon his follower's lips, but the King stooped hastily, raised the arras well on high, and signed to the chamberlain to hold it up and cast the light into the narrow way he was about to traverse.

Then with one heavy thrust he threw open the door, and without a moment's hesitation passed in with his sword advanced, to be followed quickly by the chamberlain, who raised the light above his head, to throw the King's shadow right before him, so that his mock semblance, looking black, solid, and grotesquely dwarfed, moved on in front till it struck against the angle of the wall where the passage turned sharply to the left.

Here with sword advanced the chamberlain approached as closely as he could, fully expecting attack from a hiding foe; but the King passed boldly on, with his shadow before him, till the next angle was reached, their footsteps sounding hollow, dull, and strange in the confined space.

The King walked onward like one well accustomed to traverse the place, and in another few minutes the great candle his follower bore was casting the dwarf shadow upon the heavy door that blocked the end.

"A false clue, Hurst," said the King gruffly. "The secret of this place is still our own.—No, by my faith!" he almost roared. "The light, man—lower—and look here!"

For there, plain to see, was the ring of a heavy key in the lock of the massive door, and as the King seized the latch and raised it with a click, the door swung inward easily upon its well-oiled hinges, followed by a puff of the soft night air, which would have extinguished the light had not the King hastily closed the door again.

"Gone, and by this way!" he growled, as he turned the key, sending the bolt with a sharp snap into the socket. Then with a sharp tug he drew out the shining wards and signed to his follower to return.

Lord Hurst uttered a low sigh of relief, for he felt that the King had escaped a terrible danger, the loss of the jewel being as nothing to his life.

He backed slowly, lighting the way, till they were about half-a-dozen yards from the door, when he stopped short and raised the light on a level with a little horizontal niche close to the roof of the passage, into which the King thrust the key.

"There has been treachery here, Hurst," he said sombrely, "for a stranger would not be likely to have found that key. Simple hiding-places are often the most safe. But there," he growled, with a suppressed oath; "back into the corridor, but extinguish that light before you raise the arras, and make sure that we are alone."

The order was obeyed, the chamberlain cautiously listening, before going down upon one knee to raise the tapestry a few inches from the floor and make sure that Carrbroke was the only occupant of the great gallery, then creeping quickly out, holding the hangings upward for the King to pass, and securing the door.

"Now," cried the King furiously, as he brought one foot down with a heavy stamp, "the villains may be still within the grounds. Guard! Guard!" he roared, with a voice almost as deep as that of a raging bull; and as footsteps were almost directly heard, the enraged monarch turned upon his chamberlain and furiously bade him have the soldiery summoned and the place well searched, while many minutes had not elapsed before the alarm bell was sending its vibrating notes with a deep hum through the night air, and room and corridor echoed with the sounds of excited voices and trampling feet.

It was in the midst of the orders that were being given by King and courtier that the clashing sound of arms and shouts of angry men came from the gate and guard-room, to be followed by the news of the encounter and the visitors' escape.

And then it was as if a storm was raging through the castle, set in agitation by the bluff King, who played the part of thunder god himself, ending by stamping and raging about the outer court animadverting upon the sluggishness of his guards, till the strong body of horsemen who formed his bodyguard of mounted archers stood drawn up, ready, with their arms and armour flashing in the light of scores of flambeaux, waiting for the final order thundered forth at last by the King himself, to spare not their spurs, but ride due south and bring back the culprits alive or dead.

Chapter Thirty Six
Somebody's wound

As if to aid the fugitives' escape, the moon, which had been shining brightly the greater part of the evening, had become overclouded almost from the minute they set off, and headed by the King, who bent low over the pommel of his saddle, and at the start had seemed to drive his spurs into his horse's flanks, the little party tore over the darkened road at a furious pace, no one uttering a word.

The King led; that was sufficient for two of the party, who set their teeth and gave the horses their heads, merely taking care to rein up slightly as every now and then they came upon some terribly untended piece of the road.

"The King leads," thought the two young men, "and all we have to do is to keep close at his heels, ready if wanted, and for France."

Saint Simon was one who thought little and said less. They had had an exciting charge, mastered those who opposed them, behaved like gentlemen of France, and that was enough.

But as Denis galloped on with the wind coming cool and pleasant to cheeks fevered by the excitement that he had passed through, picture after picture flitted through his brain, dominated by that in the stable entry when he had felt his rapier glide through his adversary's neck.

Had he killed this man? something seemed to ask him again and again.

Then came the strong feeling of dissatisfaction as imaginary pictures took the others' place, illustrating the breaking open of the cabinet and the stealing of the jewel—imaginary so far as he was concerned, for no communication as to this having been accomplished had been made to him. But he took it all for granted, and though he had taken no active part in the theft—for theft his conscience persisted in calling it—the base action pressed upon him more and more, in spite of his combating it with declarations that it was an act of warfare to regain the King's own, and that it was for France.

At last as they galloped on with their horses following their natural instinct and keeping closely together as in a knot, the trouble, the worry became almost unbearable.

"Oh, if something fresh would only happen—something exciting!" Denis muttered. "I could then bear it better."

At last a thought flashed through his brain, and he started, rose a little in his stirrups, and began looking about him.

"Are we going right?" he said to himself, and he looked straight ahead now—beyond Francis, who was slightly in advance, he being on the King's left, while Leoni's horse galloped level with his own, the beautiful animal's head being almost within touch of the King's saddle upon the right.

But all was dark and cloudy, and he could make out nothing.

"The King leads," he muttered, "and what the King does is right."

Thinking this to himself, Denis rode on, perfectly unconscious of the fact that he who rode on his right was vastly troubled too, and regardless of everything else kept one eye fixed upon his liege, for he had noticed that Francis was not riding according to his wont.

He was generally upright in his saddle, and he had never seen him bend low before like this.

At first he comforted himself with the thought that it was all due to excitement and the dread of being captured after this nefarious act; for gloze it over as he would, the subtle Franco-Italian knew in his heart that though it might be for reasons of State, and to ensure the stability and future of his King, the scheme was vile. Then, too, there was all that had taken place that night, the peculiar semi-trance-like state in which the King had seemed to be plunged. There was the draught, too, that had been taken, and its effects before he had grasped the King's wrist and had led him, a passive instrument in his hands, to where the cabinet stood in the obscurity of the gallery, and had him standing there, participator of that which had followed, but in a half unconscious condition the while.

Once or twice after coming to the conclusion, and owning to himself that the state of Francis was due entirely to the draught he had administered, Leoni started nervously in his saddle, for the King had suddenly given a lurch as if partly unseated; but he regained his balance on the instant, and muttered angrily at his horse for stumbling.

They rode on now at a hand gallop, their horses' hoofs beating heavily upon the road, but not drowning the King's voice, as every now and then he made his horse lay back its ears to listen to the rider's words, which at times came angrily and fast. But they were incoherent and strange, and it was only now and then that Leoni, on his right, and Denis, on his left, caught their import, always something about the hunt and losing their quarry.

It was just after one of these mutterings that the clouds were swept from the face of the moon, passing onward like a vast black velvet curtain edged with silver, and leaving visible a third, later on a half, of the vast arch overhead, studded here and there with stars whose lustre was paled by the effulgent moon.

And now it was that, after studying the sky overhead for some minutes to make sure, Denis could control himself no longer, and involuntarily exclaimed; "Are we going right?"

"What!" cried Leoni sharply, for the King paid no heed, but galloped on, muttering to himself the while.

"Are we going right?" repeated the lad.

"What do you mean, boy?"

"The road is straight, sir, and we are riding to the north. Should we not be making for the south?"

"Are you mad, boy? What do you mean?"

"Look, sir—the stars. That must be the Bear."

Leoni was silent for a few moments, breathing heavily the while, as they rode steadily on. Then the doctor's voice came in a low angry hiss:

"Yes, boy," he said, and his voice sounded like a harsh whisper, "we are upon the wrong road; but the Count led, and I thought of nothing but making our escape."

"Are we to rein in, sir? Will you not tell him at once?" whispered Denis, leaning towards him as near as he could get.

"No; we can do nothing now but gallop on. There is certainly pursuit going on hot foot behind us—somewhere," he added, after a slight pause; "and perhaps it is in the Count's wisdom that he has chosen this way, for if we were beyond earshot when pursuit commenced, the guard would naturally divine that we should be making for some southern port. Perhaps all is working for the best."

"Ah!" ejaculated Denis excitedly, for Francis reeled again in his saddle, this time towards his young esquire, who spurred his steed level with the King's just in time to save him from falling headlong to the ground.

"Ah!" he muttered angrily. "This horse is going lame, and we shall be last. Poor broken beast, I have ridden him too hard, and—I like it not; I like it not."

"Master Leoni!" cried Denis excitedly, as the King recovered himself once more. "The Comte, sir—the Comte!"

"I know. I saw. Keep as you are now, as close as you can ride. I'll keep level on the other side. We must reach water somehow, and I will give him to drink. It is the excitement. He is ill."

"No, no, sir!" cried Denis wildly. "He is wounded."

"What!" shouted Leoni.

"My hand and sleeve are wet with blood. Look, sir, look!" For the moon was shining brightly down upon them now. "A horrible cut upon his brow!"

"Halt!" cried Leoni; and at the command the horses stopped so suddenly that but for the hands of his followers the King would have been thrown upon his horse's neck.

"Are we to get him down?" panted Denis.

"No," said Leoni, cool and stern as if, in spite of the emergency, danger was afar. "Support him that side." And letting his horse's rein fall upon the neck he drew his little *flacon* from the breast of his doublet, unscrewed the top, and passing his arm round the King's shoulders, the head fell back, and the doctor pressed the neck of the little flask between his lips, while Francis yawned slightly, and a few drops trickled over his dry hot tongue. A few drops—no more—and then the top was screwed on the flask, it was returned to its owner's breast, and he busily examined the King's forehead, after drawing back the plumed cap which had been dragged down over his eyes.

"A cut from sword or axe," muttered Leoni. "It must have been given by one of those halberdiers. He has borne it bravely, gentlemen, and like a king. Hah! My handkerchief!"

He snatched it out, just as it was, folded like a pad. "Now then, a scarf," he said. "Yours, Denis. I will unfasten it myself. You, Saint Simon, ride back a hundred yards and listen. Make out if you can whether we are pursued."

Saint Simon turned off and rode back without a word, while Leoni hastily unfastened and drew off the young esquire's silken scarf, and said with his white teeth glistening in a sardonic smile in the bright moonlight:

"Why, Denis, boy, you will be honoured to-night. You must save this scarf as an heirloom, for when you get it back it will be deeply stained with the royal blood of France."

"Hist!" whispered the lad, flushing. "The Comte will hear."

"Perhaps," said Leoni coolly; "but he will not understand. Ah, that is better: raise his head a little.—Stand still, horse!" he cried angrily; and then, as Denis raised the King's head a trifle, the white handkerchief was bound tightly over the wound, and the scarf adjusted so that it retained it in its place and formed into a turban-like cover, while the King's jewelled cap was secured by its strap to the embroidered baldric he wore.

Chapter Thirty Seven
An awkward halt

Meanwhile the strong medicament administered by Leoni had had its effect, giving the sufferer temporary energy and to some extent restoring the reeling senses, so that by the time the *al fresco* surgery was at an end, Francis began to speak with a fair amount of coherence.

"Who's this?" he said. "You, Leoni? Thanks, man. How cool and fresh the night air feels! Have I been hurt? Yes, I remember. That caitiff dog of an Englishman struck me with his partisan, and I had no time to reach him and pay him back. Thanks, doctor. Yes, I am better now. But on, on, on!" he panted, with a sudden return of the slight delirium from which he had suffered. "An end to all this. Fontainebleau! Can we reach there to-night?"

"No, sir," replied Leoni soothingly, as with his hand upon the King's rein he led his horse at a walk. "But we are well on the way for the palace. That's right. That's right. I am weary of this playing Comte, and all it means. But we shall be late, Leoni; we shall be late. They will have laid the hounds upon the boar's track. He will have broken cover, and I shall not be there with my spear."

"We will go faster soon, sir," said Leoni encouragingly; but he did not attempt to increase their speed, continuing at a walk and suddenly drawing rein to speak to Denis.

"Saint Simon," he said—"I had forgotten him."

"Coming on about a hundred yards behind," whispered Denis. "He thinks we are not followed."

"Hah!" exclaimed Leoni. "You ride on first. I will follow with the Comte. He will take up all my attention now."

"Is he much hurt?" whispered Denis anxiously.

"No; an ugly cut to the bone, but nothing to fear. Forward, boy, and keep a sharp look-out for the first road that bears off to the left. That will be the way—anywhere will be right that takes us beyond pursuit."

Denis obeyed and rode on, looking vainly for the road he sought, but finding instead several leading in the opposite direction, while at every turning he checked his horse to wait till the rest came up, for their progress was necessarily slow.

The night glided drearily on, with the paces of the horses at a slow walk growing monotonous in the extreme; and for some time past the excitement of the flight had been giving place to the first approaches of a drowsiness that was rapidly becoming invincible, when with a faint cry of joy the lad noticed, as he looked off to his right, that the faint soft light was beginning to appear in the east, becoming soon a long, low pearly band which grew broader and broader, while the stars that had brightened for a time when the moon went down began to pale.

The patches of woodland back from the road, which had been black and sombre, began to turn grey, leaves grew distinct, and before long high-up in the zenith the sky was flecked with a few tiny clouds of a soft rosy orange which gradually brightened till they glowed like fire, and then died out, leaving nothing but the clear sky, darkened in the west, but growing lighter till the eastern horizon was reached, where, plain to see, were the rapid advances of the coming day.

The birds, too, were beginning to make their pipings heard, and all at once, as if wakened by the footsteps of the horses, a lark sprang up, to begin circling round higher and higher, carolling its joyous song, and with it raising the spirits of the young esquire, as he felt that they were free once more, and at all events taking the first steps homeward and backward to the sea, which still lay between him and the rest and peace for which he longed.

It was horrible, he felt, that the King should have been injured in this ill-starred expedition; but now it was to be at an end, and as the lad thought this in the dewy freshness and cool air of the hour before sunrise, he began to enjoy the beauty of the pleasant woodland country through which their horses paced. But he looked back from time to time, to see Francis more upright in his saddle, with Leoni riding knee to knee, and Saint Simon grave and silent fifty yards behind.

Still they passed nothing but some foot-track or rugged lane—nothing in the way of a high-road—and the lad was about to draw rein at last to seek counsel as to their further proceedings, when at a turn of the lane he caught sight of a spreading clump of trees and what seemed to be a village green, about which clustered a few humble cottages, and an inn whose sign projected from a tree trunk that overhung the road.

Denis checked his horse now and waited till the others closed up.

"Shall I see if the people are awake," said the lad, "and ask them of our way?"

"No," replied Leoni coldly. "Ask nothing; but go and summon the people. Ah, there is some one stirring there! Look—coming out from the door. Ride on and tell him we want rest and refreshment—a chamber, too, for a gentleman who has had a fall from his horse. Denis, boy, we are in a perilous strait. I dare not let the King go further until he has had some hours of rest and sleep."

Chapter Thirty Eight
The King's horses and men

The landlord of the little inn welcomed his visitors eagerly, for he had never before had guests of such degree, and when not observed he gazed open-eyed at their rich habiliments, for there had been no time to don their travelling garments. Everything had been made to give way to the opportune moment for securing the jewel and making their escape.

All the host studied was about how many gold pieces he would be able to charge this noble gentleman who had had so unfortunate an accident through his horse stumbling upon the ill-kept road, while he and his wife did everything they could in their attentions, in the hope that their visitors might prolong their stay.

Leoni bit his nails to the quick as he paced up and down, watching the road from the King's humble chamber, expecting every minute to see a mounted guard coming to arrest them, and in spite of his longing to be upon the road he dared not suggest such a thing to the King in his intervals of consciousness, when he questioned about his state and where they were, for his hurt was too serious for any risk to be run.

So Leoni tended his wounded sovereign night and day, while, quite as impatiently as he, Denis and Saint Simon tried to while away the time by giving extra attention to the horses, and feeding them up ready for a severe test of their powers when they once more continued their flight.

They too watched the road each way without attempting to leave the inn, lest troubles should arise and they not be there.

It was late in the afternoon of the fourth day, and the impatience and anxiety of the King's followers had grown unbearable; but they had this consolation, that the wound was doing well, and that though weak Francis was conscious and ready to talk as much as Leoni would permit about Fontainebleau and the journey home.

But he always avoided making any mention of the jewel, or of his dissatisfaction at having attempted so wild an escapade.

It was, then, late in the afternoon of this fourth day, when after Francis had had a light meal he sank into a profound and restful sleep, thanks to Leoni's dressing of the wound; and as soon as his attendant had satisfied himself that the sleep was deep, he went down to the shabby little room occupied by Denis and Saint Simon, who sat dolefully comparing their quarters with those they had so lately left.

"He is better, then?" cried Denis, springing up as Leoni entered; and then he looked wonderingly at Leoni, who stood perfectly still, rapt of manner and silent, gazing fixedly at him with that expressionless stony eye, while with the other he seemed to be looking Saint Simon through and through.

"Yes," said the doctor at last, as if dragging himself back from where his thoughts had wandered away; "better—much."

"He is ready to start, then?" said Denis eagerly.

"No, nor near it. We are quite lost sight of here in this lonely place. I think we can do so with safety, so we will stay another night. I dare not risk another breakdown on the road."

"Oh," ejaculated Denis, "you surely do not advise that we should keep his—the Comte in this squalid place another night?"

"Not from choice, boy, but from necessity. Another such a night as he has just had, and he may be fit to start. To leave to-day would aggravate his wound."

"Oh," cried Denis impatiently, "while at any moment Henry's people may have obtained a clue and surround this place!"

"We are playing for high stakes, boy," said Leoni gravely, "and we must take all risks."

The King did not awaken until late in the evening, seeming so much rested and clear that Denis's heart leaped with excitement, for he began to speak calmly, declaring that he was ready to start.

"No, sir," said Leoni. "Believe me, not yet. Let us see what to-morrow brings." And he reached out his hand to take his master by the wrist; but with an impatient "Pish!" Francis snatched his hand away and sprang to his feet.

"Absurd!" he cried. "I am quite fit to start, for the pain has left my wound. It would do me more harm to stop fretting here. Order the—"

He said no more, but made a snatch at the wall and would have reeled and fallen had not Saint Simon acted as the sturdy buttress he was, and lowered him easily into a chair.

"That giddiness again," cried the King, with a sigh. "The doctor is right. Early to-morrow morning, then, gentlemen," he said, with a peculiar smile. "Leoni is king now, and reigns in our stead. I like not his palace, but we shall be safe here."

The evening passed on. Leoni was with the King in his chamber, and Denis and Saint Simon were seated gloomily together in their humble room, and the latter was from time to time sipping and making wry faces over a stoup of the bitterest, sourest, harshest cider that was ever drawn from tub, when there was the loud clattering of horses upon the road coming at a sharp trot; and as the young men sprang to their feet a loud command was heard, which was followed by the stamping and shuffling of hoofs as a troop of horsemen drew rein shortly in front of the little inn.

"Caught!" said Saint Simon abruptly, and his hand sought the hilt of his sword, while Denis followed his example, just as the door was thrown open and Leoni rushed in.

"The King's guards," he cried, "and resistance will be in vain. Gentlemen, I am ready to give my life, as you are yours; but even if we die for our master's sake, what then? We should only leave him a prisoner in Henry's hands, to bear the brunt of his trouble all alone."

"You mean that we must surrender?" cried Denis angrily.

"Yes," said Leoni, looking at him fixedly, and with a smile upon his lips, "and I give you good counsel. It must be so. Hah!" he whispered harshly, as he caught the boy by the breast. "Hark!"

He loosed his hold, stepped lightly as a cat to the window, and peered through a tiny opening in the partly fastened window-shutter, to make out dimly a little crowd of horses and men in the cloudy night.

But his ears made up for the want of penetration of his eyes, for just then a sharp order rang out and the horses, which had been taking their turns to lower their muzzles to the water in the long trough in front of the inn, raised them, dripping, and a couple of minutes later the troop was in motion again, with the hoofs of the chargers rattling and gradually dying out upon the road.

Denis was in the act of drawing a long deep breath of relief, hardly believing that they had escaped, when their host appeared at the door.

"The King's men, gentlemen," he said, "from Windsor; but it was only to give their horses water," he added sadly. "They would not come in to drink, and I expect," he continued dolefully, "when I go to look I shall find the trough empty, and an hour's work before me to fill it from the well. But they are the King's men, gentlemen; any other travellers would have paid, as you do, gentlemen, generously and well."

"Let me pay, then, for this," cried Denis, light-hearted as he was at the thoughts of their escape, and he slipped a broad piece of silver into the man's hand, sending him on his way rejoicing.

That night Denis dropped into a deep but at the same time a thoroughly uneasy sleep, in which at times it seemed to him that he was being pursued, at others that he was the pursuer, while people were constantly getting into his way, shouting out lustily, "You cannot pass!" He was in terrible anxiety too about his master, who was just ahead, urging on his horse, not apparently along an ordinary respectable country road, but through what seemed to be absolutely interminable galleries of a palace. He wanted to tell him to turn either to the right or to the left, and by that means escape from what appeared to be a labyrinth; but unluckily he could not get his horse abreast of that of his master, and the wind was blowing so hard that his voice would not carry. He was just about to shout "France! France!" when he woke up, with the perspiration standing on his brow and the conviction full upon him as he reached for his cloak and sword that real danger did threaten his lord, when Leoni seized his arm.

"Come, boy," he said, and he led him into the room where Francis and Saint Simon were talking.

And then sounds below caught the boy's ear, the trampling of horses and the *burr, burr,* of deep-toned voices, one of which said angrily:

"We had traces of the fugitives up to this place. Did they come here?"

"No," was the landlord's prompt reply.

"Well, we must remain here for the night."

"But, sir, I have no room in my poor inn for such a company as yours."

"What you have will serve," was the response, and the speaker entered the inn, striding past the host.

Francis heard these last words.

"We must come to a great resolution, gentlemen," he said calmly. "We must separate. Singly you may get through. You will leave me here as I am ill. I will follow as best I can. Go."

"Never, Sire," said Leoni, and his one word had two echoes in the little room.

"But—" began Francis, and he stopped, for there was a noise on the stairs, and the landlord was heard exclaiming:

"I assure you, sir, that the room is not fit—"

"Well, there is a light in it anyway."

"It is empty, sir."

"I see a light under the door."

"But my guests cannot be disturbed."

"You said that the room was empty just now. Peste! Your word seems doubtful. I will see for myself."

The landlord was silent.

"Stand out of the way, old man, and let me pass, if you value your head."

The door was pushed roughly open, and the Captain of the Guard strode in.

"Found!" he cried. "I shall save my credit at Court.—Gentlemen," he went on, with the utmost courtesy and bowing low, "his Majesty the King, disappointed with your abrupt leave-taking, has commanded me to escort you back to his palace."

"It is impossible," cried Leoni sternly. "The Count was seriously wounded as we left the gates. You see for yourself. He is faint and weak."

"I am very sorry, sir," replied the captain sternly, "but I have his Majesty's orders."

"But not to brutally slay the King's guest. I am a *chirurgien*, and you may take my word."

The captain took a candle in his hand and held it over the rough pallet where Francis lay, and satisfied himself that Leoni's words were true.

"Is the injury bad?" he said quietly.

"Bad, but not dangerous if he is left undisturbed."

"And if I consent to defer our departure till the morning, what then?"

"I cannot say for certain, sir," replied Leoni, "but I think it may be possible, with care."

"Very well," said the captain; "but I give you warning, gentlemen, that any attempt at an escape—"

"Bah!" ejaculated Leoni contemptuously. "Are we likely to leave our master?"

"Perhaps not," said the captain, with a bluff laugh, "but you might try to take him."

"In a litter?" said Leoni mockingly.

"There, we must not bandy words, sir," said the captain. "It is my duty to tell you that an attempt at escape may be at the cost of some of your lives. We will stay here the night. But now, gentlemen, I have one unpleasant duty to perform."

"Our swords!" cried Denis hotly.

"No, sir," said the captain, with a smile. "His Majesty would not desire that I should call upon you to suffer that indignity. My instructions were that in your hasty departure the other night one of you took by mistake something—papers, documents, I don't know exactly what—but something to which his Majesty attaches great importance."

"I hardly understand you," said Leoni coolly.

"Perhaps one of your friends does, sir," continued the captain. "Of course it was taken by mistake."

"This means, I presume, that you consider yourself bound to search us?"

The captain bowed.

"Pray do so, then, but incommode my patient as little as you can. You have an easy task, sir, for our valises were left behind."

As Leoni said, it was an easy task, for all offered themselves freely to the officer's inspection, and soon after the latter signified that he was satisfied, and was about to leave the room. But as he reached the door he stopped short and turned to Leoni.

"One moment, sir," he said. "Can you and will you answer for the Comte here, who seems to be insensible to what is going on?"

"He is," said Leoni, "from the effects of his wound."

"Then will you speak for him? And you, gentlemen, will you all give me your word that you are not bearing off any paper or despatch belonging to his Majesty?"

"Certainly," replied Leoni, "and my friends will too. We have neither paper nor despatch belonging to your King."

The captain bowed, and left the room, to set a couple of his men as sentries at the chamber door; and as the occupants of the humble room stood listening to the King's heavy breathing, for he had fallen into a deep sleep, they heard the tramp of footsteps outside, sounds which made Leoni glide on tiptoe to the window and cautiously look out.

"Prisoners indeed," he said softly, with a bitter smile, as he returned; and as in the dim light of the two candles burning on the table Denis met the doctor's eyes with a stern reproachful look, he shuddered slightly, for they looked to him more strange and fixed than ever, having so strange an effect upon him that he could not put his reproach into words.

"Well," said Leoni lightly, "calmness is the best remedy for a trouble. Gentlemen, I will watch by our master's side; you are young, and had better go back to your chambers and try to sleep. Of course it would be madness to attempt to escape."

Chapter Thirty Nine
A Death Warrant

"Well," said the King, on the following evening, "you have them prisoners?"

"Yes, Sire."

"Safely?"

"They are back in their old apartments, sir," replied the chamberlain.

"What, not imprisoned?"

"No, Sire; they are carefully watched, but they are still your Majesty's guests."

"Absurd!" cried the King fiercely. "This man can be no ambassador. He is a marauder, a masquerader, who came to my court to act the common thief."

"But the letter, Sire, of which he was the bearer?"

"Is as false as everything else concerning him. My guests!" cried the King fiercely. "My prisoners! This man shall die."

"But that will not restore the jewel, Sire."

"What!" cried the King angrily. "Have you not got it?"

"No, Sire. They were carefully searched, but it was not found."

"Then he shall be forced to confess where it is."

"I have not told your Majesty all yet," said the chamberlain.

"Then why have you not?" cried the King fiercely. "Speak out, man; speak out!"

"Your Majesty checked me," replied the chamberlain deprecatingly, "The Comte was—"

"The Comte!" cried the King contemptuously.

"Then this member of the Valois family, as you believe he is."

"But no—absurd! Let him be the Comte de la Seine; one who has come here under false pretences, a pretender. Whoever he is, he is my enemy, fate has placed him in my hands, and he shall die—ay, if it costs me a war with France. But mark me well—he dies as the thief who under the mask of a French nobleman entered my palace to plunder. The world shall see in this matter only the just punishment of a crime." And as he spoke the King drew towards him paper and seized a pen. "Short and sharp punishment," he said, "and in thus acting I clear the way to the throne which by rights is mine."

The chamberlain stretched out his hand in an imploring gesture, the while a mocking smile played about the King's lips.

"Sire," he said, "hesitate now. Think well of what you are about to do. Heaven could let no good come of it, and the day will dawn when you will rue the committal of a crime."

"Hurst!" exclaimed the King angrily; but the chamberlain dropped on one knee.

"Your Majesty, let me plead for this stranger who came to your Court—"

"As a thief."

"No, Sire; as a patriot who had determined to obtain the jewel which in the old time belonged to his ancestors' crown."

"That is naught," said Henry. "This man shall die." And he raised the pen once more.

"You who are so great a king, Sire, should be magnanimous here. This night, Sire, is your own, to do good or ill; but it will be the darkest of your reign if that warrant is signed."

"But why do you intercede?" asked Henry, and he threw himself back in his chair. "Francis is nothing to you."

"The life of a noble prince, Sire, is much to all the world, and—"

"You know him?" interrupted the King sharply.

"Last year in Paris, Sire, he befriended my brother, who could speak nothing of him but good; and I have not told you, Sire, that he is very ill."

"Bah!" cried the King.

"Deadly sick from his wound, Sire."

"His wound!" said the King, starting.

"Yes, Sire. In the daring escape, when two of the guards and Sir Robert Garstang were wounded, the Comte was struck down by one of your brave halberdiers."

"And serve the villain right," cried the King impetuously. "Brave fellow! has he been rewarded?"

"No, Sire. That is left for your Majesty to do."

"And it shall be done, on my royal word," cried the King. "Wounded and sick, say you?"

"Yes, Sire; I have seen him, and he is very weak."

"Well," said the King, "you have done your part in your appeal. But I have made up my mind to this." And as he spoke the King drew himself up in his chair once more and seized his pen.

Hurst watched as if fascinated, seeing the King commence to write, and then toss the pen aside as he finished, while afterwards he was about to summon the officer of the guards without, but checked himself, extending his hand to Hurst, who bent over it.

"I will not doubt you," he said, handing him the warrant. "Deliver it to the governor." And then with a wave of the hand he dismissed the chamberlain, who withdrew.

Outside the chamber, Hurst proceeded a short distance down a corridor, and then gazed at the document by the light of a swinging lamp.

"The death warrant of the King of France," he mused, as he noted the words condemning the Comte de la Seine to die, and then the formula: "By the King. Given at our Court at Windsor—Henry R."

He went on slowly along the corridor till he had passed beyond the King's private apartments, and, as if drawn by some attraction, made his way in the direction of the chamber where Francis was lying suffering from his wound.

"Bad, bad, bad," he muttered to himself. "I must be right, and Francis was ill-advised, if advised at all, and not led by his own impetuous nature to play such a trick as this. Well, he gambled with his life, and he has lost. What is it to me? I have my duty to perform. But I would give something now for the instinct of the prophet, to be able to see what this will mean in the future to France and to my own country when it is known."

He walked on dreamily, and then started, for he found that he had unconsciously drawn near to Francis's chamber, and he hesitated, half disposed to go in and see how he fared; but he frowned and went on.

"No," he said, "I have my own head to think of, and my movements may be misconstrued by the most jealous man that ever sat upon a throne."

He was passing slowly on in the gloomiest part by the door, when he started, for some one had silently glided out of the opening and plucked him by the sleeve.

"My lord," whispered a voice.

"Ah!" exclaimed Hurst. "You are the doctor, the Comte's follower with the strange eye. What of your master? How is he now?"

"Bad," said Leoni softly.

"So much the better," said Hurst bitterly. "Insensible?"

"At times, my lord."

"Better still."

"You speak strangely, my lord."

"These are strange times, my man. I spoke so out of sympathy with your master. It may save him further pain."

"Further pain?" said Leoni, earning the chamberlain's term of the man "with the strange eye" by the peculiarly fixed look which was dimly seen.

"Yes, further pain. People who are insensible do not suffer, do they, doctor?"

"No, my lord; but what do you mean?"

"What is the meed of a thief who robs a king? Is it not death?" cried Hurst fiercely; and as he spoke he stretched out one hand and tapped it sharply with the folded warrant that he held.

"Hah!" ejaculated Leoni harshly, and then almost as fiercely as the chamberlain he whispered, "Would he dare to raise his hand against the ambassador of France?"

"No, sir," said the chamberlain coldly, "but against the thief of the night, who abused his hospitality that he might steal. Hark ye, man; if you have your master's interest at heart, tell him to try to make his peace with the King by telling him where the jewel lies, for it must be somewhere concealed. Let him give it up and crave the King's mercy, before it is too late. Do this, and it may save your life as well."

He turned away, leaving Leoni standing motionless a short distance from the door, where he remained without stirring until the chamberlain's footsteps had died away.

Chapter Forty
A boy's ruse

The doctor lost no time in thought, but returned to the outer apartment which he had quitted only a few minutes before, to find that Saint Simon had joined Denis and was watching by the bed where Francis lay insensible.

"We must act at once," he said, as they joined him and he gazed at a narrow window through which the moonlight came. "Our King is in danger of his life."

Denis's hand went to his sword.

"We will fight to the last," he said, "and die."

"Boy!" exclaimed Leoni contemptuously. "Fight and die! Better act with craft and live. What! Would you fight an army? Bah! It is not by that means that we can save his Majesty from this perilous pass."

"Then how?" asked Denis. "Order me to do anything and I will obey."

"I know," said Leoni thoughtfully; "I know." And he took a pace or two up and down the apartment with his eyes fixed on the floor, while the two young men watched him narrowly, seeming to be endeavouring to read his innermost thoughts, the ideas which surged within.

"There is but one thing to be done," said Leoni at last gravely. "Francis is ill and closely guarded, and his life is doubly in danger, for Henry's intentions are lad." And as he spoke he looked hard at Denis, who said not a word.

"And what is that one thing?" asked Saint Simon.

Leoni thought a minute or two before replying.

"It is this," he said at length quietly. "We his followers are free to go where we list, and Francis must be saved. I, alas, can be nothing in my plan; but you," he went on, looking direct at Saint Simon, "or Denis, might save the King."

"How?" exclaimed Denis again, as he firmly met the speaker's peculiar gaze.

Leoni turned from him, walked slowly to the outer door, opened it as if about to pass out, and then closed it again, to return quickly to his two companions, and whispering softly in so low a voice that it was hard to hear:

"By taking his place while he escapes, and personating him as he lies here bandaged, his face half hidden in the shadows of the heavy hangings of the bed in this darkened room."

"I am ready," said Saint Simon huskily.

"And I!" cried Denis. "But—the Comte?"

"I have thought of that," said Leoni. "He is too ill to understand what is done, and I can mould him to my wishes in every way. We are free, as his servants, to come and go from the chamber, and there may be ways by which we can escape—three of us—that is, the Comte and two followers, while one brave devotee assumes his master's aspect as a wounded man. It may be days before the discovery takes place, and by that time all may be safe. Denis, boy, will you do this thing and be for the time being the simulacrum of him we serve? Good: your face speaks. I knew it. It is not a question of likeness, but of wearing a heavy bandage that will nearly hide your face."

There was silence for a moment, and then Leoni spoke again.

"What about the way?" he said. "It is night now, but if we could gain the grounds—but how?"

"The secret passage, sir," whispered Denis. "It availed once, why not again?"

"The passage!" cried Leoni. "No; once used, they will guard it safely now. But stop; they do not know that we escaped that way, and it might prove as sure an exit as it did before. I have seen no guard in that corridor since our return."

"Nor I," said Denis eagerly.

"But how to pass the gates?" said Leoni thoughtfully.

"There is no need," cried Denis. "Follow the narrow alley leading downward to the river, and take the boat of which young Carrbroke spoke. The river! Surely you could escape that way."

"Boy," whispered Leoni ecstatically, "you are the deliverer of France! Hah!" he added, in tones full of regret. "And you will not be with us! The river—yes. They would never dream that we escaped that way. Quick, then. There is not a moment to be lost. You will not flinch?"

"I? No!" whispered Denis proudly.

"Quick, then! The darkness is the best disguise." And leading the way into the sleeping chamber, he busied himself with torn-up linen and scarf, preparing the semblance of bandages, while Denis unbuckled his sword-belt and hurriedly threw off his doublet.

A few minutes sufficed for the skilful hands of Leoni to strap and bandage the gallant lad's features, leaving him standing on one side of the bed while he went to the other to draw back the coverlet.

In obedience to the thought that flashed through his brain the lad bent quickly forward, caught at the King's hand and raised it eagerly to his lips, half rousing him, to mutter in his sleep, while Leoni took out and unscrewed his little flask and applied it to the King's lips.

"Drink this, sir," he said, and in strict obedience to his medical attendant, the sick man drank till the vessel was withdrawn.

"Ah!" exclaimed Francis wearily. "I am not well, Leoni. We pay dearly for our adventure. But we will hunt to-morrow at Fontainebleau. Is it not so? Call the Master of the Chase."

"You may do so, sir. But you feel stronger now?"

"Yes, yes."

"Then come, sir." And Leoni snatched the cloak which Denis had thrown on a chair and wrapped it round the King. "We will start at once, sir."

"Yes," said Francis, "we will start at once—at once." And he leaned heavily on Leoni's arm, while the latter drew the heavily plumed hat which the boy handed him lower over the King's features.

Denis accompanied them to the door.

"Farewell," he said.

Leoni turned and gazed at him, and for a second the saturnine expression faded and a look of tenderness came over his features.

"Until we meet again," he whispered.

Then the door closed and the lad stood wondering whether the plan would succeed, whether the King would on the morrow be far on his way to the sea.

The next minute he was in the inner chamber by a mirror, smiling at himself, before plunging into the King's place, turning on his side, and drawing the coverlet right up to his ears.

Chapter Forty One
A visitor for a patient

The time up to the closing of the chamber door had been one of wild excitement. There was the disguise, and then the scene of preparing Francis for another flight, his helplessness, and the calm, unresisting way in which he had yielded himself to Leoni's hands.

Then came the departure, the farewell of Leoni, whom at times he seemed to shrink from with dislike, almost with dread, but only to feel himself won back again, attracted by the doctor's manner and his manifest liking for his young companion.

Then there was the closing of the door, which seemed to cut the lad off from his friends and leave him, as he threw himself wearily into the bed to lie there alone in the darkness, face to face with a horror which chilled him through and through.

For in his chivalrous excitement which thrilled him with a feeling that he was about to do a most gallant thing in the service of his King, he seemed to have no time to think; but now in the silence and gloom of that solitary inner room, there was time for thought, time for his feelings to be harrowed by the knowledge of what was to come, and as he lay there he began to picture to himself how it would all be.

How soon he knew not, but before long some one would come, miss the King's attendants, inquiry would be made, and possibly the supposed Comte, lying wounded in the bed, would be sharply questioned as to the whereabouts of his doctor and gentlemen.

"What shall I do?" thought Denis. "I must keep up the semblance of being the King. I am supposed to be very ill, and I can pretend to be insensible. That will all gain time if I refuse to speak; and those who come will never for a moment think that the King's attendants have left him helpless here—far less fancy that they have escaped.

"But have they escaped?" thought the lad; and in his excitement the perspiration broke out upon his brow, as he lay wondering whether they had found the private passage unfastened and won their way through to the gardens, so as to pass unnoticed along the alleys and down to the river steps and boat.

"No," he thought. "Impossible. The people here would surely have securely fastened up that way, and the King has been captured; and with such an enemy as Henry what will be his fate?"

For some time he gave these thoughts firm harbour, but at last his common sense prevailed. The idea was absurd, he told himself. If the little party had been seized while making their escape the whole castle would have been in an uproar, full of wild excitement, with the hurrying to and fro of steps, especially the heavy tramp and clash of the guards, instead of which all was horribly still, while the candles burning in a couple of sconces were hidden from his sight by the heavy hangings of the bed, so that he lay there alone in the deep gloom.

There were moments when the shadows cast by the lights seemed to take form and move, making him feel that he could lie there no longer, that he must spring out of bed to face bravely these weird and shadowy forms, and convince himself that he really was alone, and merely a prey to a childish superstitious dread brought about by the horror of his position.

It was hard to bear, and required a heavy call upon his manliness to force back these fancies and prepare himself to play his part when the crucial time came of some one visiting the room and finding that the Comte's attendants were no longer there.

"It is for the King of France!" he muttered, when at last the dread and horror of his position had culminated in a feverish fit that seemed as if it would end by his springing out of bed, tearing off the mockery of his disguise, and hurrying through the outer chamber into the corridor to seek the company of the nearest guards.

"It means hastening the discovery," he muttered, "but I can bear this no longer. It is too much."

He lay panting heavily for some few moments before a reaction came, following quickly upon the one question he asked himself, contained in that one little word:

"Why?"

He began breathing more easily the next moment, for the weak boy had mastered, and manliness was coming to his aid.

"Oh," he muttered to himself, "am I to be as cowardly as a girl? It is too childish. Afraid of shadows, shrinking from lying alone in the dark! Why, I shall fancy next that I shall be afraid to lie here with the sun shining brightly, through the panes. What difference is there between the light and darkness? I can make it black darkness even at noonday if I close my eyes. I know why it is. I am tired and faint. There is no danger—for me. The danger is to the King. This is only a trick, a masquerade. Sooner or later I shall be found out. But what then? I am only a lad, and this King Harry would be a bloodthirsty monster if he had me slain for what is after all only a boyish prank. I have nothing to do but lie here quite still, as if a sick man, and very bad. They will find out at last. Well, let them. I am utterly tired out with all I have gone through. My head is as weary as my bones, and now all this weak cowardice has gone I am going to do what I should do here in bed, and go to sleep.

"Oh, impossible! Impossible!" muttered the lad wearily. "Who could sleep at such a time as this?"

He rose upon his elbow and said those words in a hoarse whisper, as if he were questioning the shadows that surrounded the great curtained bed.

There was no reply from the weird and shadowy forms, uncouth, strange, and distorted; but he answered his piteous, despairing question himself.

"I can," he said, "and—"

There was a pause of a few moments, and then he muttered between his set teeth:

"—and I will."

With a quick movement he drove his clenched fist two or three times into the great down pillow, making it purl up into a hillock, upon which he laid his cheek, and into which it softly sank, while, closing his eyes, he strove to force himself into a heavy sleep, till his strong effort joined with his bodily weariness, and he sank into a deep dreamless trance.

How long this lasted he never knew, but all at once he lay wide awake and wondering, striving to realise where he was, and what the meaning of that heavy distant tramp, tramp, as of soldiery coming nearer and nearer, till it ceased outside the farther door in obedience to a hoarse command.

There was another order, followed by a close fusillade-like sound of the butts of halberds planted upon the floor. Then a few moments' silence, and as the lad strained his eyes in the direction of the doors, that farthest was suddenly flung open and the outer chamber was filled with light which emphasised the gloom of the inner, where, fully alive to his position, Denis lay still, closing his eyes and pressing his face farther into the pillow, as a stern voice shouted as if in warning, for all to hear: "His Majesty the King!"

Chapter Forty Two
In the gloomy gallery

Leoni was the moving spirit of the adventure of what he felt to be another daring attempt to escape; for Francis, under the influence of the medicament that he had administered, was like a puppet in his hands; while Saint Simon, big, manly, and strong, ready to draw and attack any who should bar their way, spoke no word, but followed his leader's every gesture watchfully, suggesting nothing, doing nothing save that exactly which he was told.

As they stood outside the door and began to move along the corridor, the place looked so lonely and the task so ridiculously easy, that the scheming, subtle doctor's heart smote him with a feeling of remorse.

It seemed to be so cruel, so cowardly, to escape and leave that brave lad, who was ready to sacrifice his life in his master's service, alone there with his despair, waiting for the discovery that would probably end with his death.

"Pish!" said Leoni to himself. "What is the boy to me? Nothing more than a pawn upon the chessboard of life, one of the pieces I am using for the sake of France—France, my country, for which I have ventured this. For what is this gay butterfly? King? Yes, the King upon the chessboard, whom it is my fate to move; and where I place him, there he stays. It is I, I in my calm, grave, unobtrusive way, who am the real King of France—now nearly at the pinnacle of my ambition, or shall be when I have achieved these last moves. And yet I am not happy. It jars upon me cruelly that I should have to leave this boy. Pooh! Absurd! I will not think about him," he muttered; and then with a silent mocking laugh, "And yet what is he? Only, as I say, a pawn, which the necessities of the position force me to sacrifice."

These thoughts flashed like lightning through his brain, as, grasping the King's arm with one hand, he waved the other in the air as if in the act of casting all these thoughts behind him. But he winced the more, for the thought of Denis alone there in the King's chamber clung to him and seemed to press him down.

But there was stern work awaiting him, for he would not, he could not believe that their escape could be as easy as it seemed. The corridor leading to the great gallery near the King's apartment appeared perfectly deserted; neither guard nor gentleman in attendance seemed at hand to hinder their approach to the arras which hid the secret door. But he did not believe and he would not trust so impossible a state of things.

Stopping suddenly close up to the panelled wall, he signed to Saint Simon to close up.

"Take the King's arm," he said; "he needs support. I am going forward. If you can make me out and the signal I give, follow quickly on. But wait till I raise my hand."

He walked swiftly on, almost gliding like a shadow over the wall, for his footsteps made no sound, while as he passed one candle which gave out a feeble light a curious gleam flashed from one of his eyes.

The next moment he was past, and right in the King's gallery, still without seeing anything to hinder his signalling to Saint Simon, and reaching safely the spot opposite to the secret door.

"If I were alone," he thought, "I have but to cross here, pass behind the arras, make my way to the riverside, and then somehow I could, I would, reach France, with my country the richer for this night's work. But there is the King," he muttered softly; "there is the King." And he pressed himself back against the tapestry, looking in his sombre garb, in the faint light of the great place, like one of the needlework figures in the hangings.

But his heart was beating fast, for all at once and quite unexpected there was the sound of footsteps, so slow and measured that he knew they must be those of a sentry; and the next minute a tall figure, dimly seen, came in his measured way along the gallery, as if to pass him, while Leoni's hand slowly glided towards the hilt of his sword and clutched it fast.

He held his breath and nerved himself for the cat-like leap he was prepared to make as the sentinel came abreast, for he felt that it was impossible that the man could pass him without his being seen.

But to the watcher's intense astonishment the sentry stopped short in the centre of the gallery, when he was about a dozen yards away, turned upon his heel, and began to retrace his steps. Leoni on the instant judged that the man had come to the end of his beat, and if this were so the task seemed easy, for by seizing the minute when his back was turned and he was at the full extent of his monotonous tramp in the other direction, it seemed to the doctor that it would be easy to step across the gallery, raise the arras, and pass into the secret way.

"One at a time," muttered Leoni; "one at a time. Easy for us; but can I make my chief piece obey me and move alone?"

The disposition was upon the watcher of the sentry to glide back at once to where he had left Saint Simon and the King; but he felt that he must make sure in this crisis of the adventure before he took his next step, and he waited, closely pressed up against the tapestry, looking more than ever like an embroidered figure, as the sentry halted far down the gallery, softened by distance into a mere shadow, turned, and resumed his pacing.

The task seemed harder than ever to stand pressed there against the panelling, watching the coming of the stalwart guard, and it took all the doctor's nerve and self-command to stand there so absolutely still of body, while his nerves and thoughts were moving with an intensity that literally thrilled.

"Coming towards his death," said Leoni mentally, as the man came on and on, gradually ceasing to be so shadow-like and dim as he advanced. "His life or mine. His life or mine. His life or mine," something within him seemed to keep on saying, till the end of the sentry's beat appeared to be quite over-passed and he was coming nearer, so near that Leoni felt he saw him at last and the crisis was there, when the man stopped, hesitated for a moment, then began pacing back just as before—but not quite, for almost as soon as his back was turned Leoni's command over his nerves and muscles ceased, and he began to glide silently along by the tapestried panels to reach Saint Simon and the King at last.

No word was spoken now but the single one "Follow," as Leoni softly took the King's hand and led him over the ground he so lately had traversed, pausing after a time as the trio came within sight of the sentry, and standing close up against the wall, to wait till the man reached his nearest point to the secret door to turn in his automaton-like fashion and begin marching back.

Leoni waited till the sentry half covered the distance he had to traverse, and then led the King swiftly and silently till they were nearly opposite the panel door, to pause once more—three shadowy figures now—to wait there during the most crucial time, for the great test was now at hand.

Could he trust the King to remain silent till the man turned back—if he did turn back without distinguishing that he was not alone in the gloomy gallery?

But Leoni was a man of resource, and to meet this difficulty he bade Saint Simon lie down at full-length close to the wall, while he pressed the King behind the pedestal of a statue standing in a niche a few yards away.

It was a great risk, but the King seemed plunged in a deep sleep, and at a time like that something had to be risked. It was the daring of the plan that carried it through, and the fact that the sentry's perceptions were dulled by habit. Hence it was that he came on, gazing introspectively and seeing nothing but his own thoughts, which were of the near approaching time when he would be relieved, and return to the guard chamber, supper, and sleep.

Leoni hardly breathed as once more he watched the man come on nearer and nearer, apparently to his death, for this time Leoni softly drew the keen stiletto that he wore, and crouched ready to ensure silence and save the King if he were driven to the last extremity. But that was not to be.

The man came to the full extent of his paced-out beat, turned, and marched back, while before he was half the distance to the other end the doctor had glided across the gallery, raised the arras, and pressed the boss, fully expecting to find that the door was fast; but it yielded silently, and the doctor's heart leaped as he drew in a long deep breath of cool moist air.

Dropping the arras, he stood for a moment gazing after the shadowy sentry, feeling startled to see how far he was still from the end of his beat; and, acting contrary to the mode he had planned in his determination to seize this opportunity if it could be done, he glided swiftly across to where the King was standing, and caught him by the arm.

"Come," he whispered, with his lips to Francis's ear, when the King yielded as if he were a portion of the speaker's self, walking with him silently till they were half across the gallery, when all at once a bright light threw up into bold relief the figure of the sentry at the far limit of his tramp, and the two fugitives stood out plainly before Saint Simon like two black silhouettes upon the distant glow.

"Lost!" sighed Leoni, as, utterly unnerved, he stood tightly pressing the King's wrist, unable even to stir, but listening to the sounds of voices which came weirdly and whispering along the gallery—challenge, reply, and order of the changing guard.

Before recalling the fact that the bearers of the light were hardly likely to discern them at so great a distance, he recovered himself and pressed on towards the door and raised the tapestry, when without word of direction Francis passed through, followed by Leoni, and the arras was dropped.

"Saint Simon," muttered the doctor, as without closing the door he led the King onward for about a dozen yards, before returning to the open door with the intention of kneeling down to raise the hangings slightly and watch.

"Must I leave him behind—another?" he muttered; and then he started, to clap his hand to his dagger again and prepare to strike, for there was a faint rustling sound from the open door and then the faintest of faint clicks, followed by the expiration of a heavy breath as from one who could contain it no longer.

Leoni stood with his arm raised on high and his stiletto pointing downwards. The next moment it had dropped to his side, for from out of the darkness in front there came the whispered words:

"Are you there?"

"Saint Simon!" cried the doctor, not beneath his breath, for he was too much excited by his surprise to control his emotion, as he stretched out his left hand to grip his follower by the arm. "I did not expect this," he muttered.

"Too dangerous to stay," said Saint Simon.

"Yes, and you were right; it was bravely done."

"But what about the garden door? It will be fast."

"The saints forbid!" muttered Leoni. "Follow and attend the Comte. I will go on first and see."

He glided on with extended hands, expecting momentarily to touch the King, but did not overtake him till the little landing was reached, where Francis was standing at the head of the flight of steps.

Leoni pressed past him and began to descend, holding his master once more by the hand, which he dropped as soon as they were at the foot, and then passed on rapidly with his pulses throbbing and in a state of ungovernable excitement such as he had not felt since the commencement of the adventure.

But this was of short duration. Schooled now by previous experience, Leoni ran his hand along close to the angle at the top of the wall upon his left, expecting moment by moment that it would come in contact with the ledge. He was quite right. It did, and glided into the niche, when a chill seized upon his heart and made it cease its heavy beat.

The niche was empty!

By the King's orders the outer door must have been locked, and they were prisoners as fast as ever, unless some other scheme could be devised.

For a few brief moments Leoni gave way to despair. Then with an angry ejaculation he pressed on with extended hands, covered the few yards more that had to be passed before the door was reached, touched it, and swept his hands towards the lock, and once more no longer in full command of his faculties, he uttered a faint cry of joy.

The key was in the lock.

Chapter Forty Three
King Denis refuses

Denis's heart beat wildly for a few moments, as he asked himself should he be asleep or waking; but the heavy beating calmed down at once as he heard the King's slow footsteps in the outer room, and then the question in the now well-known voice:

"No attendants?"

"No, Sire. I presume he is asleep."

"Then I must awake him," said the King sternly; "but my business is with him alone. Go, and retire the guards. I will summon you when I have done."

"But, your Majesty —"

"Silence! Can I not defend myself were it necessary against a wounded man? Go, and at once!"

The chamberlain, whose voice Denis had recognised at once, retired in silence.

There was the trampling of the guards, the closing of the outer door, and then as Denis lay listening all was still, while he began counting the slow heavy beating of his heart.

"What will follow now?" he asked himself.

He knew at once, for there was a slight cough, a heavy step, and the King strode through the dividing door into the chamber, stopped as if looking round for a moment, and then stepped round to the side of the great canopied bed, drew forward a chair, and seated himself between the recumbent prisoner and the window. Then he coughed again, but sharply and angrily this time.

"You hear me, Comte de la Seine?" he said haughtily.

It seemed to come naturally to the young esquire how to play his part — to gain all the time he could; and he slowly raised one hand and let it fall heavily back upon the coverlet.

Henry was satisfied, and his tones bespoke it, as he said:

"It is well, sir. I have stooped to pay you this visit—here this night, to remind you that by the way in which you have repaid my hospitality you have forfeited your life."

Denis raised his hand again, so that it came out of the shadow thrown by the curtains into the light cast by the candles right across the bed; and as the King sat there as if watching the effect of his words, the hand was waved carelessly in the air before it was allowed to descend.

"Hah!" cried the King. "You are a Frenchman, sir, and you behave with all the flippancy of your race. I understand your gesture. It means recklessness. You, so to speak, tell me that you do not value your life. You defy me. But you will alter your tone when you are called upon to march in the middle of my guards to the headsman's block, and suffer there for your crime."

There was a quick impatient gesture of the hand again.

"We shall see," continued the King, with his voice growing deeper, suggestive of the hot anger that was burning in his breast. "And now listen to me, M. le Comte de la Seine, as you call yourself. But you have not deceived me. I know everything, even to the reason why you have stooped to play the part of a common cutpurse."

Denis raised his hand again with an angry gesture, and Henry continued more loudly:

"I repeat it, sir," he cried; "a common cutpurse; and please understand that you are quite at my mercy. No one can save you but I. Now listen. Men call me merciless and tyrannical. Let them. I am also just, and can be merciful when I please. Are you ready to accept my mercy?"

Denis raised his hand again quickly.

"Hah! Good! Then it is in your power to act in a way that will command this mercy, possibly my forgiveness, and the continuance of the feeling of friendship that you, so brilliant and talented a man, have won."

Denis raised his hand again, as if in deprecation, feeling in spite of his perilous position something like amusement at the success attending the playing of his *rôle*.

"Oh yes," continued the King; "you have proved yourself a man brilliant, courtly, and in every way fitted for the high position you held before you stooped to the wretched chicanery and folly which brought you to this pass. Now, sir, I tell you I am ready to be merciful and spare your life, but upon conditions; and these stipulations which I shall make, I tell you, you as my prisoner are bound to accept. You came here under false pretences to steal a jewel that was England's by the right of conquest, making to yourself the excuse that originally it belonged to France. Is not this so?"

Denis raised his hand again.

"You do not speak," said the King. "Well, knowing as I do that you were badly wounded by my faithful guards, and are now suffering severely for your crime, I am willing to accept a motion of your hand, a gesture, as your acceptation, as a reply. You see, sir, that all through this mad escapade Providence was working a means of compassing its righteous ends. You have fallen completely into my power, and either you submit to my terms or die."

Denis raised his hand quickly.

"You mean an appeal for mercy," cried the King. "Wait till you have heard my terms. They are these. I have here," he continued, unfolding a paper, "a complete renunciation on the part of France of the city of Bordeaux with the towns and territories embraced by Guienne, lands that were won by the good sword of my predecessors, to have and hold for three hundred years, but which you now occupy on sufferance and by the magnanimity of the English throne, which has mercifully withheld itself from seizing them by an act of war."

Denis's hand, now fully in the light, was extended for a moment, but sharply withdrawn, for the fingers to begin tapping impatiently upon the coverlet.

"Ah, you hesitate!" cried Henry. "Let me tell you that it is no time for hesitation, and that I shall brook no argument, accept nothing but a full and sufficient resignation made now upon this paper, which needs but your act and deed made fully by the addition of your royal name."

Denis raised his hand slowly, and let it fall heavily upon the bed.

"Hah!" cried the King, in a tone which evinced triumph and intense satisfaction, as he rose to his feet and walked slowly to a side-table standing beneath one of the sconces, upon which were writing materials ready to the visitor's hand. "I am glad," continued Henry, "that you are acting so wise a part. I might call in my chamberlain and others of my people to witness your surrender, but I will spare the feelings of a brother monarch who is completely in my hands. Your signature, Sire, will suffice." And as he spoke he took up and dipped a pen and seized a book, to bear them in company with the paper he held to the side of the bed, where he spread the paper upon the work.

"Now, Sire," he continued, "at this moment we are enemies. Take this pen and add your royal name where I will place my finger, and I give you my kingly word that I will wipe out from the tablets of my memory the whole of your dastardly action, and become henceforth not only your brother of England, but your willing ally against all enemies who may rise up in an endeavour to imperil our thrones. There, Sire; I presume you are not too weak to write. Come: take the pen."

Denis, who was now nearly at his wits' end how to continue the comedy, and beginning to flinch in his dismay at having gone so far, raised his hand slowly and closed his fingers upon the pen, while with a sigh of satisfaction Henry placed his index finger, upon which a large gem was glittering, upon the blank spot beneath that which he had written upon the paper.

"Stop!" he cried suddenly. "I had forgotten. It is not written down there, but for it I will take your kingly word. You promise me to restore the jewel reft from my cabinet and hidden somewhere you best know where. Surely you can speak enough for this—the fewest words will do. You promise by your kingly word and all that is holy to restore that gem?"

He ceased speaking, and to one of those present the silence in that room seemed more than awful, till Henry spoke again.

"You hear me, sir? One word will do, and that word, Yes."

The answer made Henry start back in amaze, for, desperate now, and nerving himself to meet the crisis which might mean the sacrifice of his life, Denis with a quick flick of his fingers sent the fully feathered pen flying from the gloom of the hangings where he lay far out into the room.

"What!" roared Henry. "You refuse?"

"I refuse," said Denis, in a hoarse whisper.

"But why?" cried Henry, half suffocated by his anger.

"Because," cried the boy defiantly, "I am not the King." And with a quick movement he threw back the coverlet, sprang from the bed, and tore off his bandages, to stand there in the full light in white shirt and trunk hose, scattering the wrappings which had disfigured his face, just as, startled in his turn and fully expecting an attack, Henry took a couple of steps backward and drew his sword.

Chapter Forty Four
The escape

For a few moments excitement got the better of the grave subtle doctor, and he was within touch of flinging open the door and hurrying Francis out into the grounds. But drawing in a deep breath he was cautious the next moment as some lurking beast of prey.

The key was turned by slow degrees without a sound, and the door drawn carefully inward till there was a slight crack, through which the night wind came in pleasantly to his heated brow, and he paused for quite five minutes, listening; then gradually opening more and more, he satisfied himself that there were no concealed guards among the bushes, waiting to spring upon him and make him prisoner when he stepped outside.

His next act was to remove the key to the garden side of the lock. This done, "Now," he whispered, and Francis, who seemed more than ever under his control, stepped quietly out, followed by Saint Simon; after which the door was cautiously locked, and Leoni slipped the key into his pocket.

There was another pause, which made Saint Simon utter a low deep growl.

"What is it, boy?" said Leoni.

"The boat! The boat!" whispered the young man. "We are losing time."

"Perhaps gaining it, my dear Saint Simon," was the reply. "Youth is rash; age is cautious. Our progress must be slow and sure."

He took and pressed the young man's hands as he spoke, before leaving him to take a few strides for observation along the path, and then returning, musing to himself that all seemed too easy, and that at any moment there might be some sudden check to their progress.

Back once more, he bade his two companions follow, leading them slowly and cautiously on, sword in one hand, stiletto in the other, as advance-guard, Saint Simon, similarly prepared, forming the rear; and then on and on they went downward through the bushes, which ever and again brushed against their sleeves, and twice over startled and arrested by a sudden dash as of an enemy; but it was nothing worse than a startled bird, blackbird or thrush, roused from its roosting sleep by the disturbers of its rest.

And so downward along the winding, well-marked paths, with nothing to hinder their progress, no guards to arrest, and Leoni strong in the belief that some great check must come, settling in his mind that the encounter would be down by the landing-place when they tried to set free the boat.

In this belief when they were nearly there he stopped short, laid his hand upon the King's shoulder to press him aside, and whispered to Saint Simon to join him in the front.

"There may be watchers there," he said. "Be well on the alert."

The next minute as they moved forward the head of the stone steps was reached, lying in the darkness of the clouded night nearly hidden by a great overhanging willow, whose pensile twigs brushed the roof of the waterside summer-house supported upon slimy water-worn piles, to one of which the boat-chain was attached, the rusty iron creaking faintly against the ring-bolt as the skiff swung softly to and fro, influenced by the swift stream.

"Hah!" sighed Leoni to himself. "Fate is with us yet. Who says our mission is unrighteous?" And a feeling of exultation rose within his breast, only to be crushed-down directly after by what seemed to be a heavy weight of misery, beyond which he seemed to see the reproachful eyes of the King's esquire, sacrificed that he might succeed.

"Into it and unloose the chain, boy," whispered Leoni, eager by action to change the current of his thoughts.

Saint Simon quickly sheathed sword and dagger as he stood on the lowest step and reached out to draw in the boat, into which he stepped, making the chain rattle as he drew it through the ring, and his leaden utter an impatient:

"Hist!"

The next minute the freed boat was grinding against the step, and Leoni steadied it by planting a foot upon its side.

"Now, boy," he whispered, "seat yourself, and be ready with the oars— good! Now rest one on the step here and keep the boat steady.—Quick, sir! Step in, and sit down at once."

The King obeyed without a word, and no sooner was he seated than Leoni followed, and took his own place between Francis and Saint Simon, whom he relieved of one of the oars.

"Push off!" whispered Saint Simon, who held the oar that rested on the steps.

"One moment's thought," whispered back Leoni, speaking over his left shoulder, as he glared around for danger, his ears twitching the while like those of some wild animal which felt that there was peril in the air.

"Now," he said, in a whisper just loud enough for the young man to hear, "if we go upward it is farther into the country, but harder work, for we are against the stream. If we go downward it is towards the capital, and the work will be light, for the stream will bear us on.

"Yes," he said, after a pause, "if we are pursued and the boat is missed they will think that we have taken the easier way. No, boy, ours is no time for ease; hard work and safety must be our motto now. Push off and row with me slowly and steadily onward against the stream."

Saint Simon bore heavily upon his oar and with a thrust sent the boat's head outward; and directly after, dipping as lightly as they could, they pulled together with a wonderful regularity for such unpractised hands out towards the middle, till a scattered light or two appeared from beyond the trees, showing where the castle lay.

And then onward in silence for a few hundred yards along between the dimly seen silent banks of the black river, for the clouds seemed to have lowered and there was not a star.

All at once a movement on the part of the King took Leoni's attention, and he drew in his oar, to bend forward and then rise in the boat, for Francis had sunk slowly sideways, fast asleep; while, with the action of a careful mother bending over her child, the strange subtle doctor carefully readjusted his cloak to guard him from the night air, before resuming his seat with a sigh, and taking up his oar.

"A trifle, Saint Simon," he said playfully. "There are times when we have to protect our master with our swords, but we must not forget such little things as this."

"Ah!" ejaculated Saint Simon, with a groan.

"Why, what's the matter, boy? You don't resent having to row the night through like some poor slave?"

"No, no. I was thinking about poor Denis. Doctor, don't think me weak. I loved that boy."

"Say love," cried Leoni warmly. "Bah, man! Henry may be a tyrant, but he could not be so base as to hurt a boy like that. Row for our lives while I prophesy what I believe in spite of bitter despairing thoughts. We shall live to see our brave young companion safe again."

"Bravo, doctor! Your medicine has given me heart. Row? Yes. I can do it now till my arms refuse to stir." And on the boat glided, kept closer to the shore where the eddies played and the full force of the stream was missed.

And then on and on hour after hour, with a few intervals of rest where the waters whispered and they made fast to some overhanging bough and spent the minutes thinking that horsemen might be near, scouring the country where they could approach the banks on either side to cut off the fugitives, though not a sound was heard.

And so on till day broke and they made fast amongst the trees in the most secluded place they came to, not daring to expose themselves where they might be seen.

They had no trouble with the King, for, weak with his wound and half stupefied by the drug Leoni had administered, he slept on hour after hour through the pleasant morning and through the heat of noon, his resting-place quite cool beneath the shadowing trees and with his brow fanned by the soft summer breeze. He did not even stir when, kneeling in the boat, Leoni moistened and drew off the bandages to dress his wound, washing them in the stream and drying them in a patch where the hot sun heated the bows of the boat, but still slept on as if restful and comforted by the chirurgeon's skilful hands.

"Better or worse?" whispered Saint Simon, while the task was in progress.

"Better, boy, and healing fast. He will sleep for hours yet, and waken quite himself towards evening; but then," added the doctor, with a sigh, "we have another difficulty to face, if we are not taken."

"Ah! What's that?" cried Saint Simon quickly, and Leoni smiled sardonically, making his companion wince at the peculiar look in his eyes.

"I was thinking, boy," he said, "of how you are going to spread the white napkins and the silver cups for our master's banquet, for he will be hungry, ravenous, after his long fast. You see, he may be displeased to find the banquet cold."

Saint Simon stared at him with open eyes and mouth.

"Why, you are laughing at me," he said.

"Well, why not?" replied Leoni. "Surely, after all my slavery of brain, when success shines down upon me I have a right to smile."

"Success!" cried Saint Simon bitterly. "Why, you have failed."

"Hah!" said Leoni, with a peculiar smile; and then after a short pause, "Well, boy, what are we to do for food? This water is beautifully limpid and clear to quench our thirst, but it will not appease hunger."

"I'll go ashore at the first hostelry we see, and buy what we want," replied Saint Simon.

"And expose us to fresh capture? No, boy; we have had enough of hostelries. Every one within reach of the river will be searched. We shall have to fast till we are far enough to venture ashore."

"And the King?" said Saint Simon.

Leoni looked at him curiously, and slowly placed his hand within his breast to draw out the little golden flask, which he tapped with his finger-nails.

"Three parts gone," he said; "but enough left for the Comte's use. A few drops will quell his hunger; double the quantity will make him sleep in peace. When you can bear your fast no longer, you shall have a few drops in water if you are a good boy."

"Bah!" growled Saint Simon. "I can bear hunger like a man."

The day glided by in perfect peace, the two rowers resting from the past night's labours, and the King sleeping as quietly as a child; while from time to time as Saint Simon glanced at him sadly, thinking of how he and Leoni had been the cause of all the trouble to his friend, he could not help a growing feeling of admiration within his breast as he saw how able the doctor's ministrations were, as shown by the way in which he had treated his master's serious wound.

It was during one of these musing fits, when he was wondering, to use the homely phrase, how Denis was getting on, that Leoni, after a long silence, spoke out decisively.

"We will wait till it is dark," he said. "It will not be long now—and then row on through the night. It looks so clear that I expect we shall have the moon to help us on our way. To-morrow morning we shall be obliged to risk landing somewhere on the left bank, and then make our way due south, walking till the King is weary—of course after one of us has bought food of some kind, for he will never walk without. Hah!" he continued, as he bent over the sleeping King and carefully examined his face. "He is dreaming a good deal now."

"How do you know?" asked Saint Simon.

"By the motion of his eyes."

"Why, they are shut, sir."

"Yes, but look how they are turning about beneath his lids. He is going through some imaginary scene—hunting perhaps."

Singularly enough, as the doctor spoke in a whisper, Francis proved the correctness of Leoni's surmise, for he exclaimed:

"Yon bosky piece—quick! Lay on the hounds!"

Leoni drew back with a smile, and met Saint Simon's wondering eyes.

"Yes," he said; "he is getting to the end of his deep sleep. It will not be long before he wakes, and I should say just at dark. Ah, good! It is lightening in the east. Yonder comes the moon. We will start at once; but I must cover him again. The mist is rising in the meadows, and it promises a damp night."

As he spoke he bent over the King to draw his cloak about shoulder and throat; but at the first touch of his hands the King started up and caught them fast.

Chapter Forty Five
The Balas Ruby

"Who's this?" cried Francis sharply, and in a much firmer voice. "Hah! You, Leoni?"

"I, M. le Comte."

"Bah! The Comte! But what is it? Have I been asleep and dreaming? Where are we? What are we doing here?"

"Making for Fontainebleau, sir."

"Yes, Fontainebleau!" cried the King eagerly. "But like this—in a boat?"

"Yes, sir—" began Leoni.

"Say Sire, man! I have done with this masquerading folly. Speak out plainly. That mummery is at an end. Why are we in this boat?"

"Escaping from King Henry's vengeance, Sire."

"Hah!" cried the King. "I do not understand. Yes, I remember now. It all comes back. There was some question of that—oh yes, I remember—the fit of madness. But was I not wounded?"

"Yes, Sire; but your injury is healing fast."

"To be sure. I feel better, after long weeks of horrid dreams. Well, that is all over. It was while escaping. But tell me—I am growing confused again—what mean you? That we are escaping now?"

"Yes, Sire; soon to be in safety and on your way to your own great land."

"Ah!" cried the King, in a tone full of satisfaction. "That is good. I would that I had never left it upon this quest. But how dark it is getting!"

"Yes, Sire; but it will soon be lighter," said Leoni quietly.

"Make it lighter in my dark brain, man, if you have it in your power," cried the King impetuously; "for one moment I see clearly; the next, I am confused again. Yes—that is what I wanted to think of. Is Saint Simon there? But where is my young esquire? On your life, man, don't tell me he is dead!—Hah! Is that the truth?"

"No, Sire," said Leoni sadly. "I pray that he may be alive and well."

"May be alive! What do you mean, man?"

"That it was his and our duty, Sire, to save you from King Henry's anger. You were his prisoner, and at all costs had to be saved."

"Yes, yes; I had to escape. I have a dream-like memory of something of the kind, though it is all confused."

"Yes, Sire; from your wound."

"Hah!" cried the King. "But what is that to do with young Denis? Was he cut down too?"

"No, Sire; quite uninjured when we saw him last."

"When you saw him last? Then where is he now?"

"A prisoner at the castle, Sire. The brave lad volunteered to take your place while we endeavoured to save our King."

"To take my place! Do you mean to say, then, that he personated me?"

"Yes, Sire; to lie as if wounded on your bed."

"He did that?" cried the King; and Leoni slowly bent his head.

"Then he has the making of a king within his breast. Brave boy!" cried Francis; and he was silent for a few moments, while bending over the side of the boat he scooped up the clear cold water in his hand and drank again and again.

"Hah!" he cried. "That gives me power to think. Did I understand you aright that I am escaping and have left that boy to bear the brunt of my folly, to suffer for my madness imprisonment and maybe death?"

The doctor bent his head.

"Leoni," cried the King passionately, "is this acting like a king?"

"Sire, it is not for you to ask, nor yet for you to judge of this. Your brave young esquire felt it to be his task, and he volunteered to play his part, as either of us would have done. It was to save your life, your servant's duty at a time like that."

"And you tell me that it is my duty as a king to sacrifice that boy just entering the dawn of his young manhood so that I might live?"

"Yes, Sire; for your subjects' sake."

"I am the King, and judge of this. A thousand times no! It shall not be."

"Sire, it must. What is one young life compared with yours?"

"Everything," cried the King, "if I am to live in peace."

"But, your Majesty, it is too late to think of that."

"Never too late while there is life," cried the King. "Loose the boat and take those oars."

"What would your Majesty do?" cried Leoni.

"Go back to Henry and meet him face to face. Let him work his will on me if he dares. But he shall not injure a hair of that brave boy's head. Bah! He would not have dared."

"You are mistaken, Sire."

"In what?"

"In King Henry's intentions. He meant your death."

"What! In cold blood to slay a brother king?"

"Not a brother king, Sire, but the Comte de la Seine, who had entered his Court in disguise."

"Impossible, Leoni! I repeat, he would not dare."

"Sire, your death warrant was made out."

"What!"

"I saw it, Sire, in Lord Hurst's hands; and he told me indirectly what was to take place."

"Leoni!" cried the King.

"Those are the simple words of truth, Sire. That death warrant, signed by the King's own hand, was the mainspring of my action. Was I not justified in doing anything to save your life?"

The King was silent.

"Leoni!" he exclaimed at length. "I am faint with hunger. Is there no place near where we can get food?"

"There is a farm we passed a little lower down, Sire," replied Leoni; "but we dared not stay for fear the pursuers might be searching either bank."

"Let them search and find if they will," cried the King. "I must have refreshment before I do more."

"Your Majesty wishes us to row there and take our chance of being discovered?"

"Yes," said the King, "and at once. But stay. You are certain that the Count's death warrant was signed?"

"Yes, Sire; sure."

"Bah! If I declared myself there would be an end to that?"

"No, Sire."

"What!" cried the King.

"Henry doubtless has his ends and would gladly have you dead. If you declared yourself now he would laugh you to scorn and call you impostor, cheat."

"Hah!" cried the King, grinding his teeth. "Let him if he dare! But I will not believe it of him, going as I shall now, for nothing shall stay me from hurrying back to save that poor lad's life."

"But, your Majesty, let me implore you!" cried Leoni.

"Implore, then, but you will find me deaf."

"For your own sake, Sire!"

"It is for my sake I go—mine honour as a king."

"For the sake of your servants, then, who have risked so much!"

"I cannot! I will not," he cried. "I will go."

"For the sake of France, the country you so dearly love!"

"It is for the sake of France I go, to prove myself worthy the name of her King. You urge me to perform a dastardly act in fleeing at a time like this."

"Remember, Sire, the reason why you came."

"I do," said the King, standing up proudly in the boat, as the edge of the moon began to lift above the low mist that lay upon the river and adjacent meads, lighting up the King's face, animated now into stern beauty by the spirit within which spoke, "and think of it with shame. Listening to your words, I blinded myself into the belief that it was right, that it was a brave and a gallant act to wrest that Crown jewel from King Henry's hand; but I see more clearly now that my mad enterprise has met with its merited fate, and go back I will as a chivalrous knight, ask my brother King's forgiveness, and save that brave boy from his cruel fate."

"But, Sire, remember! Remember Fontainebleau and France."

"I do; and I remember too that your plot has failed."

"But it has not failed, Sire," cried Leoni, rising now; and as he stood erect there was a look of triumph in his face which gave him, as it were, a reflection of the kingly majesty before which he stood. "It has not failed, but ended in triumph and success."

"What!" cried the King fiercely. "You speak in riddles. Tell me what you mean."

He seemed to tower over his follower, who, apparently humbled, crouched before him with lowered head and outstretched deprecating hands, with which he covered his face as if asking mercy. But the next moment he sprang up once more, just as the King angrily repeated himself:

"Not failed!" he cried. "Tell me what you mean?"

For answer Leoni threw back his head and held one hand on high full in the light of the moon, which flashed and scintillated from the many facets of a brilliant gem.

"Hah!" cried the King excitedly. "What have you there?"

"That which we came to seek, Sire. The Balas ruby—the fateful gem of France!"

Chapter Forty Six
In borrowed plumes

Denis stood for a few moments panting heavily, not daring to take his eyes from those of the King, who stood there speechless with astonishment. Then by an effort the boy wrenched his gaze from where it was held, as he thought of his own sword; but the weapon was on the other side of the bed, and as he realised it the thought came that this was a King—one who had but to utter a word to bring in his guards.

"Tricked again," said the King at last; "and by you, boy! Francis's esquire! Where is your King?"

"Beyond your reach, Sire, by this time," said the boy boldly, nerved as he was by the feeling that he had gained much time, and that his words were true.

"Escaped?"

"Yes, Sire."

"Ah!" ejaculated the King. "And I see now this was another ruse. How like a Frenchman! He was not wounded after all."

"He was, Sire," cried the boy indignantly, "and dangerously too."

"But that jewel—where is it now? On its way to France?"

"No, Sire; I can answer for that."

"Then you have it."

"No, Sire, I have it not; and I am sure—my life on it—it never passed into his Majesty's hands."

"You lie, boy!" cried the King fiercely.

"I am a gentleman of France, Sire," said the boy haughtily.

"A gentleman of France!" cried the King scornfully. "A member of a gang of thieves!"

"I am your prisoner, Sire," said the boy boldly, "and I know what is bound to be my fate. I am no member of a gang of thieves, but one of my

King's esquires, bound to do his duty as his Majesty's servant; and I have done mine—no more."

"Ah!" cried the King, making a quick advance towards the boy, who made an involuntary movement towards his rear, but checked it on the instant, drew himself up proudly, and folded his arms across his breast.

"Pish!" said Henry impatiently. "I was not going to slay you, boy." And he thrust his sword back into its sheath and caught the lad by the shoulder. "Then that was the King of France!"

"Yes, Sire."

"I knew it," cried the King, "and Hurst was right. And you have been deceiving us all here, lying bandaged in that bed, while he has been placing himself beyond our reach, bearing away that fateful gem?"

"Yes, Sire; but my word for it, his Majesty the King has never laid hands upon the jewel, and is not bearing it away."

"Well!" exclaimed the King, with his eyes rolling and his cheeks puffed out; and then, loosening his fierce grip upon the boy's shoulder, he staggered back to the nearest chair, dropped into it, and laughed.

The next minute the mirth died out of his half closed eyes, and a scowl appeared upon his brow, as he fiercely gazed in the eyes that did not for a moment blench. But the frown died out in a look of admiration, as he said sharply:

"You springald, to play a part like this, with the executioner's axe hanging above your neck and waiting to fall. Why did you do this?"

"To save my master, Sire."

"Hah! To the risk of your own life."

"Yes, Sire."

"Speak out, boy—the naked truth. Are you not afraid?"

"Horribly, Sire," replied the boy slowly. "The duty is harder than I thought."

"Hark ye," cried the King; "are all French boys like you?"

"I hope so, Sire."

"Do you? Well, boy, I don't believe they are. But speak, and don't turn white like that—a gentleman of France, as you call yourself—a king's esquire, should not be afraid to die."

Denis was silent perforce, for no words would come.

"A daring young dog!" muttered the King, in a tone so low that it hardly reached the listener's ears. "Look here, sir," continued Henry, "you have forfeited your life and stayed me from showing mercy to your master. Now, sir, would you like to win it back?"

"Gladly, Sire," cried the boy, "but—"

"But what?" said Henry sharply.

"I will not do anything to betray my King."

"Wait till you are asked, boy," said Henry roughly, as he kept his eyes fixed admiringly upon the lad, who faced him still with a wondrous command of nerve. "You know that I have the power of life or death?"

Denis bowed his head slowly.

"Well, then, a king cannot stoop to slay even an enemy if he is brave. I will give you your life on one condition."

The boy started, and the King smiled.

"Not to sign a paper which gives me Bordeaux and Guienne, but to be my faithful servant and serve me as you have served your master to the end. I want followers like you. Be English, even if you have French blood flowing in your veins. Well, why do you not speak? Is not mine a kingly act?"

"Yes, Sire, and I am grateful."

"Well, why do you hesitate? Enter my service. The star of the Valois must be setting fast when its representative can stoop to such a deed as this."

The lad shook his head.

"What! Do you not understand? I will find work for your sword. Serve me faithfully, and rank shall in time be yours. Do you forget that your life is still at stake?"

"I cannot buy it, Sire, by betraying my master. Francis is my King."

"And fortunate in having followers like this," said the King to himself, as he rose, turned sharply from where the boy still stood with his arms crossed upon his breast, fighting hard for the resignation that refused to come, while his heart now beat slowly and heavily, as if in the march that ended in the scaffold and the axe.

The next minute the King had flung open the outer chamber door, as if to show to the boy his fate, for there stood the captain with the guards drawn up on either side, their armour gleaming and the lights they bore flashing from their halberds' heads.

But the boy stood firm, seeing as it were through the glittering pageantry of the English Court the gleaming fields of far-off France, a sparkling river, and the grey steeple turrets of an ancient French *château*. It was home, with all he loved therein.

It was momentary, and the vision was dissolved by the King's loud voice, as he cried sharply:

"Who's with you there? Hah! Hurst! Look here, man."

"Your Majesty!" cried the chamberlain, looking at the boy in astonishment.

"Behold my royal visitor!" cried Henry mockingly. "This is the way my courts are kept."

"I do not understand, your Majesty," cried the chamberlain, trembling for what was next to come.

"But I do, man!" cried Henry. "Here is our sick and wounded prisoner."

"A ruse—a trick!" said the chamberlain excitedly.

"Yes—French," cried Henry, with a mocking laugh. "The bird has flown, and left another in his nest. There, young popinjay, young daw— look at him, Hurst! He has cast his borrowed plumes." Then turning to Denis: "Put on your own feathers, boy. You will come with me. Bring him to my apartments, Hurst."

"As a prisoner, Sire?"

"No," said the King, still fixing Denis with his eyes, and speaking to him as much as to the chamberlain. "He is my guest still, though his master is gone. See that you use him well."

Chapter Forty Seven
Francis is a King

To have seen King Henry seated at his supper in that eventful year, and on one particular night, it would have been impossible to suppose that not many hours before he had been indulging in so fierce a storm of passion, such kingly rage, that not one of his most trusted courtiers and counsellors had dared approach for fear of consequences that might ensue.

It was the lion's feeding time, and the food had evidently been good and satisfying. The music too in the minstrels' gallery had been sweet and pleasant to the ear. The Court jester had for a wonder excelled himself in his strong endeavours to put the King in a good humour, and uttered no less than three samples of his wit which had made the King roar, inasmuch as in the tail of each joke there was a slightly poisoned sting which had gone home to the three noblemen for whom they were intended, my Lord Hurst, the King's chamberlain, getting the worst dose.

There had been a good deal of whispered wonder running through the great dining chamber, especially below the salt, where the King's gentlemen were seated who had for long been disappointed at the absence of royal favour and promotion they had been hoping for since they came to offer their services at Court; and though all who were well within the scan of his Majesty's eyes spoke softly and with a stereotyped Court smile upon their countenances, they said more bitter things by far than any that had been uttered by the King's jester, their remarks being dipped in envy, as they asked one another whether this French boy to whom the King was showing such favour—this French *champignon*, "impudent young upstart"—was to be the new favourite now, and one and all said to themselves that which was too dangerous to confide to another, that the King must have gone a little mad over the fit he had on discovering the loss of his favourite jewel, which had been carried off—so rumour said—by the so-called French Ambassador. This, joined to the second escape, must have turned the royal brain; otherwise he would never have displayed such sudden favour to one who had played so daring a prank as the impersonation of the wounded man.

But all the same this great favour had been shown, and there was the young upstart of an esquire seated on the King's left, where all through the evening he had been the recipient of the greater part of the royal conversation, responding in French, with a little English which made the King roar, and encouraged him to continue his rather lame efforts at English conversation with an accent that could be called nothing better than vile.

The evening had passed away, and, wearied out at last, the King himself had relieved his feelings with more than one unroyal yawn—signals these of the time approaching when the gentlemen of the bedchamber would have to be in attendance, and another of the Court days be at an end.

Henry was about to rise, when the chamberlain came quickly behind his chair and whispered something close to his ear, looking hard at Denis as he spoke.

So meaning was his glance that the boy, who in spite of the royal favour had been on pins all the time, took fright at once, ready as he was to associate everything informal as being in some way connected with those who had escaped. The next moment the lad's hands had turned cold and damp, while a giddy sensation attacked his brain, for the King had suddenly exclaimed:

"Hah! The Captain of the Guard with his reports?"

"Yes, Sire. I have told him to wait at the door of your private cabinet. Will you receive him there?"

"No," cried the King bluffly. "Bring him in here, and see that he has a cup of wine.—Now, my young masquerader," he cried banteringly to Denis, "there's news for you. Scores of my guards have been scouring the riverside, and they have come to announce that the prisoners have been secured, for our sick friend the Comte was certain to break down before he had gone far. Well, why do you look like that?" he continued, as he noticed the change in the young esquire's face. "There, there: I am not so savage as they say, and whatever happens it is nothing to you, boy, for somehow— there, never mind. Here comes my friend the captain."

For there was the heavy tramp of feet, and the stalwart Captain of the Guard, in half armour, huge buff boots, and pointed morion set well back upon his head, strode up to the King's table, dusty and travel-stained, to sink upon one knee, the plates of his armour grinding together with a strange sound as he went down—a sound repeated as the King signed to him to rise.

"Well, captain," cried the King bluffly, "what have you to report? You have captured the French pigeons which escaped their cage, and brought them back with all that they took away?"

"No, Sire," said the captain shortly.

"What!" roared the King, in a voice of thunder; and there was utter stillness in the great chamber as, in no wise abashed, the captain went on:

"Six companies of horse, Sire, have searched every road and every village on the way towards London, and six more companies have harried every place on both sides the river from here to—"

"Bah!" roared the King. "Out of my sight! Go!"

The captain saluted, and began to walk backwards, the rowels of his spurs clinking, while his armour crackled loudly as he made his way; but before he was half the distance towards the door he was brought up short by the royal thunder which exploded with one sharp crack about his ears.

"Stop! At eight to-morrow let the outer court be filled with my archers of the guard and my horses ready. I will take up this quest myself."

He rose to go, as the captain again saluted, and there was a sharp rustling of garments throughout the great chamber as the courtiers who had been present at the supper rose, when to the surprise of all the great door was once more thrown open, and one of the Court functionaries stepped quickly forward and in a loud clear voice announced:

"His Majesty the King of France."

There was a peculiar thrill running through the great chamber, and then a heavy bang as Henry in his astonishment gave vent to his feelings in a truly English way, for he brought down his clenched fist upon the table with a thud which made the silver flagons leap, and one, the tallest on the table, thin and weak with age, missed its footing and came down upon its side, seeming to bleed the rich red wine in a little pool.

The next moment, with bandaged head erect and flashing eyes, Francis appeared in the doorway, resting upon Leoni's arm, Saint Simon slightly behind on the other side ready to support his master should he want his help.

But none was needed. Francis stood for a few moments gazing towards the upper table where the King was standing, and his quick clear glance took in the position in a moment, for he had seen Denis standing a little to Henry's left.

Then with a quick movement Francis thrust back Leoni's arm and walked proudly up towards Henry's chair bowing slightly once to right and left as he swept with disdainful eye the now silent throng.

Then, to use the good old grandmotherly term, a pin might have been heard to drop, as Francis pressed forward till close up to where Henry stood, and before the English monarch could recover from his surprise his visitor had laid his hands lightly upon his shoulders and kissed his cheeks.

It was all done in the most courtly way, and only as one of the grandest gentlemen in Europe could at such a time have given the salute, while its reception was as marked and English as it was the reverse of friendly. For the King was so utterly taken aback by this change in the state of affairs that for a few moments he could not speak. When he did find words they were of the gruffest and most matter-of-fact that an Englishman could vent.

"So then," he cried, "you have come back?"

"Yes, my brother," replied Francis, and his voice sounded musical and soft, as the gesture he made was graceful and easy. "I, the King of France, have come back to you, my brother of England, to ask your pardon for my mad folly and grave mistake. See here," he continued, after a slight pause, and he once more looked round the tables at the glittering courtiers, while he held out fully in the light the scintillating ruby that had attracted him to the English shores. "I am no believer in magic or the dark art, but there must be something strange and fateful in this stone, magnetic perhaps, but he what it will, it led me here, knowing as I did the history of its loss; and now I have brought it back to its rightful owner, to its proper resting-place. It is yours, my brother of England, won in the far back past on the battlefield. I for the moment have held it once again in this right hand. Sire, I return it now, asking once more your forgiveness of the past, your renewed hospitality to a sick man for the night."

He ceased speaking, as Henry made a snatch and caught the jewel from his hand, when, light as the action was, it was sufficient to make his now exhausted visitor stagger. He would have fallen but for the King's strong arm, which saved him, and helped him to the seat Henry had just vacated.

"Quick, here!" he shouted. "Wine for my brother of France!"

There was a quick movement, but Henry's hand was the first to snatch one of the silver flagons from the table and hold it to the fainting King's lips, as he drank with avidity, uttered a sigh, and then rose with a smile.

"Am I a prisoner?" he said.

"No," cried Henry in his deepest tones—"my brother and my guest."

As he spoke he caught Francis by the hand and half supported him on his right, as he turned now to the excited lookers-on.

"My lords and gentlemen," he thundered out, "are we to be out-distanced in chivalry and generosity by the King of France? No!" he almost roared, as he turned to Francis. "Sire," he cried, "it was to win back that stone to the Crown of France that you risked your life and liberty, coming almost unarmed to my Court and bearing it away. I, Sire, can but admire your daring and the gallantry with which you carried out your quest to its successful end. And, Sire, I honour far more the gallant act of chivalry, that bravery which forced you back to my Court to make this honourable amend. Francis, my brother, I cannot take the gem. It is the jewel of France, and you shall bear it there. Keep it, Sire. It is yours."

Chapter Forty Eight
Leoni's secret

The festive days were few before Francis, now the honoured guest of Henry, left Windsor on his return to Fontainebleau, for he was still weak and suffering from his wound; but it was a pleasant time, especially to the King's esquires, after a little cloud had cleared away and the sun of two young lives once more was shining bright and clear.

It was towards the evening of the day succeeding the events of the last chapter, when Denis caught sight from one of the windows of the King's gallery of Carrbroke walking in the gardens below, looking moody and strange, while all at once, as if conscious that he was being watched, he glanced up at the window and caught sight of Denis looking out ready to wave his hand.

The English lad frowned, turned his back, and began walking away, while, stung to the heart by his reception, the blood flushed in the French lad's face, and drawing back from the window he ran along the gallery, to descend into the court, reach the garden, and make his way to that portion of the pleasaunce where he had seen his English friend. It was some time before he could find him, but at last he came suddenly upon him in a secluded portion nearly surrounded by a grey stone wall covered with growing plants.

"Ah, there you are at last!" cried Denis.

Carrbroke turned upon him angrily and clapped his hand to his sword.

"You have come to fight?" he cried. "Well, it is death here to draw. Come out into the park, and I'll show you how I act towards a thief."

"A thief!" flashed out Denis, imitating his companion's action. "This is cowardly from you. But no, I will not quarrel. You do not know."

"Not know! Do I not know that in my confidence and belief in our French guest, whom my father had honoured, I foolishly trusted you with the secret of the King's private way—and for what? To help you and your friends to steal."

"No," said Denis gravely; "you don't know that, for it is not true. I did tell Leoni—"

"Ugh!" ejaculated Carrbroke. "That man's horrid eyes!"

"Yes," said Denis, with a peculiar smile; "that man's horrid eyes—thoughtlessly, I suppose, of the secret way, when I believed my duty called; perhaps you would have done the same. But I had nothing to do with the taking of the gem. Pah! I hated it all through, but as the King's esquire I had to fulfil my duty to my master. Believe me, I did not help to take the jewel. I felt that I would rather have died. Will you not believe me, Carrbroke?" And he held out his hand.

"I feel I cannot," cried Carrbroke.

"Does it take a king to forgive?" said Denis, with a smile. "To say those words, I forgive you, when there is nothing to forgive?"

"Oh," cried Carrbroke hoarsely, and he looked sharply round to see if they were observed, before snatching and tightly grasping Denis's extended hands.

A few minutes later the two lads were walking together arms on shoulders, in full sunshine of their young nature, that light seeming to be at the zenith, while the ruddy orange sun itself finishing its daily rounds was slowly sinking in the west.

"Hah!" cried Denis. "I am glad we are friends again. I know it looked black against me, and—"

"Oh, don't!" said Carrbroke. "I thought we'd agreed that all that was buried, never to be dug up again. But look here, we must have it now; there is one thing I want to know."

"What?" said Denis, with a peculiar mirthful look in his eyes.

"It is very horrible," continued Carrbroke. "I did not mean to ask you, but I feel I must. Of course your Leoni believed he was doing right for the sake of France, and to serve his master, but I never understood where he managed to hide the ruby. Do you know?"

"I did not know till yesterday."

"Ah, did he tell you then?—But no, I will not ask you to break his confidence."

"It is not to break his confidence, for he did not tell me," replied Denis. "I learned it from Saint Simon, for he saw it on the boat."

"Saw the ruby in the boat?" cried Carrbroke. "Why, how did it get there?"

Denis was silent for a moment or two, and then whispered something, with a peculiar smile upon his lips as he placed them near his companion's ear.

"What!" cried Carrbroke, starting back and staring in wonderment at his companion. "He hid it there? Then that accounts for his peculiar fixed look."

"Yes. He was fencing when a young man, and his adversary's rapier point completely destroyed his left eye."

"Ah!" whispered Carrbroke, beneath his breath. "I see. Then the eye is false—made, you say, of gold, enamelled to look exactly like the other, a little hollow globe."

"Yes; an *étui*, we may call it now, but never meant to conceal that gem."

"Horrid!" cried Carrbroke.

"Yes," said Denis quietly; "but believe it if you can."

"Oh," cried Carrbroke, "I believe; but if he had liked it could never have been found."

A week later the parting of the two lads was like that of brothers, and it was full of promises of what they would do when they met again.

Perhaps they encountered later on at the Field of the Cloth of Gold; but history only says—